THE MELTING POT
and Other Subversive Stories

Also by Lynne Sharon Schwartz

Lynne Sharon Schwartz

THE
MELTING POT

AND OTHER
SUBVERSIVE STORIES

1817

HARPER & ROW, PUBLISHERS, New York

Cambridge, Philadelphia, San Francisco

Washington, London, Mexico City, São Paulo

Singapore, Sydney

These stories originally appeared in slightly different form in the
following magazines:
"The Subversive Divorce,"*Confrontation*
"So You're Going to Have a New Body!," *Mother Jones*
"The Two Portraits of Rembrandt," *Moment*
"The Last Frontier," *Witness*
"Killing the Bees," *Tikkun*
"What I Did for Love," *Prairie Schooner*
"The Sound of Velcro," *Fiction Network*
"The Painters," *Other Voices*
"The Thousand Islands," *North American Review*
"The Infidel," *Michigan Quarterly Review*

Last stanza from "Advice for Good Love" in *Love Poems* by Yehuda
Amichai. Copyright © 1979 by Yehuda Amichai. Reprinted by
permission of Harper & Row, Publishers, Inc.

FIRST EDITION

DESIGNED BY RUTH BORNSCHLEGEL

COPY EDITOR: MARJORIE HORVITZ

Library of Congress Cataloging-in-Publication Data
Schwartz, Lynne Sharon.
    The melting pot and other subversive stories.
    I. Title.
PS3569.C567M4 1987 813'.54 87-45074
ISBN 0-06-015814-X

87 88 89 90 91 HC 10 9 8 7 6 5 4 3 2 1

Contents

The author wishes to thank the John Simon Guggenheim Foundation and the National Endowment for the Arts for their generous support during the writing of many of the following stories.

And advice for bad love: With
the love left over
from the previous one
make a new woman for yourself,
then with what is left of that woman
make again a new love,
and go on like that
until nothing remains.

—Yehuda Amichai,
"Advice for Good Love"

The Melting Pot

Rita suffers from nightmares. This morning's: she is summoned from San Francisco to New York for her grandfather's funeral, where she causes a catastrophe. She enters the chapel with her Russian-born grandmother, Sonia, on her arm, she sees the sea of men and women segregated by a carpeted aisle—solid people, bearers of durable wisdom—and her legs become immovable weights. Everything in her hardens, refusing to move towards the women's side, where she belongs. Even her teeth harden. Sonia, a scrawny, vinegary woman in perpetual haste, tries to drag her along, but Rita cannot be moved. Suddenly from the closed coffin comes a choked, rising moan almost like a tune, the voice trying to break out in protest. Rita's grandmother gasps in horror, clutches her chest, and collapses. All the mourners look at Rita and gasp in unison, like the string section opening a great symphony. One by one, they topple over in shock, both sexes heaped together, mingling. Rita's teeth clench in the dream, biting the hands that fed her.

She wakes up and holds on to Sanjay, who grunts in his sleep. The nightmares dissipate more quickly when he is there. He is a very large, smooth man and she clings to him like a rock climber. In the limbo of waking she cannot even remember which house they are in, his or hers—for they are next-door neighbors, only a wall between them for six years. They live in similar narrow row houses with luscious little flower beds in front, on a sunny San Francisco street lined with eucalyptus trees.

Sanjay, a seeker of practical solutions, thinks the ideal solution to Rita's nightmares would be for them to marry. Why should they live on opposite sides of the wall, like those silly lovers of legend? They are not children, there are no watchful parents hindering them.

"One day soon it will strike you," he says now and then in half-humorous, half-cajoling way, a man of many charms, "that it is the right thing to do. It won't happen when we are making love, but at a more trustworthy moment. Maybe after you have asked me for the fifth time to fix your dishwasher, or after I have consulted you for the ninth time on how some fourth cousin can satisfy the immigration authorities. Some very banal moment between us, and you'll suddenly know. You will want to belong to me forever."

Rita usually laughs. "You've seen too many Fred Astaire movies." But she is afraid. She doesn't want to belong to anyone forever. She has grown up watching that. And she is afraid she won't know how to fit herself in, fit with another life. She looks at their bodies, which do fit sleekly together. Parts of them are the very same color, side by side. The palms of his hands are the color of her thighs, his cheeks the color of her nipples. "What would our children be like?" she says lightly. "What would they call themselves?"

She is not really worried about possible children or what they would call themselves. She mentions it only to deflect his yearnings, because Sanjay has three children already, grown and married. The oldest, who has gone back to India to study his roots, is Rita's age, twenty-eight. It is only natural that Sanjay's fatherliness should appeal to her, a fatherless child— that and his size and bulk, his desire to possess and protect, his willingness to fix her dishwasher and to accept the silences during which she tries to extricate herself from her history. His willingness to accept her history itself. But marrying him seems so definitive.

Now she sits up, leaning on her elbows. The room is suffused with a pre-dawn tinge of lavender. It is Sanjay's house. Of course. There are the faint smells of cumin, coriander, anise—bitter and lush. They are strongest in the kitchen but waft through the other rooms as well. Sanjay's daughter comes two afternoons a week to cook for him. She was born right here on Russian Hill, but she cooks the way her mother did. She doesn't know that her father and Rita eat her food in bed. Sanjay cannot bring himself to tell his children he sleeps with the young woman next door, although he is ready to present her as his wife.

"Why do you let her do that?" Rita asked at the beginning, three years ago. "Doesn't she have enough to do, with the baby and all?"

"I don't ask her to. She insists, ever since her mother died. She's very old-fashioned." A soulful pause. "And she's such a good cook."

"What do you cook when you're alone?"

He made a wry face. "Hamburgers. Tuna fish."

Besides the lush smell, she sees it is Sanjay's house by the shadowy bulk of the large chest of drawers, the darkened sheen of the gilded mirror above it, the glint of the framed photograph of his wife on the chest. When Rita first came to his bedroom Sanjay used to turn the photograph to the wall. As a courtesy, she assumed, for he is a man of delicate feelings, of consummate discretion; but she wasn't sure if the courtesy was directed to her or to his late wife. Now, grown familiar and cozy, he sometimes forgets. Rita has always imagined that she reminds him of his wife, that he wants her because of a resemblance. With the picture facing front, perhaps they two are communing through her body.

Well, all right. Rita is used to being a link, endlessly malleable. She is used to reminding people of someone, and to being loved as a link to the true loved one. Even at work, she helps people locate their relatives, and at times she is present at the reunion and watches them embrace. When they finish embracing each other they often embrace her too, as the link. She helps them find ways to stay here. If they succeed in becoming citizens, then Rita is the bridge they pass over to their new identity.

"Immigration law!" Her grandfather, Sol, expected the worst when she started. "You'll see," he grumbled over the phone, wheezing long-distance. "You'll be always with those refugees, you'll wind up marrying one, you with your bleeding heart. And who knows where they come from, what they—"

"Enough already, Sol!" Sonia's rough voice in the background. "Enough!"

"Sometimes these people have to marry someone just to stay in this country," he explains to his granddaughter, the immigration lawyer. "They see a pretty young girl with a profession, what could be better?"

True enough. In three years Rita has had several tentative suggestions of marriage. But she tries to find those desperate souls a better way. She reminds them that they came here to be free, free, and that marriage to a stranger is no freedom. Besides, there is Sanjay.

Sanjay works all day in a laboratory, or la*bor*atory, as he calls it; he wants to cure hemophiliacs, bleeders. (Contrary to popular notion, hemophiliacs do not bleed more intensely than most people, only longer.) Sanjay knows almost all there is to know about genes and blood. Indeed, he has the exile's air of knowing all there is to know about everything. Yet he has been here for nearly thirty years, is a citizen, and, unlike Rita's jittery clients, seems very much at home. His face has taken on a West Coast transparency. His courtly speech is sprinkled with the local argot. Still, Rita suspects, even knowing all there is to know about her, he sees her as his entryway to the land of dreams. His bridge. His American girl.

*   *   *

Rita's present life is, in her grandfather's view, one of disobedience (like her nightmares), but as a small child she was quite obedient. She submitted when he found her costuming paper dolls in her bedroom on a Saturday afternoon and unhooked the scissors from her thumb and forefinger, reminding her that Jews do not cut on the Sabbath. Nor do they color in coloring books, trace pictures from magazines, turn on the lights, the toaster, the radio, or the television, use the phone, cook, sew, drive. . . . The way Sol explains it, they are defined by what they are forbidden. There are things they must not eat and not wear, not do and not utter. The most constricted people are the most holy, relieved from confronting the daily unknown with bare instinct, for happily, every conceivable pattern of human event and emotion was foreseen centuries ago and the script is at hand, in old books in an old tongue. She submitted. But she was allowed to read. *A Little Princess* was her favorite story, where the orphaned and hungry heroine is forced to live in a lonely freezing garret, until a kindly Indian gentleman feeds her and lights a fire in her room and finally rescues her altogether, restoring her to a life of abundance.

For the most holy people, the most holy season is fall, the most beautiful. Also the most allusive and most amenable to introspection, with its amber light, its sounds of leaves scuttling, brittle as death, on the pavement, its eerie chills at sundown, and its holidays calling for renewal, guilt, atonement, remembrance, hope, and pride, one after the other in breathless succession. It is the season to think over your past deeds and ask forgiveness of anyone you might have injured, for only after asking a fellow creature's forgiveness may you ask God's. God has a big book and keeps his accounts: Your fortunes in the year to come depend on your actions in the year just passed. (Karma, thinks Rita years later, when she knows Sanjay.) It is the season when Rita is required to get out of her jeans and beads and into a dress. Shoes instead of sneakers. Sweating great beads of boredom, resistance seeping from every pore to form a second skin beneath her proper clothing, she trails her grandfather to the synagogue to sit with the women in the balcony (so as not to distract the men) and listen to him sing the prayers in a language she cannot understand.

Her grandmother the atheist also conforms, sits in the women's balcony behind a curtain and fasts on the Day of Atonement, and this not merely out of obedience, like Rita. Sonia finds her identity in opposition. She conforms in order to assert her difference in the New World, as in the Old World others asserted it for her, in the form of ostracism and pogroms. But within the family's little conforming circle she has to assert her difference too, and so while her husband is out at the synagogue she fixes herself a forbidden glass of tea. Her wiry body moves quickly around the kitchen, as if charged with electrical current. Snickering like a child, she raises the steaming glass by the rim and drinks, immensely pleased with her mischief, her high cheekbones gleaming.

"You might as well have a sandwich while you're at it," says Rita, at eleven years old not yet required to fast, to choose between her grandparents, obedience in bed with defiance.

A sandwich would be going too far. They destroy the evidence, wash and dry the glass and spoon and put them away; luckily he doesn't count the tea bags, hardly the province of a holy man.

What is the province of a holy man? God, of course. Wrong. Rules. Sanjay could have told her that. His family's rules fill at least as many books. Rita's grandfather loves rules, constrictions, whatever narrows the broad path of life and disciplines the meandering spirit for its own good. The lust to submit is his ruling passion. It is part of the covenant with God: Obey all the rules and you will be safe. Sol takes this literally. He seeks out arcane rules to obey and seizes upon them, appropriates them with the obsessiveness of a Don Juan appropriating new women. Nor is that enough; his passion requires that others obey them too. His wife. His granddaughter. For the family is the pillar of society. The family is the society. And if a member disobeys, strays too far beyond the pillars, he becomes an outcast. At risk in the wide world, the world of the others. "Them."

So Rita rarely hears him speak of God. And Sonia mentions God with contempt, as one would speak of the meanest enemy, too mean even to contend with. "What God says I'm not interested in!" she shouts bitterly when Sol nags her back onto the little path of submission. "I'm interested in what people do right here on earth!" Alone together, Sonia and Rita never tire of cataloguing the discrepancies between God's reputation and his manifest deeds. They, obey in their hearts? It is to laugh. And laugh they do, showing their perfect teeth, as enduring as rocks. Of course they are women, their minds fixed on the specific. Perhaps they cannot grasp the broader scheme of things.

"What would be sins?" Rita asks her grandfather, thinking of Sonia's tea.

He pats his soft paunch thoughtfully with both hands. "Lying to your grandparents. Thinking wicked thoughts. Being unkind to people."

This sounds fairly mild. She tries to enumerate her greater sins but can think of none that any God worthy of the name would take notice of. With a new assassination almost yearly, the portraits of the dead promptly appearing on the walls at school, can God care that she listens to the Supremes on a Saturday afternoon, she and the radio muffled under a blanket? She asks her grandmother about sins but Sonia waves her arm dismissively, an arc of contempt scything the air. Rita infers that God, rather than mortals, has a lot to answer for, though she doesn't know what in particular is on her grandmother's mind besides the general wretchedness abounding. Poor people ride to Washington on mules. Long-haired students in Chicago get beaten by police. Rita passes the time in the balcony constructing cases against God on their behalf. Her father was a lawyer, she has managed to glean; she invokes his help. The cases are very good, watertight, with evidence starting from Abraham; no, Abel. But no matter what the jury decides, God remains. That is his nature, she gathers, to be there watching and judging, always alert for a misstep, but not helping.

*   *   *

Light is coming in at the window, a Pacific coast autumn light, creamy, soft-edged. As it slides up his face, Sanjay wakes, and Rita tells him about her bad dream, for she cannot shake it. She tells him how in the dream her father's father, the most obedient servant of his Lord, is taken, even so. How his obedience did not shield him in the end, and how she, by her disobedience rooted in a certain juxtaposition of genes, causes a shocking event, rivaling the one that convulsed the family twenty-six years ago.

"Heredity," says Sanjay sleepily, "doesn't work that way. You make too much of it." He has exchanged the faith in karma for the science of genetics. And he wants to help. He wants her to turn around and live facing front. Odd, since he comes from a country imprisoned in history, while she is the young West Coast lawyer. Sometimes it seems they have changed places.

"And don't you make much of it? Don't you tell me you get glimpses of your father's face in the mirror when you shave, but with a peeled, American expression? I feel my mother when I brush my hair. In the texture of the hair."

"That's different. You can inherit hair but not destinies."

He sounds so sure. . . . "I think in the dream he was trying to sing. Did I ever tell you that my grandfather used to sing in the synagogue?"

"I thought your mother was the singer."

"Her too. That was a different kind of song. He ran the store all week, but on Saturday mornings he was a cantor, he led the prayers. Then when I was about seventeen, he had some minor surgery in his throat and he never sang again."

"Why, what happened?"

"Nothing. He was afraid."

"Of what?"

"Well that's exactly it. Something cosmic. That his head might burst, I don't know. It was just too risky. The absurd thing was, he had the operation to restore his voice. We never heard him sing again. So what do you make of a man who loves to sing and sings for the glory of God, then refuses to sing out of fear?"

"In his heart he still sings. He sings, Safe, safe." Sanjay composes a little tune on the word.

Rita smiles. "I thought immigrants always sang, Free, free."

"Not always. We"—he means his brother and himself, who came here to be educated and returned home only to visit—"we sing, Away, away. New, new." He yawns, and then, in a lower key, "Guilt, guilt."

All the indigenous American tunes, thinks Rita. But she is still smiling. He has a way of making heavy things feel lighter.

He has a mild grace that buoys him through life. Maybe she should marry him after all. She is so malleable an American, she could become anyone with ease. And it would be a way to live; it would be safe, safe. She might even let her hair grow long and smooth it down with coconut oil, start frying wheat cakes and clarifying butter and stepping delicately down the hills of San Francisco as Sanjay's wife did, holding up her long skirts.

That was how Rita first saw them, the Indian gentleman and his wife. It was the day of her graduation from college, which her grandparents flew west to attend. Afterwards, she took them across the bay to San Francisco, to show them her new apartment. For she was staying on. Through a friend, she had found a summer job in a Spanish record store, and in the fall she would start law school.

While Sonia tore through the rooms like a high wind, Sol stood at the front window, holding the curtain to one side and peering out as though he were in a hostile country, a place you could get yourself killed. Though not much of a traveler, he had been here once before, briefly.

"Who are your neighbors?" he asks, gesturing with his chin.

"I don't know. Which ones?" Rita comes over to peer out too.

It is an Indian couple, the man tall and broad, with heavy eyebrows and longish hair, dressed impeccably, even a bit flam- boyantly, in a light gray suit. Rita likes the suit and likes his walk, stately, meditative, achieving a look that is both scholarly and debonair. By his side is a slight woman in a green and gold sari, holding his arm. Her head is lowered, so Rita can barely see her face. She holds the sari up skillfully, climbing the hill.

"I guess they're an Indian couple."

"Indians?" Her grandfather's voice rises. Bows and arrows?

"From India. You know, Gandhi, Nehru, no eating cows. That's what the women wear."

"I know what India is. I read the papers too, Rita. I'm not as ignorant as you think."

"Sorry, Papa."

"How do they live? Nice?"

She shrugs. "I guess so."

"Yes. They're not the same as the colored."

"Oh, Papa, don't start."

The Indian couple is moving unusually slowly, their heads cast down. They look like a devoted pair; they walk in step, rhythmically. As they turn into the front yard next door, to the left, he swings the gate open for her.

Much later, when Rita tells Sanjay about the first time she saw him, he says they might have been coming from the doctor; it was the month when his wife had some tests. The tests said yes, but it would probably not get really bad till the end.

It is strange, Rita thinks now, that she was with her grandfather when she first saw Sanjay.

*   *   *

A scene from one of Rita's silences: Her great-uncle Peter, her grandfather's twin brother, is a philanthropic dentist—he fills the cavities of Orthodox Jewish orphans for free. Also he checks Rita's teeth. Her grandmother drives her to his office for a checkup every six months, on a Sunday morning. The tiny waiting room is crowded with old people—fifty years old at least; where are the orphans of legend? They wait in the little waiting room which smells of dental supplies—sweet, medicinal, like wintergreen—until all the paying customers have had their turns, which may take an entire Sunday morning. Rita and Sonia share many qualities of temperament, notably the impatience gene. They wait with difficulty. Though they like to talk, they find no solace in the small talk that accompanies waiting. They leaf through magazines, they go to the superbly clean bathroom smelling of mouthwash, they pace the tiny waiting room. Sonia, unable to be confined, goes out to walk around the block. Rita cannot take such liberties since it's her mouth waiting to be examined, and her uncle might take a notion to sneak her in between the creaky patients. Her grandmother walks fast, round and round the block; Rita imagines her tense, bony body crackling like November twigs. Sonia's short auburn hair is alive in the breeze, and her fierce mind works on the fabric of the past, ripping stitches, patching.

At last it is Rita's turn. Her great-uncle, bald and moon-faced, rotund in his sparkling white jacket, round-collared like a priest's, beckons, the outstretched hand making a swift fluttering motion, giving the impression that she has been dilatory, that she has kept him waiting. He greets her using a Hebrew name that no one ever uses. She feels he is talking to some invisible person in the room. "What a pretty complexion," he says, in a way that suggests perhaps it is not, a consoling way. And, "What strong white teeth!" In a stage whisper, over her head: "She must get those from her mother."

"I have strong white teeth too," Sonia says with savage energy. "When have you ever had to fix anything in my mouth?"

Sonia dislikes her brother-in-law passionately. All the dislike she cannot expend on her husband she transfers to his twin brother. Peter and Sol are cautious people, supremely timid in the face of life. Yet they came to the New World as infants and know only by hearsay what they escaped. Sonia, who came later, remembers, and finds their timidities an indulgence. Her family are extravagant-tempered Russians whom Russians never accepted as such, which is why they journeyed so far. Genetically defiant people with hyperactive brains, willful, angry, ebullient. Their bones snap, the veins in their temples throb. There is nothing they cannot feel passionate about, and so they lavish huge and frightful energies on life and live long, propelled by their exuberant indignation. Rita is fascinated by them and bored by her grandfather's docile family. She sees the two sides of the family as opposing teams, opposing stances towards life. When she is older she sees her grandparents in an incessant game of running bases: they throw the ball back and forth—the ball is truth, how to live—and she, Rita, must run between them, pulled now to the safety of rules and traditions, now back to the thrills of defiance and pride.

Once she is in the funny chair, Peter gives her avuncular rides up and down, chattering affectionately, almost too affectionately, as if he is trying extra hard. There are whispered words with her grandmother, exchanges Rita doesn't grasp except that Sonia wants none of his proffered commiseration. "You can't trust one of them, not one," he mumbles. "That's the way it is, that's the way it will always be."

"Shh, shh," Sonia hushes him in disgust. "Just do her teeth, no speeches." Sonia always sticks up for her; with crackling Sonia she is utterly safe.

"Such beautiful dark hair." He does seem to like her, in the brief time he has available. Yet he calls her by the wrong name, which you do not do to someone you like. That's not who I am, Rita wants to cry out, but there is something peculiar and mysterious about who she is that keeps her silent, open-mouthed like an idiot. She sometimes gets glimmerings of losses below the surface, like sunken jewels that divers plunge and grope for in vain. They might be memories of a different climate, or the feel of an embrace, or a voice, feelings so fleeting and intangible she can hardly call them memories. But they have been with her since she can remember—wispy vapors of another way she might once have been, another mode of feeling the world, as believers in reincarnation sense their past lives.

That's not who I am, she wants to cry out, but she can offer no more, she knows nothing more, and anyway he is all frothing joviality and patter, while his hands nimbly prepare the instruments. Rita is enthralled by the rows of false teeth lined up on the cabinet, pink gums and ivory teeth, the many different shapes waiting like orphans to be adopted, for mouths to come by and take them in, ready to be pressed into service chewing and forming the dental consonants. Unspoken words and stories are hiding in the teeth.

"So. Are you going to play Queen Esther this year?"

"No." She rinses and spits. "The teacher said I should be Vashti."

"Well, Vashti is good too. She was very beautiful."

"She gets killed in the beginning. I was Vashti last year."

"Finished?" asks Sonia impatiently.

Fortunately Rita's teeth are excellent, she can be disposed

of in five minutes. Rocks, he says every time. She has rocks in her head. And he tells her that her teeth, like her grandmother's, will last a lifetime. Good news. Sharp and hard, they bite, they grip, grind, gnash, and clench. They make the words come out clear. Sonia grinds her teeth all night, Sol remarks at breakfast. Good, Rita thinks. They will be useful in times of stress. They will help her chew hard things and grind them down, make them fit for swallowing.

*   *   *

When Sanjay's wife died, Rita paid a neighborly call, as her grandfather taught her to do. Solomon was conscientious about visiting the bereaved. He would enter their houses with no greeting (that was the rule), seat himself in a corner, open a book, and pray as though he were alone in the room and the universe, which in a sense he was, for all around him people continued to speak, eat, and even make merry as survivors will.

The rules behind her, no book to guide her, Rita brings a rich, fruity cake to Sanjay and greets him. They have exchanged greetings on the street, she has inquired with concern about his wife, but she has never been in his house before. She notices he has some Indian things—a big brass tray, a lacquered vase with an array of peacock feathers, and several photos of Allahabad, his home town, a very holy place, he tells her, where two holy rivers meet. One photo shows masses of people, the tops of heads, mostly, bathing in a holy river banked by two fantastical buildings, castles out of a tale of chivalry. Otherwise it is a San Francisco kind of house—airy, with thriving plants and colorful pillows. It smells spicy.

They become friends. They go to an occasional movie, a restaurant. He asks her advice about relatives who need green cards. She asks if he can fix her dishwasher. She loves the way he moves, his great weight treading softly, the smooth sound of his voice and the way after all these years he keeps pronouncing certain words in the British fashion—"dance," "record," "laboratory"—his slow, very inquisitive eyes and hard mouth.

Finally, after several months of decorous behavior they meet by chance on the street one evening and get to talking. Something feels different. Ripe. His eyes and his speech are slower, more judicious than usual, almost ponderous. He asks her into his house and she smells the sharp spices. He gives her some stuffed chappattis his daughter brought over that morning; he insists on warming them in the oven first. Delicious. The bread is important; it is, she understands, part of the seduction. Standing very erect, shoulders squared, like a man about to deliver a speech, he says, "Well, Rita, I have never courted an American young woman before, so you'll have to forgive my . . . ineptness. But it seems time, to me. And you? Will you?" She nods. He looks so safe.

Upstairs, the furniture in the bedroom is weighty, built for the ages. It reminds her of the furniture in her grandparents' apartment. Married furniture. The first thing Sanjay does is turn his wife's photograph to the wall.

Rita lets herself be undressed. "Oh. Oh," he says, touching her. When he takes her in his arms she feels an immense relief —at last!—as if she has been freezing for years and suddenly a fur coat is thrown over her, the kind of coat shown in photos of Russian winters, and she realizes she has wanted him from the moment she saw him from the window three years ago, looking out with her grandfather. She can feel his immense relief too, but that, she imagines, is because he has not held anyone in his arms in months. Oh God, she hopes it will not be . . . like that.

No, he is in no hurry. He proves to know a lot about women. Maybe in a past incarnation he was a woman—she can almost believe it. Also, from the way he touches her, she feels how he must have loved his wife. She wonders if she feels like his wife, if maybe all women feel alike, after a certain point. In his arms, Rita forgets who she is. She could almost be his wife. And then she falls immediately asleep.

When she wakes, the bedside lamp is on and Sanjay is weeping into the pillow. He looks up and sees her watching. "I'm sorry. Forgive me." He stops abruptly.

Is this all she will ever be, a link to the beloved dead?

"Really, I'm terribly sorry, Rita. I thought you were sleeping."

"It's all right, Sanjay, it's all right." What else can she say?

She does not sleep much that night but watches him sleep. For hours, it seems. She has shielded herself so far, but now it envelops her like a shower of gold threads, of red powder, and she sees that love is the greatest defiance of all. She is afraid of it.

She has to leave early, go home to the other side of the wall and change, pick up her cap and gown. She is graduating from law school that very day. Sanjay says he wants to be there, so she gives him a ticket—she has them to spare since her grandparents are not flying out this time. Sol's heart is too irregular.

Just before she leaves to take her place in the line, he slips her a tiny candy wrapped in silver paper. "For luck."

She starts to unwrap it.

"No, no. You eat the paper too."

She trusts him infinitely. She eats the paper. Silver, sweet, delicious. Bits of it stick in her teeth, making the taste linger.

*   *   *

When he announces months later that he loves her and wants to marry her, that he has thought it over and waited to speak until he was quite sure, she takes the information skeptically.

"Why? Can't you believe that I loved her and now I love you?"

"I don't know."

"You must have loved other people. I don't think about them."

"But I haven't."

"Maybe, maybe not. You do love me, though," Sanjay says.

"I know. Must I see a problem in that, perhaps?" This is comical, she thinks, this interrogation. He can be so matter-of-fact, even imperious. There is a sliver of amusement in his eyes, too. Whatever he is, she loves.

"I never felt this before. I don't know what to make of it."

"Come now. You must have. American girls . . ."

"I was busy with other things."

"What things?"

She can't tell him how she spent her college years. It's too crazy. Not yet, anyway. So instead she says something hurtful. "You're too old for me."

He seems impervious, tilts his head carelessly. "That can't be helped. And anyway, you don't really mind."

It's true, she doesn't. Quite the contrary.

*   *   *

Rita and Sanjay find that their backgrounds have a number of things in common. A preponderance of rules for proper behavior is one, especially rules about not consorting—eating or sleeping—with members of another caste. This, like pioneers, they have both left behind. Arranged marriages is another. This one does not seem so far behind.

"So you never really knew her before you were married?"

"We knew each other, but not in the way that you mean. The families met several times. We spoke. It's not really so preposterous. The idea is that you come to love each other. We trust in proximity to breed love."

Rita frowns. He is still trusting.

"It sounds very unromantic, I know. But it doesn't exclude romance of a kind."

"Does it work? I mean, for most people?"

"Well, more than you'd expect. Some love each other with a goodwill kind of love. Some even have passionate love. But there are other ways to love besides those, more ways than are recognized here. You can love someone simply because she's yours, part of you. You've accepted each other and you don't question it. My parents were like that. Are still like that."

"And what about you? What kind of love was it?"

He closes his eyes. The pain of loss, regret? Or merely impatience. "Why do you keep asking? You know the answer."

She knows. The goodwill kind, the passionate kind, the

totally accepting kind. Often, those first three years, she saw them walking arm in arm down the street, their steps falling together in rhythm. Belonging.

"You were lucky. Did she know, the first night, what she was supposed to do?"

"Not precisely. She was a very sheltered girl."

"But you knew, I presume?"

Sanjay takes a deep breath and his face begins a little performance—his face has a great repertoire of expressions. His eyes roll, his forehead wrinkles, his lips curl. "What do you think?"

"Was she appalled?"

"No."

Rita would like to know, in graphic detail, exactly how Sanjay made it clear what was expected. She is not a voyeur by nature; rather, she is mystified by the transmutations of love—how indifference turns into love, love into indifference and even worse. But it is useless to ask. He doesn't tell. It must be too precious. Yes, because he does love to tell stories about his parents, his brothers and sisters and cousins. She has heard comic stories about bicycles capsized in the mud and a flirtatious widowed aunt, stories of school pranks and festival antics, and painful stories about a baby sister who died of diphtheria on the day Gandhi was shot. But no stories about his wife.

"I know what you're thinking. But people can love more than once, Rita. After all . . ."

"I know, I know." Yet she knows only in the abstract. She feels generally ignorant on the subject. She thinks that what she saw, growing up, was not love but a species of belonging.

Her grandparents' marriage took place in 1927 and was also arranged, though not as strictly as Sanjay's. The couple was introduced; they took several walks together over the Brooklyn Bridge; they went to a few movies and even to an opera, *Madame Butterfly*. This was all quite ordinary. But the wedding itself was extraordinary. The father of the groom had collapsed and died two days before. No matter; the rules say ceremonies must take place as scheduled, like Broadway shows. And the bride did not refuse; she had not yet learned how. But she had her doubts, surely, Rita thinks. For it is hard to imagine the Sonia she knows being so compliant. Surely she must have been astounded, felt that such a beginning did not augur well and maybe she had better pull out before it was too late? But it was already too late.

"Can you picture that wedding?" she queries Sanjay.

"Well, quiet, I'd imagine. Very quiet."

No doubt. A dearth of dancing, the musicians laboring to rouse an unappreciative crowd. Rita's various aunts and uncles, disguised as young people, gathered around linen-covered tables, eating sweetbreads and drinking sweet wine while salt streams down their faces. The children fretful and confused—no one is urging delicacies on them or swinging them through the air. Her own father not yet an outcast, not even born, a gleam, as they say, in his father's very gleaming eye. As her grandparents toast their life together, the groom weeps under the harshness of his own discipline. He can barely drink and cannot eat. He does not need to eat. Self-pity and self-satisfaction are his feast—for this ordeal will make him a better person, bring him favor in the eyes of his God. What kind of eyes could they be?

Very quickly the couple has an indissoluble connection, a son. Sonia's first decade of marriage is a depression, then comes the war.

Throughout their married life there are many changes in the world. The maps of Europe, Africa, and Asia change drastically. There are immense shifts of population, new technologies, cures for diseases; wonders and horrors as usual. The twentieth century. But—and she has to admire his tenacity— Rita's grandfather's world remains the world he grew up in, a small world left over from the youth of the century, a bit cramped and crowded, like a room to which new pieces are added but from which nothing is ever thrown away, a thoroughly benign and safe world, according to his stories—for he is, yes, a storyteller, with a magnetic eye, bluest of blues, and a magnetic voice.

"Our house was the place where all immigrants stopped

first," he says. "And no matter how crowded we were, when they opened the door, whoever came in I welcomed them with open arms. I was only a child. But I felt the call of blood."

Open arms. He lives, Rita comes to understand, by appropriation. He takes in, processes, categorizes, labels, and provides a commentary. To have any act unexplained or unexcused, anyone left out of the scheme, can put the world in an imbalanced state, as taunting and intolerable as an unresolved chord in his singer's ear.

So he narrates the fortunes of each arrival, one by one: loves, travels, business ventures, progeny. And in his stories—long, highly dramatized, and gripping—never a harsh word is spoken between sister and brother, parent and child, husband and wife, only happy grateful immigrants making good in the promised land, learning the customs and the lingo. He has an instinctive way of skimming over pain or crisis, alighting mostly on moments of epiphany when generosity and breadth of spirit are revealed, moments when virtue triumphs over self-interest. What everyone fled from is never mentioned above a whisper, and never at all in the presence of "them," the others, the ones who can never be trusted, who pursue and destroy. The moral is always the same: The family is the pillar of society. There are no distinctions when it comes to family. A cousin? "Like my own brother!" (A granddaughter? "Like my own daughter!") And when a member strays beyond the pillars he becomes an outcast. Formerly appropriated, now vomited up.

Since Sol's stories extol righteousness, Rita asks why, then, he and his brother don't go out, this minute, and work for civil rights and for an end to the war in Vietnam. If they fled from the draft on one continent, shouldn't they protest it on another? Sol listens because she is a clever speaker, and when she becomes too annoying he waves her away like a mosquito. Her uncle the dentist points out that all the boys in the immediate neighborhood are going to college, not Asia. Once, her great-aunt, the dentist's wife, loses patience. "Protest, protest!" she mocks, eyeing Rita as she would a stranger who has jumped the line at the bakery. "She should be glad she has a roof over her head."

What could it mean? Rita knows her parents are . . . well . . . dead, it must be. The subject is taboo. It is as if she is Sol's and Sonia's child. This is her roof, isn't it? Her grandfather tells his sister-in-law to shut her big mouth. Sonia goes further and throws her out of the house, and the incident is closed. Everyone goes to bed with a headache.

Undaunted, at fourteen years old Rita thinks she too can appropriate the world, make it over to fit her vision. Not all immigrants are so well assimilated, she finds out. She feels for those beyond the pillars, maybe because she is darker than any Jew she knows and has never had a chance to play Queen Esther. With an adolescent's passion to convert, she wants her grandfather to feel for them too, and to agree that breadth of spirit does not mean obeying the most rules but scorning them all, except for the rules of the heart. She wants him to thrill to the uneven rhythms of heroic outcasts, anarchists: "I might have lived out my life talking at street corners, to scorning men. I might have died unmarked, unknown, a failure. Now we are not a failure. This is our career and our triumph. Never in our full life could we hope to do so much work for tolerance, for justice, for man's understanding of man as we do now by accident. Our words—our lives—our pains—nothing! The taking of our lives—lives of a good shoemaker and a poor fish-peddler—all! That last moment belongs to us—that agony is our triumph!" She finds this in a book about famous trials of the century, and shivers with passion.

But Solomon hears it impassively, and in response, launches into one of his own speeches—clears his throat and prepares his oratorical voice. "Ours, Rita, is a religion of ethics. A man's devotion to God is shown in how he treats his fellow man, beginning with his own—his children, his grandchildren"—he smiles fondly, justly pleased with himself on this score—"his neighbors." (Sonia puts down the skirt she is hemming, tosses aside her glasses and stalks out of the room.) "In other words, *mamaleh*, charity begins at home."

Very well, and where is home? Everywhere, she lectures him in turn. He calls her a bleeding heart. Whatever he cannot appropriate, whatever refuses to go down and be assimilated— outsiders, heinous deeds, gross improprieties—he ignores, which means it ceases to exist.

He has been unable to appropriate, for instance, his son's marriage to a Mexican immigrant, which took place in far-off San Francisco, California, in 1955. This Rita learns through piecing together family whispers. If Sol had had his way, ostracism—the tool of his enemies—would not have sufficed; according to the rules, his son would have been interred in absentia and mourned for a week, and neighbors would have visited him and Sonia while they sat on wooden boxes, wearing bedroom slippers, with the mirrors in the house covered by bed sheets. But he didn't have his way. Sonia refused to do it. It was the beginning of her refusals.

That her mother was Mexican is one of four or five facts Rita knows about her. Her name was Carmen. She was a singer—strangely enough, like Rita's grandfather, but singing a different kind of song. Rita would like to know what kind of love her parents had and how they came to marry, but she never will. It was certainly not arranged.

*   *   *

Rita's dream foresees her grandfather's funeral because he is not well, Sanjay suggests reasonably. Perhaps, she shrugs. She is not really seeking explanations. It is certainly true that Sol's fears have caught up with him, and that there are not enough rules to cover them adequately. Once sturdy, he has become in old age what he calls "nervous." He sees death coming, and his nervous system is in a twit. He has spells of weakness, shortness of breath, panic; all activities have to be gauged in advance as to how taxing they will be and the chance of mishaps. He monitors his vital signs with loving care, as solicitous of himself as a mother. The path has narrowed till on the vast new continent there is hardly room to place one foot in front of the other. Safe, safe. Rita hates the way he lives. She wants him to get up and do something—sing, pray, sell sports-wear, anything but pave the way for death, be the advance man.

But for safety he must keep himself as confined as possible, especially since Rita and Sonia have slipped out of his control. He would not be so "nervous," he claims, if he could oversee what they were doing at all times. Of course, this cannot be. Rita is far away, doing God knows what and with whom, and Sonia has to manage the store. Sonia began to elude him long ago anyhow. For the first three decades of their marriage she obeyed, and then something happened. It was as if she had sealed up her disobedience the way pioneer women canned fruits and vegetables for a later season, and then she broke it out in abundance, jar after jar releasing its briny fumes. Years ago, members of the congregation reported that they saw the cantor's wife, her granddaughter beside her, driving his car on the Sabbath, a cigarette in her invincible teeth! Where could they be going? There was even talk of replacing him, but it came to nothing—they pitied him, first his great tragedy with his son and now unable to control his family.

Sonia, once tame, has reverted to the ways of her family. Anarchists, though not the grand kind. No, they fit very well into the elastic New World. Except that they argue passionately with the clerks of bureaucracies, they walk on the grass, they refuse to wait on lines, they smoke in nonsmoking areas, they open doors labeled authorized personnel only, they zip through traffic jams on the shoulders of roads or in lanes blocked off by orange stanchions. It is part of their passion, their brand of civil disobedience. Sol is horrified and Rita is amused, even though these are gestures only, to show they will not take the law from anyone, for they know who the lawgivers are. Clay like all the rest. They obey what they like, laws unto themselves. They are in fact (some of them, at any rate) lawyers. They came here in installments, three boys and three girls from Kiev. The girls became seamstresses, the boys lawyers. The girls went to facto-ries, to sit on a cushion and sew a fine seam, while the boys were sent to school—the New World not so unlike the Old in that regard.

Three dressmakers make three lawyers: stitch, stitch. The dressmakers live in small apartments in Jewish ghettos with their husbands, small businessmen like Rita's grandfather, while their brothers prosper in modern assimilated suburbs. Then in 1959, the only child—a son—of one of the girls is stabbed to death in far-off San Francisco, California. That is truly lawless. The family, convulsed, will grieve in unison. That is not the kind of lawlessness, the kind of anarchy they intended, no, never, never! His mother will stop recognizing the world, any world, New, Old, all the same to her.

The family fears she may never return to the realm of the living. Days go by while she sits on a hard kitchen chair with her eyes fixed on nothing. She will not change her clothing or eat or sleep. When spoken to she will not respond, or else shakes her head, or at the most says, "Not now." It seems she is waiting for something, someone. Perhaps she is remembering how she refused to mourn her son when he married out of his faith—was it for this, so she could mourn him now?

Meanwhile her husband, accompanied by his twin brother the dentist, will fly out to the unknown western territories to settle his son's affairs and see that justice is done—a most adventurous trip, which he would not undertake for any other reason, but shock has made him a father again. The former outcast as a corpse is unobjectionable. And what, of all things, will he discover in the shadow of the Golden Gate but a child! Just two years old. If he had known, maybe . . . The child has been staying with her maternal uncle and his wife (her mother being in no condition to take care of her), but really, it is very difficult. They own a bar, a nightclub, actually—he is the bartender, his wife the waitress. (And there Rita's mother sang her Spanish songs. A vision in sequins? A floozy? She will never know.) No place for a baby. Without a moment's hesitation, Solomon transcends himself (possibly for the baby's blue eyes, which reflect his own), to perform the one daring act of his life—he takes her back. He takes her in. It is an act that could speak best for itself, but he cannot resist the ready phrase, a Jewish Polonius.

"It was the call of blood," he explains to Sonia as he enters carrying the child on one arm, suitcase and briefcase dangling from the other. She stares at him in the stupor that has become her mode of existence. Nothing surprises her. "Here," he says more naturally, holding out his burden like an offering. "Better take her to the bathroom. Her name is Rita." He thrusts her at Sonia. "Take a look at her eyes. Like skies."

A good name, Rita. It can derive from either set of genes. And there are plenty of dark Jews, her grandfather will declaim, presenting her to the family and the neighbors, the little bilingual prodigy. Yemenites. Ethiopians. The sons of Ham. Anyway, she is not all that dark. Some regular Jews are swarthy. Anyway, there she is, and her grandmother takes her to the bathroom, feeds her, clothes her, and lo, a miracle sprung from tragedy, Sonia returns to life like Sarah in Genesis, fertilized in old age. Soon the neighborhood women start coming back to the house for fittings. They stand stiffly, only their mouths moving, as she pins folds of fabric around them, the pins stuck in her tough teeth. Rita plays with dolls at their feet, and not all her dolls are blonde. One is quite dark, with glossy black hair—Sonia understands the demands of a pluralistic society. That doll is not Rita's best baby, however. Her best baby is a blue-eyed blonde she calls Nita, to rhyme. The clients fuss over her, how cute, how bright, congratulate her grandmother on this unexpected boon, but their tone is very odd, not utterly pure. Ambiguous, like Rita.

For Sonia, though, there is no ambiguity. She accepts their goodwill with nonchalance—the pins in her mouth make it hard to speak in any case—and in their presence ignores Rita. When they leave she clasps her close, then talks, talks, low and fast like someone who has saved up words over a lifetime. She talks as if she is talking to herself—much of it a small child can hardly understand. So many things that she thinks and feels, but not the one thing. Of Rita's parents she never speaks, but she returns to life, and best of all, learns to drive. She neglects the housework that exasperates her, and together they breeze through the tangled city like tourists. Even when Rita is a big schoolgirl, she will wait for her and greet her at the door at three-fifteen: "Let's take a ride, okay?"

They ride through exotic neighborhoods of Greeks, Asians, blacks, Hispanics, Russians—there they eat pirogen and caviar and borscht. A passionately discontented woman, angular and veiny, Sonia is most content at the wheel of the dark green Pontiac. A born voyager. Short, straight-backed, she sits on a pillow and stretches her neck like a swan to peruse the traffic. Her driving style is aggressive, arrogant, anarchic. And Rita by her side is her natural passenger. Nothing can shock or frighten her, so thoroughly does she trust her grandmother, so closely are they twined, having accepted each other on first sight with no questions asked, like Sanjay's parents—neither the U-turns in tunnels nor the sprinting across intersections nor the sparring with buses and trucks. Sonia is omnipotent, fearless. Queen of the Road. Defying the rules about the Sabbath, she takes Rita to, of all places, the beach, where in all kinds of weather they wet their feet in the surf and build sand castles and Sonia tells stories—not morality tales like Sol's but true stories without morals—of what lies across the openness of the Atlantic, and she tells Rita that they came here to be free, free.

Now Rita longs for those forbidden afternoons at the edge of the Atlantic. Like a child, she would like to incorporate her grandmother, swallow her, as her grandfather lived by appropriating. Appropriation is the tactic of the lost and the scared. Oh, if only Rita could swallow her whole, if only she would go down, she could have Sonia forever with her. Safe at last. Then she would never clutch her heart and die as in the nightmare, leaving Rita standing alone, severed.

*   *   *

While Sanjay and Rita are watching a Fred Astaire and Ginger Rogers movie on television one evening, her phone rings. Rita speaks to her friend who still works in the Spanish record store in the Mission district. When she hangs up she says, "I've just been invited to a wedding. Rosalia's brother Luis. Would you like to come?"

"I never knew you could speak Spanish like that." They have been lovers for almost a year.

"Oh. Well, I need it, you know, for my clients."

"But you speak it like a native. I thought you were only two years old . . ."

"I learned when I was in college. Do you want to go to the wedding? It'll be fun. Lots of music and dancing."

"Sure."

She sits down and touches his hand. "I used to go out with her brother, years ago. He's very nice. Gentle, you know, like Rosalia. I'm glad he's getting married."

"You never mentioned it before."

"Well, it was nothing, really. We were kids. There's no way it should bother you."

"It doesn't. Only I sometimes realize I know so little about you. You tell me so little."

Sanjay develops an interest in her past loves. Like her curiosity about his wife, his is not lascivious in nature. Rather, he wants coherent social history. What has her life been all about? And generically, what are young American women's lives all about? a question that has never occupied him before.

She is not a typical case, Rita tries to explain. But it's a matter of optics, of the precision of the lens. To a fifty-year-old naturalized Indian widower, she is representative enough. He wants his American girl, Rita thinks. And he wants the real thing.

"Did you ever sleep with any of your clients?"

"No! Anyway, by the time I had clients I already knew you."

"Well, what about at law school?"

"One student." She grins, teasing. "One professor."

"A professor!"

"Is there any more paratha?"

Sanjay reaches for the plate on the floor. "Yes, but they're cold by now."

All during these absurd conversations they eat his daughter's food. Rita feels funny about that, but Sanjay says nonsense, his daughter made it to be enjoyed. Food is for whoever is hungry.

"I don't mind them cold. Thanks. You'll be relieved to know I wasn't in his class at the time."

"But a law professor. A jurist! He must have been so much older."

"He was seven years older, Sanjay. What about you?"

"I may be old, but at least I'm pure!" He laughs loud belly laughs. His whole body shakes. The bed shakes. Rita feels safe, wrapped up warm in his laughter. He is so domesticated, so easy to entertain. Pure: he says he never knew any women besides his wife. Before he was married, two prostitutes. They don't count.

"We'd better start at the beginning. What about in college?"

"This is getting very silly. Stop."

"Aha! Now we're getting somewhere."

"Just Luis, for a while."

"Why a Chicano?"

"Why not? Now stop. Really. It's annoying."

"Because there's something you're not telling me. Why won't you marry me? You're footloose. Then you'd know where you belong."

The Indian gentleman next door wants to rescue the poor orphan girl, give her food and warm clothes and light a fire in her garret. And she would not be cast out if she married him, as her father was. It's thirty years later. And it's Rita. What can you expect? They are prepared for almost anything from her. They believe in nature, not nurture, and she believes with them.

But she has never told anyone. She shakes her head.

"Is it terrible?" Sanjay asks. He is not fooling around anymore. She sees his age in the set of his face. His lips are parted. His cheeks are sagging in a kind of resigned expectation.

"Yes."

He hands her more stuffed bread. "Well, eat something while you tell me, then." To her surprise, his eyes, however old and sympathetic, have turned lustful. He is waiting to hear about a frenzied, tragic love affair. Rita stares right into them as she speaks.

*   *   *

She was seventeen. There was talk in the house about where she would be sent to college. Oh, how she kept them young, kept them abreast of things. She said to her grandmother in the kitchen, making the fish for Friday night, "You have to tell me now. Or I'll go away forever, I swear it."

"Big shot!" Sonia says, her fingers plunged deep in the bowl of chopped fish. "Where will you go? And with what?"

"There's always a way for a girl to make a living, Grandma. This is 1974, after all," and she smirks brazenly. "I know plenty of places I can stay."

A look of doom streaks over Sonia's face, and it is not so much prostitution she is thinking of as certain types of irregular living conditions: dope fiends, drifters, hippies, pads. Rita is bad enough already, with her ideas, her gypsy clothes, her unexplained forays into Manhattan, her odd-looking inky newspapers, the closely typed petitions she brings home indefatigably for them to sign; but at least she sleeps in her bed every night and takes showers. . . . At the same time, the vision of such irregularity holds a fascination for her grandmother, Rita can tell. She sees enticement seasoning the horror in her eyes, orange flecks against the green. Sonia might have tried it herself if she hadn't been so tired, sewing in the factory. Sometimes she even signs the petitions, after Sol goes to bed.

"You're not going anywhere," Sonia says confidently, blinking away her enticement, slapping the fish into ovals, and she shoves the bowl in Rita's direction for help. "Just to college like all your cousins."

"But I'm not the same as them. I have a right to know what I am, don't I? All these years you would never answer me. But I'm not a child anymore. It's my life."

There is something different, this time, in the way she says it, or maybe Sonia is simply worn down—Sol will be going to the hospital for his throat operation very soon; there have been doctors' appointments, consultations; he lays down the law in an ever hoarser voice. "You can't ask this of me!" she groans, but they both understand she means the opposite. Rita waits, her hands growing cold in the bowl of fish. She forms an oval and places it in the baking pan.

"They were separated. They never could get along. I knew. I used to speak to him all the time. No one could stop me from using the phone." She looks at Rita curiously. "I even knew about you."

"What about me?"

"That they had you! But I didn't tell him. That's what he wanted, not to know anything. Like he was dead. So let him not know, I thought." Sonia sits silent, not moving, a hostile witness in the box.

"So?"

She sighs as though she had hoped for a reprieve, that this much would be enough. "So he went over there to get something. They had an argument."

"And?"

She wipes her hands carefully on a dish towel. Then she takes the towel and holds it up to her face, covering her face. Her words come muffled through the towel. "She stabbed him."

"She what?"

"With a knife." She weeps behind the towel.

Rita is weirdly calm. Of all the scenes she had invented, never anything like this. Much more romantic, her visions were. Lost at sea. Activists kidnapped by the Klan. Wasting disease. Cult suicide. Yes, her nights have been busy, but all wrong. "I don't believe it."

"Don't, then. You asked. You pestered me for years."

"It's not possible. He must have been stronger than her."

"But he didn't have the knife," she wails. "Oh, my baby." Shoulders heaving, towel over her face.

Suddenly Rita cannot bear that towel anymore and snatches it away. Her grandmother's hollowed face is wet and blotched and smells of fish. "No. That can't be the whole story. He must have attacked her first."

Sonia gives the maddest laugh, a witch's cackle. "He? The gentlest boy who ever breathed?"

Rita could almost laugh too. Their child, gentle! But she also knows they do not attack. A picture is coming into focus, a kitchen, a hysterical woman who looks like an older version of herself, waving a bread knife; a pale man trying to wrest it from her. But she's too quick, too fierce. . . . Oh God, already she's becoming a type, a caricature. Leave her be. Leave that room altogether, before it gets bloody. . . . What about the baby . . . ? The baby is in another room, mercifully sleeping, yes. Go back, try again, try it in the living room. The scene has endless possibilities, bloody ones, Rita could labor over it for years. Give up the rest of her life to screening it every possible way: He said . . . No, she said . . . She grabbed . . . No, he . . .

"Wasn't there a trial? Didn't the facts come out at the trial? I bet she was a battered wife." Yes, lately even juries have learned to sympathize. Her poor mother, black and blue? Sonia looks baffled—this is beyond her imaginings. "I'll find out the truth," Rita shouts. "I'll visit her in jail." Where she languishes, thinking only of her lost baby.

"She's not in jail."

"No?"

"Finished. Six years and out. Good behavior! Rita, everyone said it, even her brother, what kind of woman she was, how she treated him so terrible. He was a good man, the brother. He wrote us a letter about . . . I felt sorry for him."

The outrage. She killed Rita's gentle father and she walks the streets free. "She never looked for me?" Now, now, she feels tears. This is the real outrage. Sonia feels it too.

"We wouldn't have given you up anyway. You were my reason to go on living. Two years I waited to see you." She covers her face again, this time with her hand and only for an instant. "And then I got you for good." As she gazes at Rita, her brow, for once, is calm. "You're just like him."

Me! thinks Rita, with my murderer's face? It must be a torment to have me around, reminding everyone. And what is just like him? They never say. Now more than ever she wants so badly to see him, it is almost like a sexual longing—she will die, just shrink and evaporate, if she cannot see him, touch him. She does not recognize the feeling till much later, though, when she knows Sanjay.

("When I know you," she says. "When I know you.")

For her mother Rita does not long—she feels she has her already, in her bones, her blood, the coarseness of her hair. In some essential, inescapable way, she carries her around.

"Why did they get married?" she whispers to Sonia. Why does anyone?

"Ha!" Sonia is recovered now, is getting back to her work. She must know these spasms of grief intimately after so many years, the way people know their attacks of epilepsy or asthma—the shape of their parabolas, and the intensity. She must have learned how to assimilate them into her days and proceed. It strikes Rita that she has never seen her grandmother idle. From dawn onwards Sonia scurries about, shopping, cooking, sewing, driving. Then at ten o'clock she falls exhausted into her old stuffed chair in the living room to read novels under a solitary lamp, while Sol calls every ten minutes, "Come to bed already!"

"Why did they have me?"

"Come on with the fish, Rita. It'll be midnight at this rate before we eat."

There is only one place she wants to go to college: Berkeley. Her grandfather is sure it is because they have the most hippies there. Her grandmother knows better, but in the end Rita gets her way. They are old and weary, no match for her in her new wisdom. For what scope and vision she suddenly possesses! Now she understands why her grandfather cleaves to the rules and her grandmother cleaves to him, all the while raging against God and driving like a maniac. She understands why the family, those stolidly decent people, look at her with a blend of pity and suspicion—it's not the color she is, no, it's that at any moment she may show her true colors. . . . She understands so much, it feels at night as if her head will burst with understanding and with blood. Only the one thing she wants to understand she doesn't.

She will find her and make her tell how it was. How to think about it. Until she knows, between her and the rest of the world is a wall of blood, ever fresh, never clotting, and she will never cross it into a life.

Her mother must have been a Catholic; as a girl she must have knelt and confessed to puny childish sins—lying, being unkind, thinking wicked thoughts. Maybe the Christ in her village church dripped with crimson paint and so she got used to spilled blood, it didn't seem alien and horrifying. It doesn't to Sanjay; he is used to handling it, but what does it tell him?

("Stop torturing yourself. It's only a physical substance, a liquid. It carries things, but not the kinds of things you mean. Don't tell me I traveled halfway across the world to find a mystic."

He's getting to sound like a Jew, thinks Rita. They are changing places.)

When she goes away to school her grandparents are afraid she will become a hippie, a druggie, but instead she spends her free time in San Francisco, the Mission district, where the Mexicans and Chicanos live, looking and waiting. A deranged sort of looking—she doesn't really want to find. She wants to be found. She learns Spanish—relearns—and it nestles lovingly in her mouth. Her tongue wraps around the syllables like a lover returning from exile to embrace his beloved, feeling the familiar contours. People say she sounds like a native speaker. She learns it so she can ask around for her, but she never asks. She doesn't even know her mother's name. Carmen, yes, but not her last name. Useless to ask for her own last name. Her mother does not seem one of the family. She would not have kept it.

("How did you expect to find her? What did you think you were doing?" Sanjay is incredulous. The Rita he knows is so sane, so sensible, aside from the nightmares. So presentable. It would be his pleasure to bring her home to meet his family, once they had gotten used to the idea of a half-Jewish, half-Mexican American lawyer twenty-two years younger.)

What did she think she was doing? Wandering around the Mission looking for a woman who looked like her, who would be looking in turn for a girl like Rita. Only the woman isn't looking. She has never looked. Luncheonettes, candy stores, bars—Rita can't get to like the food she buys as her excuse for being there, heavy and beany, maybe because for her it is the food of despair. She reads the names of singers on posters outside cafés, she reads the personal ads in newspapers, she even studies the names alongside doorbells in dingy, flaking old buildings. Crazy, she knows it. No explanation or story could change the fact. Like God in the trials she staged as a child, it remains: One lives having killed the other. It would be the same fact if the roles were reversed.

Nothing ever happens except some men try to pick her up, and once her pocket is picked in a movie line, and she makes friends with a girl who works in a record store and goes out with her brother for a few months. Rita is drawn by the easy friendliness of the family. She sees a life there that she might retreat into, but she would have to tell so many lies, and even so she would never fit in, never feel quite right. By what right is she anywhere, she the most contingent of contingencies, a superfluous mystery? So she breaks it off. And with that, the quest breaks off as well. Enough. She is worn out, like a soldier after battle, like a battleground in the night. For a month, over Christmas vacation of her junior year, she goes home to do nothing but sleep, grinding her teeth.

When Sonia asks anxiously what she plans to do after college, she says she will apply to law school. Because she is tired of her obsessions, tired of the parents she can't remember and who have left her this hard inheritance to swallow, tired of breaking her teeth on it. However hard she gnaws, the mystery won't crack. World without end, she is two years old, and in the next room is some kind of dreadful racket going on that will not let her sleep, some kind of screeching not at all like the singing she is used to, and maybe it is all a bad dream, but the next thing she knows she is in an airplane with two strange men who are interchangeable and who weep, and it is a miserable trip, she wets her pants, she throws up.

"Rita, Rita." Sanjay takes her in his arms. "Lie down and rest. Give it up."

Lying there, Rita wonders once again who she would be had she been left with her aunt and uncle in the bar. Maybe then her mother would have rushed to her when she got out of jail, like a doe flying to her fawn, and sheltered her and told her . . . everything. Or would she have done as the mother eel, who flees to the other end of the world and leaves its young behind, groping in slime? Maybe she could have become a nightclub singer too? But she has no voice—she would probably work in a store like Rosalia. Or go off to New York to search for her father's family, who would appear exotic and a little alluring. She might speak English with a rippling musical accent and move and dress and feel about the world in a different way. She could be almost anyone, and anywhere. Even now, there are times when she thinks of her name and who it stands for, and it feels like looking in a mirror and seeing a blank sheet, the sheet covering a mirror in a house of the bereaved. But she is this, and here, this person in Sanjay's arms.

She thought he would be horrified, repelled by her. Instead he has fallen asleep holding her, his arm draped across her middle like a sash. She watches him sleep for a while, then gets up and tiptoes around the bedroom. She takes a good look at the photograph of his wife. Yes, there is a certain resemblance. The result of nature, history, the migrations of people, and love.

It is strange that with all the hours she has spent in this bedroom she has never poked around. She opens the dresser drawers, one after another, but all she sees are Sanjay's socks and underwear and handkerchiefs neatly and predictably folded. Then, on a shelf in the closet she finds a pile of saris, also neatly folded, all colors, generous, deep colors, gold threads running through the fabrics. She chooses a red one, the bridal color. But she can't figure out how to get it on right. It is fun, this dressing up; she did it as a child. Vashti. Finally she gets the sari on in a makeshift fashion, not the way Sanjay's wife used to wear it. In the bottom drawer of the night table she finds little jars of powders—red, amber, green, blue—and she plays with them, dabs them on her hands, puts some green on her eyelids. She has seen women with a spot of red in the center of the forehead, but she is not sure what it means, maybe a symbol of Hindu caste or rank; she doesn't dare do it. She appraises herself in the mirror. Queen Esther, at last. Behind her in the mirror she sees Sanjay roll over and open his eyes. He blinks and the color drains away, leaving him yellowish.

"Rita? What are you doing?"

"How do I look?"

"That's not how it goes. Don't, anyway. Take it off. It's not right."

She steps to the edge of the bed, presenting herself. "Fix it. You must know how it goes. You must have seen it done a million times."

"I don't. Do you know how to tie a tie?"

She tries to dab some red powder on him, but he moves out of reach. He won't play. "Please, Rita. Stop."

She yanks off the red sari, the bridal color, rolls it into a ball, and weeps into it.

"But I love you," he protests, a frightening look of middle-aged acceptance on his face. He does not show any shock at what she has told him—that is what is frightening. Will time do that to her too, and then what will she have left? "I do, Rita." If she didn't know him, his smile might seem simpleminded. "You don't have to masquerade for me to love you."

But she cannot believe it. It costs so much.

The Subversive Divorce

They had expected to stay married, that is, to live in a plague-ridden land uninfected, immune to the prevailing currents. In their early youth, divorce had been a germ confined to movie stars and misfits, and over the years marriage, like a layer of fuzzy insulation, had kept them wrapped in that safe climate. Till from their own involuntary clawing the insulation grew frayed, and let in the tainted air.

The trouble was a mutual and consistent failure to say or do the right thing at the right time. It was a failure, they recognized in less feverish moments, springing from the premise of marriage itself, which licensed the expectation that each would say and do the right thing in all seasons. In bouts of hoarse shouting and tears, the air between them whipped by gusts of words, they tried to transform each other into more fitting people, without the slightest effect, save that they came to take a perverse pleasure in thwarting expectation.

Then would come a truce. They would recklessly reveal the ingredients of an ideal mate like chefs revealing a secret recipe, and each one would try to cook it up out of the provisions at hand, would try even to procure the absent ingredients from the air. But like inept loaves, their efforts fell flat; like cuts of meat, they were overdone or underdone, with sauces too thick or too thin. When they served these failed dishes there were stinging scenes of reproach. By the end, even if one of them did happen by instinct or accident to say or do the right thing at the right time, the thing was unacceptable, coming as it did from someone already proven to be wrong.

The words of reproach were made more terrible by their banality. For in a process of verbal erosion, theirs became a primitive language, a once-advanced civilization reduced to scratching stick figures, rock scraping rock. I can't take this anymore, it's ruining me, how did I get into such a mess. If one of the teen-aged twins was around, the words would be hissed through teeth scored by nighttime grinding. Go, then, go. I'm not keeping you.

Despite the evident meanings of the words, married life would continue: dinners, children, jobs, recreation, domestic maintenance, and even making love as usual. They liked each other; what they loathed was the distortion of identity marriage produced, marriage so public and powerful, marriage imposing its rites, grinding away the personal in the service of an inferred higher good. Making love by its nature does not permit very much distortion of identity, yet insofar as they were simultaneously married and making love, a certain element of distortion, of institutional service, crept in.

Then one evening when both their son and their daughter were out, leaving them to rant unrestrained, at the instant that he shouted, I can't take this anymore, and she responded, Go, then, go, she realized that this time she meant it. Why right then is a mystery, the pretext being no more virulent than most. She knew only that if she consented to mean what she said, she would never again need to take part in this fevered dialogue.

They both quieted, a welcome hush like the sudden cessation of a truck grinding garbage just outside the window. They had been standing, the better to rage; they sat down to gaze at each other across a coffee table like harmless, relieved strangers who have rushed to the same sheltered doorway in a downpour. Okay, okay, he said in an astonished calm.

Divorce, they well knew, began with physical separation. But she had never, even in the most noxious of spells, felt she had the right to uproot him from his family, nor had he any more wished to be so uprooted. And certainly she could never leave her children. No more could he, but . . . a mother is a mother, he conceded in this polite conversation of strangers in a doorway.

Look around, she said. There's no hurry, now that we've decided. And after a pause, feeling an embryonic wifely panic, added, Meanwhile, we might as well keep our system running as usual. To avoid total disorder?

The domestic system, aspiring to justice, had been meticulously and with great boredom worked out during the era of working such things out. It was not, to her, a thing to be tossed aside lightly, even in the face of divorce.

The system, he said judiciously, existed to support a marriage, which no longer exists. A system runs on expectations, and if we're divorced we hardly have the right to expect very much of each other, do we? That is the whole idea.

His reasoning saddened her, given the climate, heavily scented with sweet expectation, in which they had been married. Though it was less saddening than the prevailing weather.

Look, I don't want total disorder either, he said more sweetly. I'll abide by the system. I promise! This more sweetly still.

But can you still promise? If we're divorced?

They would have to approach the divorce from another path. Money, which made them groan. What money they had was all commingled. The money was as married as they were, if not more so, and how to disentangle it seemed beyond any household remedy. Why not let it remain commingled for the moment? After all, the money was not quarreling uncontrollably, it was not weeping in the shower or behind the wheel of the car with the radio tuned to rock lyrics which, however inane, managed to strafe the exposed heart. And neither one of them was likely to abscond or, heaven forbid, contemplating remarriage. Well, what luck! they exclaimed. Too good to be true! smiling like strangers in a mood of wonder becoming friends in the doorway, sensing some tenuous future connection. So many divorces snagged on money, turning good people vindictive. While in theory, divorce might remove all need for vindication. The war would be over by decree, and like the clouding dust of combat, marriage would settle; you could see the enemy plainly, and draw up plans for coexistence.

What about . . . ? He hesitated. I suppose you're expecting me to sleep here on the couch?

She looked hurt. If that's what you want . . .

Not at all. I'm just trying to . . . You understand, if we're going to be free . . .

Free, she echoed nostalgically, though whether it was nostalgia for her marriage or for her earlier freedom would have been hard to say. A fleeting vision of adulterous adventure next brightened her eyes, until she realized there could be no adulterous adventure, once divorced. I'm not relegating you to the couch, she replied. I never suggested anything so extreme.

They studied each other like strangers who have arranged to have a cup of coffee together after the storm passes, a gaze of acknowledgment, of anticipation of something risky yet promising, at the very least something as opposed to nothing.

Living in sin, she said.

These days they call it simply living together.

It's not quite the same as living together after we've raised two children, is it?

Well . . . He rearranged his body in the chair, shifting into a new phase of the divorce. Now that that's settled, how shall we tell the children?

They'll be sick over it.

Yes indeed. It will seem most peculiar to everyone we know.

And we shall have to explain and I hate to explain.

No one ever had to be sick over our marriage, he said, except us. Somehow marriages, unlike divorces, do not need to be explained, merely announced.

Their eyes caught and held. Do you think . . . maybe we don't have to tell anyone? Until you really move out, that is?

It was his turn to look hurt. Actually there'll be plenty of room here when they go to college, he muttered like a married man.

Maybe we don't have to tell anyone just now, she repeated, bypassing his mutterings like a wife.

He recovered the graciousness of the single. I don't mind. You do as you like.

You really don't mind if I'd rather not tell anyone?

I haven't any right to mind what you do anymore, do I? If we're divorced?

You have a right to mind when it's something that concerns you.

Everything you do concerns me.

No longer, she protested. We're divorced. And yet she was touched, even pierced, very nearly impaled by that slender arrow of love, which recalled why they had gotten married to begin with.

Noticing, he said, Marriage begins to appear as a state of mind.

I suspect marriage is something more fragile yet, namely an illusion. Divorce, whatever its snags and constraints, appears a less illusory state.

But the curious limbo of this hour may be a possible state too. This is a fairly affable conversation we're having, isn't it? The most affable in many a moon. Like unmarried people. Or previously married people. Or . . . something.

And yet they all complain so piteously of their state, without, however, envying ours.

Frankly, he pursued, what I dislike most about divorce is the word. I would like to propose that we simply think we are . . . not married.

At this point, she said, that is far too ambitious. The moment one of us rises out of our chair to perform any significant act, our relation will want to be defined. No, we have to get divorced now, despite the vulgarity of the word, for the same reasons that we had to get married years ago and not just think we were.

What were those again? he asked slyly.

Ha ha. The true marriage we imagined . . . Yet true marriage, she mused aloud, a thing that cannot exist because of the nature of human nature, would be like salt dissolving in water to make brine, like the action of wind on rock which makes sand, like red and black making brown, like a peach and a plum making a nectarine. All that fury in our marriage was the wind wailing its weariness of beating against the rock and the rock shrieking as it was pulverized, the peach crying for its fuzz and the plum for its dripping pink sweetness, the red and the black moaning as their brilliances muddied, streaming together, the salt drowning in the water and the water becoming tears, tears, tears. Thus true marriage is a brown dusty salty weeping fruit, an anomaly, a contradiction in terms, an impossibility.

But if marriage means that, he said, it would also mean sperm and egg making a child. And then the only true and beautiful and possible marriage is a child. That we have accomplished. Two. That you cannot deny.

Yes, we have served the institution. We have had our marriage.

And this is the place to leave off, for most likely this hour suspended between marriage and divorce, this so brief escape from any defined or decreed connection, affable strangers winging it in a doorway during a downpour, became the hour in which they were the least distorted and the apogee of their lives in common.

So You're Going to Have a New Body!

———— ◦◦◦◦ ————

I

Take good care of yourself beforehand to be sure of a healthy, bouncing new body. Ask your doctor all about it. He can help.

Your doctor says: "Six weeks and you'll be feeling like a new person. No one will ever know."

Your doctor says: "Don't worry about the scar. We'll make it real low where no one can see. We call it a bikini cut."

He says: "Any symptoms you have afterwards, we'll fix with hormones. We follow nature's way. There is some danger of these hormones causing cancer in the lining of the uterus. But since you won't have a uterus you won't have anything to worry about."

He says: "There is this myth some women believe, connecting their reproductive organs with their femininity. But you're much too intelligent and sophisticated for that."

Intelligently, you regard a painting hanging on the wall above his diplomas; it is modern in aspect, showing an assortment of common tools—a hammer, screwdrivers, wrenches, and several others you cannot name, not being conversant with the mechanical arts. A sort of all-purpose handyman's kit. You think a sophisticated thought: *Chacun à son goût.*

You are not even sure you need a new body, but your doctor says there is something inside your old one like a grapefruit, and though it is not really dangerous, it should go. It could block his view of the rest of you. You cannot see it or feel it. Trust your doctor. You have never been a runner, but six weeks before your surgery you start to run in the lonely park early each morning. Not quite awake, half dreaming, you imagine you are running from a mugger with a knife. Fast, fast. You are going to give them the healthiest body they have ever cut. You run a quarter of a mile the first day, half a mile the second. By the end of two weeks you are running a mile in nine minutes. Pretty soon you can run three miles in twenty-three minutes. From the neck down you are looking splendid. Perhaps when you present your body they will say, Oh no, this body is too splendid to cut.

II

You will have one very important decision to make before the big day. Be sure to consult with your doctor. He can help.

He says: "The decision is entirely up to you. However, I like to take the ovaries out whenever I can, as long as I'm in there. That way there is no danger of ovarian cancer, which strikes one in a hundred women in your age group. There is really nothing you need ovaries for. You have had three children and don't intend to have any more. Ovarian cancer is incurable and a terrible death. I've seen women your age . . . However, the decision is entirely up to you."

You think: No, for with the same logic he could cut off my head to avert a brain tumor.

Just before he ushers you out of his office he shows you a color snapshot of some woman's benign fibroid tumors, larger than yours, he says, but otherwise comparable, lying in a big metal bowl wider than it is deep, the sort of bowl you often use to prepare chopped meat for meat loaf. You nod appreciatively and go into the bathroom to throw up.

III

Your hospital stay. One evening, in the company of your husband, you check in at the hospital and are shown to your room,
which is not bad, only the walls are a bit bare and it is a bit
expensive—several hundred dollars a night. Perhaps the service
will be worth it. Its large window overlooks a high school, the
very high school, coincidentally, that your teenaged daughter
attends. She has promised to visit often. Your husband stays
until a staff member asks that he leave, and he leaves you with
a copy of *People* magazine featuring an article called "Good Sex
with Dr. Ruth." This is a joke and is meant well. Accept it in
that spirit. He is trying to say what he would otherwise find
difficult to express, that your new body will be lovable and
capable of love.

Your reading of *People* magazine is interrupted by your
doctor, who invites you for a chat in the visitors' lounge, empty
now. He says: "You don't have to make your decision about the
ovaries till the last minute. However, ovarian cancer strikes one
in a hundred women in your age group." Hard to detect until
too late, a terrible death, etc., etc.

As he goes on, a pregnant woman in a white hospital gown
enters the visitors' lounge, shuffles to the window, and stares
out at the night sky. She has a beautiful olive-skinned face with
high cheekbones, green eyes, and full lips. Her hair is thick and
dark. Her arms and legs are very bony; her feet, in paper slippers, are as bony and arched as a dancer's. Take another look
at her face: the cheekbones seem abnormally prominent, the
eyes abnormally prominent, the hollows beneath them abnormally deep. She seems somewhat old to be pregnant, around
forty-five. When she leaves, shuffling on her beautiful dancer's
feet, your doctor says: "That woman has ovarian cancer."

The next morning, lying flat on your back in a Demerol
haze, when he says, "Well?" you say, "Take them, they're
yours."

You have anticipated this moment of waking and have
promised to let yourself scream if the pain is bad enough. Hap-

pily, you discover screaming will not be necessary; quiet moaning will do. If this is the worst, you think, I can take it. In a roomful of screamers and moaners like yourself, baritones and sopranos together, you feel pleased even though you have only a minor choral part. Relieved. The worst is this, probably, and it will be over soon.

A day or two and you will be simply amazed at how much better you feel! Amazed, too, at how many strangers, men and women both, are curious to see your new bikini cut, so curious that you even feel some interest yourself. You peer down, then up into the face of the young man peering along with you, and say, "I know it sounds weird, but those actually look like staples in there."

"They are," he says.

You imagine a stapler of the kind you use at home for papers. Your doctor is holding it while you lie sleeping. Another man crimps the two layers of skin together, folds one over the other just above where your pubic hair used to be, and your doctor squeezes the stapler, moving along horizontally, again and again. Men and women are different in this, if you can generalize from personal experience: at home, you place the stapler flat on the desk, slide the papers between its jaws, and press down gently. Your husband holds the stapler in one hand, slides the corner of the papers in with the other, and squeezes the jaws of the stapler together. What strong hands they have! You think of throwing up, but this is more of an intellectual than a physical reaction since your entire upper abdomen is numb; moreover, you have had almost nothing to eat for three days. Your new body, when it returns to active life, will be quite thin.

No one can pretend that a postsurgical hospital stay is pleasant, but a cheerful outlook should take you far. The trouble is, you cry a good deal of the time. In one sense these tears seem uncontrollable, gushing at irregular intervals during the day and night. In another sense they are quite controllable: if your doctor or strange men on the staff drop in to look at your bikini cut or chat about your body functions, you are able to stop crying at will and act cheerful. But when women doctors or nurses drop in, you keep right on with your crying, even though this causes them to say, "What are you crying about?" You also do not cry in front of visitors, male or female, especially your teen-aged daughter, since you noticed that when she visited you immediately after the surgery her face turned white and she left the room quickly, walking backwards and staring. She has visited often, as she promised. She makes sure to let you know she has terrible menstrual cramps this week, in fact asks you to write a note so she can be excused from gym. Your sons do not visit—they are too young, twelve and nine—but you talk to them on the phone, cheerfully. They tell you about the junk food they have been eating in your absence and about sports events at school. They sound wistful and eager to have you returned to them.

IV

At last the day you've been waiting for arrives: taking your new body home! You may be surprised to learn this, but in many ways your new body is just like your old one. For instance, it walks. Slowly. And if you clasp your hands and support your stomach from below, you feel less as though it will rip away from the strain inside. At home, in the mirror, except for the bikini cut and the fact that your stomach is round and puffy, this body even looks remarkably like your old one, but thinner. Your ankles are thinner than you have ever seen them. That is because with your reproductive system gone, you no longer tend to retain fluids. An unexpected plus, slim ankles! How good to be home and climb into your own bed. How good to see your children and how good they are, scurrying around to bring you tea and chocolates and magazines. Why is it that the sight of the children, which should bring you pleasure, also brings you grief? It might be that their physical presence reminds you of the place they came from, which no longer exists, at least in you. This leads you to wonder idly what becomes of the many reproductive organs, both healthy and unhealthy, removed daily: buried, burned, or trashed? Do right-to-lifers mourn them?

You sleep in your own bed with your husband, who wants to hold you close, but this does not feel very comfortable. You move his arms and hands to permissible places, the way you did with boys as a teen-ager, except of course the places are different now. Breasts are permissible, thighs are permissible, but not the expanse between. A clever fellow, over the next few nights he learns, even in his sleep, what is permissible.

Although you are more tired than you ever thought possible, you force yourself to walk from room to room three times a day, perhaps to show this new body who is in control. During one such forced walk . . . Don't laugh, now! A wave of heat swirls up and encircles you, making you sway dizzily, and the odd thing, no one has mentioned this—it pulsates. Pulses of heat. Once long ago and with great concentration, you counted the pulses of an orgasm, something you are not sure you will ever experience again, and now you count this. Thirty pulses. You cannot compare since you have forgotten the orgasm number; anyhow, the two events have nothing in common except that they pulse and that they are totally overpowering. But this can't be happening, you are far too young for this little joke. Over the next few days it is happening, though, and whenever it happens you feel foolish, you feel something very like shame. Call your doctor. He can help.

A woman's voice says he is extremely busy and could you call back later, honey. Or would you like an appointment, honey? Are you sure she can't help you, honey? You say yes, she can help enormously by not calling you honey. Don't give me any of your lip, you menopausal bitch, she mutters. No, no, she most certainly does not mutter that; it must have been the tone of her gasp. Very well, please hold on while she fetches your folder. While holding, you are treated to a little telephone concert: Frank Sinatra singing "My Way." Repeatedly, you hear Frank Sinatra explain that no matter what has happened or will happen, he is gratified to feel that he did it his way. Your doctor's voice is abrupt and booming in contrast. When you state your problem he replies, "Oh, sweats." You are not sure you have heard correctly. Could he have said, "Oh, sweets," as in affectionate commiseration? Hardly. Always strictly business. You were misled by remembering, subliminally, "honey." "Sweats" it was and, in the plural, a very hideous word you do not wish to have associated with you or your new body. Sweat, a universal phenomenon, you have no quarrel with. Sweats, no.

Your doctor says he—or "they"—will take care of everything. For again he uses the plural, the royal "we." When you visit for a six-week checkup, "they" will give you the miraculous hormones, nature's way. In the meantime you begin to spend more time out of bed. You may find, during this convalescent period, that you enjoy reading, listening to music, even light activity such as jigsaw puzzles. Your twelve-year-old son brings you a jigsaw puzzle of a Mary Cassatt painting—a woman dressed in pale blue, holding a baby who is like a peach. It looks like a peach and would smell and taste like a peach too. At a glance you know you can never do this puzzle. It is not that you want another baby, for you do not, nor is it the knowledge that you could not have one even if you wanted it, since that is academic. Simply the whole cluster of associations—mothers and babies, conception, gestation, birth—is something you do not wish to be reminded of. The facts of life. You seem to be an artificial exception to the facts of life, a mutation existing outside the facts of life that apply to every other living creature. However, you can't reject the gift your son chose so carefully, obviously proud that he has intuited your tastes—Impressionist paintings, the work of women artists, peachy colors. You thank him warmly and undo the cellophane wrapping on the box as if you intended to work on the puzzle soon. You ask your husband to bring you a puzzle of an abstract painting. He brings a Jackson Pollock puzzle which you set to work at, sitting on pillows on the living room floor. Your son comes home from school and lets his knapsack slide off his back. "Why aren't you doing my puzzle?" "Well, it looked a little hard. I thought I'd save it for later." He looks at the picture on the Jackson Pollock box. "Hard!" he exclaims.

V

Your first visit to the doctor. You get dressed in real clothes and appraise yourself in the mirror—what admirable ankles. With a shudder you realize you are echoing a thought now terrible in its implications: No one would ever know.

Out on the city streets you hail a taxi, since you cannot risk your new body's being jostled or having to stand up all the way on a bus. The receptionist in your doctor's waiting room is noticeably cool—no honeying today—as she asks you to take a seat and wait. When your name is finally called, a woman in a white coat leads you into a cubicle just off the waiting room and loudly asks your symptoms. Quite often in the past you have, while waiting, overheard the symptoms of many women, and now no doubt many women hear yours. As usual, you are directed to an examining room and instructed to undress and don a white paper robe. On the way you count the examining rooms. Three. One woman—you—is pre-examination, one no doubt mid-examination, one is post.

When your doctor at last enters, he utters a cheery greeting and then the usual: "Slide your lower body to the edge of the table. Feet up in the stirrups please." You close your eyes, practicing indifference. It cannot be worse than the worst you have already known. You study certain cracks in the ceiling that you know well and he does not even know exist. You continue to meditate on procedural matters, namely, that your doctor's initial impression in each of his three examining rooms is of a woman naked except for a white paper robe, sitting or leaning on an examining table in an attitude of waiting. He, needless to say, is fully dressed. You contemplate him going from one examining room to the next; the devil will not have to make work for his hands. After the examination you will be invited, clothed, to speak with him in his office, and while you dress for this encounter, he will visit another examining room. It strikes you that this maximum-efficiency setup might serve equally well for a brothel and perhaps already does. This is a brothel surrealized.

Your doctor says you may resume most normal activities, may even do some very mild exercise if you wish, but no baths and no "intercourse." "Intercourse," you are well aware, stands for sex, although if you stop to consider, sex is the more inclusive term. Does he say "intercourse" because he is unable to say "sex," or thinks the word "sex" would be too provocative in that antiseptic little room, unleashing torrents of libido, or is it his indirect way of saying that you can do sexual things as long as you don't fuck? This is not something you can ask your doctor.

The last item of business is the prescription for the hormones. He explains how to take them—three weeks on and one week off, in imitation of nature's way. He gives you several small sample packets for starters. At home, standing at the bathroom sink, you extricate a pill from its tight childproof cardboard-and-plastic niche, feverishly, like a junkie pouncing on her fix. Nature's way. Now no more "sweats," no more tears. Your new body is complete. What is this little piece of paper in the sample packet? Not so little when you open it up, just impeccably folded. In diabolically tiny print it explains the pills' bad side effects or "contraindications," a word reminiscent of "intercourse." Most of them you already know from reading books, but there is something new. The pills may have a damaging effect on your eyes. Fancy that. Nature's way? You settle down on the edge of the bathtub and go back to the beginning to read more attentively. First, a list of situations for which the pills are prescribed. Funny, you do not find "hysterectomy." Reading on, you do find "female castration." That must be . . . yes indeed, that's you. You try to read on, but the print is so terribly small, perhaps the pills are affecting your eyes already, for there is a shimmering film over the fine letters. Rather than simply rolling over into the tub, go back to bed, fully dressed, face in the pillows. No, first close the door in case the children come in. Many times over the past weeks you have lain awake pinched by questions, pulling and squeezing back as if the questions were clay, weighing the threat of the bony-footed woman pregnant with her own death—an actress summoned and stuffed for the occasion? part of a terrorist scheme?— against your own undrugged sense of the fitness of things. Now you have grasped that the questions are moot. This is not like cutting your hair, and you have never even had a tooth pulled. The only other physically irreversible things you have done are lose your virginity and bear children. Yes, shut the door tight. It would not do to have them hear you, hysteric, *castrata*.

But of course the sun continues to rise, your center is hardly the center of the universe. Over the next few weeks you get acquainted with your new body. A peculiar thing—though it does not look very different, it does things differently. It responds to temperature differently and it sleeps differently, finding different positions comfortable and different hours propitious. It eats differently, shits differently, and pisses differently. You suspect it will fuck differently, but that you will not know for a while. Its pubic hair has not grown back in quite the same design or density, so that you look shorn or childlike or, feeling optimistic, like a chorus girl or a Renaissance painting. It doesn't menstruate, naturally. You can't truthfully say you miss menstruation, but how will you learn to keep track of time, the seasons of the month? A wall calendar? But how will you know inside? Can it be that time will feel all the same, no coming to fruition and dropping the fruit, no filling and subsiding, moist and dry, moving towards and moving away from?

VI

At nine weeks, although your new body can walk and move almost naturally, it persists in lying around the house whenever possible. And so you lie around the living room with your loved ones as your daughter, wearing an old sweater of yours, scans the local newspaper in search of part-time work. Music blares, Madonna singing "Like a Virgin," describing how she felt touched as though for the very first time. Were you not disconcerted by the whole cluster of associations, you might tell your daughter that the premise of the song is mistaken, the very first time is usually not so terrific. Perhaps some other evening. Your daughter reads aloud amusing job opportunities. A dental school wants research subjects who have never had a cavity. Aerobics instructor at a reform school. "Hey, Mom, here's something you could do. A nutrition experiment, five dollars an hour. Women past childbearing age or surgically sterile."

A complex message, but no response is really required since her laughter fills the space. Your older son, bent over the Mary Cassatt puzzle, chuckles. Your husband smirks faintly over his newspaper. He means no harm, you suppose. (Then why the fuck is he smirking?) Maybe those to whom the facts of life still apply can't help it, just as children can't help smirking at the facts of life themselves. Only your younger son, building a space station out of Lego parts, is not amused. Unknowing, he senses some primitive vibration in the air and looks up at you apprehensively, then gives you a loving punch in the knee. You decide that he is your favorite, that one day you may run away with him, abandoning the others.

VII

The tenth week, and a most important day in the life of your new body. Your doctor says you are permitted to have "intercourse." If your husband is like most men, he can hardly wait. Proceed with caution, like walking on eggs, except that you, eggless, are the eggs on which he proceeds with caution. Touched for the very first time! Well, just do it and see if it works; passion will come later, replacing fear. That is the lesson of behavioral science as opposed to classical psychology. But what's this? Technical difficulties, like a virgin. This can't be happening, not to you with that hot little geyser, that little creamery you had up there. Come now, when there's a will . . . Spit, not to mention a thousand drugstore remedies. Even tears will do. Before long things are wet enough, thank you very much. Remember for next time there's still that old spermicidal jelly, but you can throw away the diaphragm. That is not the sort of thing you can hand down to your daughter like a sweater.

VIII

Over the next month or two you may find your new body has strange responses to your husband's embraces. Don't be alarmed: it feels desire and it feels pleasure, only it feels them in a wholly unfamiliar way. In bed your new body is most different from your old, so different that you have the eerie sensation that another woman, a stranger, is making love to your husband while your mind, your same old mind, looks on in amazement. All your body's nerve endings have been replaced by this strange woman's; she moves and caresses the way you used to, and the sounds of pleasure she makes are the same, only her apparatus of sensation is altogether alien. There are some things you cannot discuss with your husband because you are too closely twined; just as if, kissing, your tongues in each other's mouths, you were to attempt to speak. But you cannot rest easy in this strangeness; it must be explored, and so you light on an experiment.

You call an old friend, someone you almost married, except that you managed in time to distinguish your feeling for each other from love. It was sex, one of those rare affinities that would not withstand daily life. Now and then, at long intervals, a year or more, you have met for several hours with surprisingly little guilt. This is no time for fine moral distinctions. He has often pledged that you may ask him for any kind of help, so you call him and explain the kind of help you need. He grins, you can see this over the telephone, and says he would be more than happy to help you overcome the mystery of the sexual stranger in your new body. Like Nancy Drew's faithful Ned.

You have to acknowledge the man has a genuine gift as regards women. From the gods? Or could it be because he is a doctor and knows his physiology? No, your knowledge of doctors would not bear out that correlation, and besides, this one is only an eye doctor. In any case, in his arms, in a motel room, you do rediscover yourself, buried deep, deep in the crevices of hidden tissues and disconnected circuits. It takes some time and coaxing to bring you forth, you have simply been so trauma- tized by the knife that you have been in hiding underground for months, paralyzed by any kind of penetration. But you are still there, in your new body, and gradually, you feel sure, you will emerge again and replace the impostor in the conjugal bed. You feel enormous gratitude and tell him so, and he says, grin- ning, "No trouble at all. My pleasure." Perhaps you will even ask him about the effects of the pills on your eyes, but not just now.

"Do I feel any different inside?" you ask. He says no, and describes in exquisite terms how you feel inside, which is very nice to listen to. This is not in your husband's line or perhaps any husband's—you wouldn't know. After the exquisite de- scription, he says, "But it is different, you know." You don't know. How?

He explains that in the absence of the cervix, which is the opening of the uterus, the back wall of the vagina is sewn up so that in effect what you have there now is a dead end. As he explains, it seems obvious and inevitable, but strange to say, you have never figured this out before or even thought about it. (It is something your doctor neglected to mention.) Nor have you poked around on your own, having preferred to remain ignorant. So it is rather a shock, this realization that you have a dead end. You always imagined yourself, along with all women, as having an easy passage from inside to out, a constant trafficking between the heart of the world and the heart of yourself. This was what distinguished you from men. They were the walled ones, barricaded, the ones with such difficulty receiving and transmitting the current running between the heart of the world and the heart of themselves. It is so great a shock that you believe you cannot bear to live with it.

Watching you, he says, "It makes no difference. You feel wonderful, the same as always. You really do. Here, feel with your hand, so you'll know." With his help you feel around your new body. Different, not so different. Yet you know. Of course, with his help it becomes an amusing and piquant thing to be doing in a motel room, and then it becomes more love, wonderful love, but you cry all the way through it. A new sensation: like some *Kamasutra* position, you wouldn't have thought it possible.

"At least you don't have to worry about ovarian cancer," he says afterwards. "It's very hard to detect in time and a terrible way—"

"Please," you say. "Please stop." You cannot bear hearing those words from this man.

"I'm sorry. I know it's hard. I can't imagine how I would feel if I had my balls cut off."

With a leap you are out of bed and into your clothes, while he looks on aghast. How fortunate that you did not marry him, for had you married him, after those words you would have had to leave him. As you leave him, naked and baffled, now, not bothering to inquire about the effects of the pills on your eyes yet thanking him because he has done precisely what you needed done. It will be a very long time before you see him again, though, before the blade of his words grows dull from repetition.

IX

Months pass and you accept that this new body, its torso ever so slightly different in shape from the old one, is yours to keep. Not all women, remember, love their new bodies instinctively; some have to learn to love them. Through the thousands of little acts of personal care, an intimacy develops. By the sixth month you will feel not quite as teary, not quite as tired—the anesthetic sloshing around in your cells must be evaporating. You resolve to ignore the minor nuisance symptoms—mild backaches, a recurrent vaginal infection, lowered resistance to colds and viruses. . . . Now that the sample packets of hormone pills are used up, you are spending about fifteen dollars a month at the drugstore, something your doctor neglected to mention in advance. Would he have told you this, you wonder, if you were a very poor woman? How does he know you are not a very poor woman? Foolish question. Because you have purchased his services. The pills cause you to gain weight, jeopardizing the thin new body and the ankles, so you run faster every morning (yes, it runs! it runs!), racing nature's way. One very positive improvement is that now you can sleep on your stomach. Your husband can touch you anywhere without pain. When he makes love to you you feel the strange woman and her alien nervous system retreating and yourself emerging in her place. You will eventually overcome her.

And before you know it, it's time for your six-month checkup. You do not respond to your doctor's hearty greeting, but you comply when he says, "Slide your lower body to the edge of the table. Feet up in the stirrups please." He does not know it, but this is the last time he will be seeing—no, seeing is wrong since he doesn't look, he looks at the wall behind your head—the last time he or any man will be examining your body. There is nothing he can tell you about how you feel, for the simple reason that he does not know. How can he? Suddenly this is utterly obvious, and as you glance again at the painting of assorted tools, the fact of his being in an advisory capacity on any matter concerning your body is both an atrocity, which you blame yourself for having permitted, and an absurdity, such an ancient social absurdity that you laugh aloud, a crude, assertive, resuscitated laugh, making him look warily from the wall to your face, which very possibly he has never looked at before. How can he know what you feel? He has never attempted to find out by the empirical method; his tone is not inquisitive but declarative. He knows only what men like himself have written in books, and just now he looks puzzled.

Why not tell your doctor? That might help. In his office after the examination you tell him—quite mildly, compared to what you feel—that he might have informed you more realistically of what this operation would entail. Quite mild and limited, but even so it takes a great summoning of strength. He is the one with the social position, the money, and the knife. You, despite your laugh, are the *castrata.* Your heart goes pit-a-pat as you speak, and you have a lump in your throat. To your surprise, he looks directly at your face with interest.

He says: "Thank you for telling me that. But not everyone reacts the same way. We try to anticipate the bright side, but some people take it harder than others. Some people are special cases."

X

A few months later, you read a strange, small item in the newspaper: a lone marauder, on what is presented as a berserk midnight spree, has ransacked the office of a local gynecologist. She tore diplomas from the walls and broke equipment. She emptied sample packets of medication and packages of rubber fingers and gloves, which she strewed everywhere, creating a battlefield of massacred hands. She wrote abusive epithets on the walls; she dumped file folders on the floor and daubed them with menstrual blood. As you read these details you feel the uncanny sensation of *déjà vu,* and your heart beats with a bizarre fear. Calm down; you have an alibi, you were deep in your law-abiding sleep. Anyhow, you would have done quite differently—not under cover of darkness, first of all, but in broad daylight when the doctor was there. You would have forced him into a white paper robe and onto the examining table, saying, "Slide your lower body to the edge of the table. Feet up in the stirrups please." Not being built for such a position, he would have found it extremely uncomfortable. While he lay terrorized, facing the painting of common tools, you would simply have looked. Armed only with force of will, you would have looked for what would seem to him an endless time at his genitals until he himself, mesmerized by your gaze, began to look at them as some freakish growth, a barrier to himself, between the world and himself. After a while you would have let him climb down untouched, but he would never again have looked at or touched himself without remembering his terror and his inkling that his body was his cage and all his intercourse

with the world was a wild and pitiable attempt to cut his way
free.

XI

A year after your operation, you will be feeling much much
better. You have your strength back, or about eighty percent of
it anyway. You are hardly tired at all; the anesthetic must be
nearly evaporated. You can walk erect without conscious effort,
and you have grown genuinely fond of your new body, accepting its hollowness with, if not equanimity, at least tolerance.
One or two symptoms, or rather habits, persist: for instance,
when you get out of bed you still hold your hands clasped
around your lower abdomen for support, as if it might rip away
from the strain inside, even though there is no longer any strain.
At times you lie awake blaming yourself for participating in an
ancient social absurdity, but eventually you will cease to blame
as you have ceased to participate.

Most odd, and most obscure, you retain the tenuous sense
of waiting. With effort you can localize it to a sense of waiting
for something to end. A holdover, a vague habit of memory or
memory of habit. Right after he cut, you waited for that worst
pain to end. Then for the tears, the tiredness, and all the rest.
Maybe it is a memory of habit or a habit of memory, or maybe
the blade in the flesh brought you to one of life's many edges
and now you are waiting, like a woman who after much travel
has come to the edge of a cliff and, for no reason and under no
compulsion, lingers there too long. You are waiting for something to end, you feel closer than ever before to the end, but of
what, you do not push further to ask.

The Two Portraits of Rembrandt

I have before me on picture postcards two self-portraits by Rembrandt, one painted in 1629, when he was twenty-three, the other in 1669, the year of his death. I have been eyeing them on and off for a long time, two years, as objects to be decoded. The message would be something beyond the obvious one about experience as registered in the flesh and the trek towards death. They seem to refer to passages, journeys, remote from Rembrandt's; they suggest something closer to home.

"The extraordinary phenomenon of Rembrandt's self-portraits," the critic Jakob Rosenberg tells us, "has no parallel in the seventeenth century or even in the entire history of art." Sixty of them, besides etchings and drawings. Years ago, in an introductory art history class, the instructor asked why, in our opinion, did Rembrandt paint himself so many times. Egotism, I promptly thought, and that was the answer a few jocular students gave. Our instructor was disheartened. "Rembrandt seems to have felt that he had to know himself if he wished to penetrate the problem of man's inner life," Jakob Rosenberg says. How obvious. How could I not have perceived that, even at seventeen?

The figure in both portraits is posed in the same way: upper body on the diagonal, head turned to face the viewer. The right side of the face is lit and the left is in shadow, but this contrast is more pronounced in the early work. In both portraits Rembrandt wears something white around his neck, while the rest of the clothing is black, first a glossy, elegant black, then, forty years later, drab and porous. From the young Rembrandt there radiates a willed elegance, an arrogance nearing defiance—youthful softness masquerading as hardness. His soft brown hair billows around his face, a long, smooth face, smoothly painted. The eyes are dark, soft, and unwelcoming, and a shadowy furrow grooves the bridge of the nose, which is straight and fleshy at the tip; the lips are rosy and curled, with the faintest suggestion of a mustache, the chin is prominent, and the space between lips and chin a shade long, a subtle disproportion adding to the general aloofness. It could be the portrait of a youth too clever for his own good painted by a discerning older person. But the painter is the youth himself, appraising his forced arrogance. A faint wonder ruffles the surface—how dare you presume to capture me, know me?

In the later portrait, all, as one might expect, is changed utterly. Rembrandt is wearing a hat, an amber beret streaked with beige. The hair is wispier, less carefully groomed; the skin has Rembrandt's characteristic mottled texture. No more smoothness, either in the subject or in the manner of presentation. The nose is fleshier and nubbier, the mouth a thin line. The fine slope of the jaw has given way to jowls and double chin: everywhere paunchy, pouchy fleshiness. He looks sad, weary, a man who has been through hard times. As indeed he has: he has seen his popularity and esteem, at their height in his thirties, gradually wane; he has seen three children die at birth; has suffered the loss of his wife, Saskia, and years later of his mistress and housekeeper, Hendrickje Stoffels; has lost his only son, Titus, at the age of twenty-nine; has been bankrupt and lost most of his possessions—enough to leave pouches on anyone's face.

Jakob Rosenberg writes that this last self-portrait exhibits "some decline in the aged artist's expressive power. His painterly skill has not failed him, but the psychological content shows a diminished intensity. The facial expression here is mild and slightly empty, when compared to all the others in the imposing group of late self-portraits," which the same critic calls, variously, mellow, tragic, monumental, reflecting "mythical grandeur and dignity," "philosophic superiority," "a deep consciousness of man's fateful destiny," and so forth.

True, there is little grandeur or majesty here, but the expression is not so much empty as subdued, in the way of a man who has withdrawn his investment in his face and liquidated it, so to speak, who is in the process of ceasing to care.

I have before me also two pictures of my father with about a forty-year interval between them, not paintings but photographs. The first is a standard graduation photo, so old that the cap and gown have almost merged with the dark background. I can just make out one sharp corner of the mortarboard floating above my father's head, pointing forward like a lance. Held flat under the light, though, the photo relinquishes the whole silhouette—gown, hat, and tassel—black eerily detaching itself from sepia. This must have been taken on the occasion of his graduation from Brooklyn Law School, when he was twenty-two or -three, about Rembrandt's age in the first self-portrait. My father sometimes said that if he had had the means— money, social class, correct ethnic background—to attend law school at Harvard or Yale, his life would have gone differently. He was not a complainer; this was a simple fact. It seems to me his life did not go so badly as it was, but what can I presume to know about his aspirations? I do know he wanted to make a lot of money and that from time to time, to my mother's horror, he would invest in risky business deals cooked up with like-minded aspirers, and lose his savings. To the end of his days he kept his dream of striking it rich. Rembrandt, who was a notoriously poor financial manager, as well as hugely extravagant in his youth, was driven in later years to an odd stratagem to stave off creditors. A contract was drawn up in which Hendrickje Stoffels and his son, Titus, were made proprietors of a business, art dealers engaged in selling the works of Rembrandt, who would own nothing himself—save his genius—and be in effect working for them. My father was not a poor manager, in fact he earned his living advising others on prudently managing their businesses, and he was not too extravagant either. But he enjoyed taking risks. Maybe it was not Brooklyn Law School that thwarted him. Maybe he too had entered, tacitly, into a contract wherein his talents were used in the service of his wife and children: an employee of a sort. In any case, the graduation picture is of a man I never knew, who hardly knew himself yet.

The connection, the curious feature, is my father's striking resemblance to the young Rembrandt—I should say my father's graduation photo's resemblance to Rembrandt's self-portrait. Even the poses are similar, though reversed—my father's left side faces the viewer and the right side of his face is shadowed—and the costumes, black relieved by the white collar. Like Rembrandt's, my father's eyes are dark, only instead of being aloof and impenetrable they are penetrating—two little glints of light, like lasers, animate the pupils. The nose, like Rembrandt's, is straight, then fleshy at the tip, the mouth has the same beautiful bow shape and haughty curl, there is the same unsettling length between mouth and prominent chin. An elongated, smooth arrogance, the blank, hard defiance of youth. Both faces are touching in their innocence and at the same time conceal what they might know, as the faces of youth can readily do.

My father did not age as drastically as Rembrandt; his cheeks remain firm in the later photo; the face is more fleshy and molded, but hardly paunchy. Because he did not suffer the wearying effects of self-scrutiny? But why should there be any resemblance, why should the comparison be symmetrical? Granted that faces in their sixties mirror the trajectory of their owners' lives, my father's life had little in common with Rembrandt's. Their similar faces took dissimilar routes to the same end. Maybe in their eighties, when the uniqueness of individual faces is subsumed under the common fate, they might again have looked alike—but neither lived that long. Meanwhile my father never lost children or wife; he was not a painter and not seeking knowledge of man's inner life; he neither achieved wide acclaim in his youth nor lost it; his business reversals were not on so grand a scale, and unlike Rembrandt, he always managed to haul his forces together and venture anew. In this late photograph (a group picture including my mother and four friends) he appears to be a calm, wise, contented man. Still handsome, in his white shirt and gray patterned tie he looks straight into the camera, one eye, as always, open slightly wider than the other, and he is almost smiling, on the verge of a full smile—but he cannot quite yield it up, as he could not quite yield up the tear I once saw in his eye. Even so, he emits benevolence. Judicious, good-tempered. Maybe not "mythical grandeur and dignity," but "philosophic superiority," yes. Is this the "real" man, sage and mellow? Does he know himself at last? I feel that although dead now, he is looking straight at me, that I am looking back at myself.

Perhaps the soul does not depart from the body at the last breath, to fly out the window and rise, but begins departing in the late years and takes its leave gradually, puff by puff, which accounts for the shrinking we notice and grieve over, the "diminished intensity" the critic complains of in the last Rembrandt self-portrait. In the late photo of my father, though, I see no diminishment yet; the face is fully alive with the abiding spirit.

My father's hand would slice the air dismissively at my analyzing pictures. I myself feel a tribal needling: all this trouble for *pictures?* He lived by the word. Pictures were a crude, provisional mode of representation and communication, happily supplanted by the advent of language. People who still looked at pictures for information were in a pre-verbal state, babies or Neanderthals. The *Daily News,* "New York's Picture Newspaper," was a publication designed for the illiterate, for "morons." Likewise *Life* magazine, which prided itself on its photography; he would not have it in the house. His newspaper of choice, the *New York Times,* contained pictures, but he probably regarded them as a concession to the occasional lapses of its readers, or proof that certain events took place, for instance that the Big Three—Roosevelt, Churchill, and Stalin—really did meet at Yalta. Other printed matter he would not allow in the house were confession magazines and *Classic Comics,* which retold great books in cartoons with captions. My aunt in Brownsville once gave me two *Classic Comics* for my birthday. I flaunted them—he wouldn't outlaw a birthday gift, but he offered to buy me the real books if only I would get the comics out of his sight. In the end I had to admit he was right, they were as nothing next to the real thing, and so for a long time I didn't value pictures either. Like him, I trusted only things that came in the form of or humbly awaited translation into words.

Or numbers. In company he liked to announce his age, a habit my mother deplored. "I'll be fifty-three years old in February!" "I'm fifty-eight years old!" "Sixty-four last February!" he would proclaim, beaming, twinkling, puffing out his chest as if the attainment of such years without showing them deserved a decoration. This was self-knowledge of a kind: he could translate himself into numbers, he kept track. My mother would grumble or slip out of the room. She would never reveal her age. When pressed, she told me she was seven years younger than he—seven must have been the highest number she thought she could offer without suggesting a questionable age gap. But part of family lore was that my parents had met in high school. When I asked how this could be if they were seven years apart, she said my father had been behind in school because he was an immigrant. He must have been very far behind, it seemed to me, maybe even a ludicrous figure?—my own school had some hulking retarded students who turned up in the same classroom perennially, like furniture. . . . Mostly I would contemplate their seven-year age difference and their meeting in high school, two irreconcilable facts, then shove it aside like a shoelace you can't unknot—today, anyway. My mother was two years younger than my father, I learned much later. My desire to know was frustrated by one type of vanity. My father, even in his immigrant state, was not far behind at all, it turns out; his type of vanity would hardly have liked my thinking he was.

Maybe it was their limitation and finiteness that he disliked about pictures. He loved what was bountiful and boundless and hated anything mean and narrow. (He hated the way he was offered food at the *Classic Comics* aunt's house in Brownsville. " 'You don't want a piece of fruit, do you?' " he would imitate. "What does she expect a person to say? Of course I don't want a piece of fruit.") Pictures were circumscribed by their frames.

A house, a tree, a cloud, added up to a landscape, and that was the end of it. The space of pictures is inner space, but he didn't look into, he looked at. Words, though, could go on forever, linear, one opening the door to a dozen others, each new one nudging at another door, and so on to infinite mansions of meditation. Nor was there any limit to what you could say; words bred more words, spawned definition, comparison, analogy. A picture is worth a thousand words, I was told in school. Confucius. But to me, too, the value seemed quite the other way around. And why not ten thousand, a hundred thousand? Give me a picture and I could provide volumes. Meanings might be embedded in the picture, but only words could release them and at the same time, at the instant they were born and borne from the picture, seize them, give them shape and specific gravity. Nothing was really possessed or really real until it was incarnate in words. Show and Tell opened every school day, but I rarely cared to show anything. You could show forever, but how could you be sure the essence had been transmitted, without words? Words contained the knowledge, words *were* the knowledge, the logos, and words verified that the knowledge was there.

Long ago, long before I knew him, my father must have had a foreign accent. I try to imagine how he sounded and hear a stranger. Did my mother, sitting next to him in high school, watch it gradually slip from him, as you watch a swimmer gradually dry in the sun, the drops first showering off, then rolling down slowly, then evaporating imperceptibly? Was there a point at which she told him, "You've got it, relax, you sound like everyone else"? One way or another, his command of the language, like Rembrandt's of his brushes, reached virtuoso proportions. Maybe—and one might suspect this of Rembrandt too, judging from the early self-portrait—he was like those stubbornly perfectionist babies you hear of, who refuse to babble, and speak only when they can produce flawless paragraphs. But fluency alone is not memorable; he was verbally idiosyncratic, selective, in such a way—or to such ears—that he leaves behind most vividly a heap of phrases, as the other left canvases, by which to know him.

My father spoke of visits to my mother's family as "going to Williamsburg," "going to Brownsville," "going to Borough Park"—the last pronounced as one word with the accent on the first syllable—rather than going to her mother's or sisters' houses. This made the visit more of a geographical venture than a personal encounter. His mode of being in the world turned on movement, getting from one place to another rather than being anywhere, something that intensified as he aged and became less mobile. Then on a family visit, immediately upon reaching the destination he would check his watch and the car's odometer and announce, "We made very good time." No sooner was he settled in a chair than he would begin calculating when he might start the return trip, plotting, again, how to make the best time. Of course, he was not well in his last years and was most comfortable lying in bed. But all his life he preferred any position to sitting; he lived in physical extremes, either frenetic movement or total repose. After supper he would lie down with the *New York Times* on the red tufted couch in the living room and wonder why my brother, at seven years old, wouldn't stop running around making noise and lie down with him. But he would stand to eat breakfast and stand, or pace, to converse. My brother and sister and I do not much like to sit either. We are most comfortable standing or lying down. Something in our genetic structure does not like to bend.

Williamsburg, Brownsville, and Borough Park were neighborhoods in Brooklyn which because of my father's frequent mention of them ("What's doing in Borough Park?" after my mother telephoned her sister) remain archetypal place names bearing the personalities of my aunts and my grandmother. Now Brooklyn boasts unfamiliar names that sound concocted: Cobble Hill, Carroll Gardens, Boerum Hill. Where are these strange places? I think, and what are their real names? I can see my father's lips compressing scornfully, rejecting the new fatuities. Greenwich Village, once Manhattan's Bohemia, he persisted in pronouncing as spelled rather than the correct "Grennich" Village. Far as he was from Bohemia, he must have heard

the words spoken; I think he persisted in the literal pronuncia-
tion to protest at least one of the area's many, to him, arty
eccentricities.

He spent his first American years on Cherry Street on Manhattan's Lower East Side, and forever after spoke the words
"Cherry Street" with a tone of disgust and hostility, a tone in
which I could feel the textures of deprivation, of all that was
disheveled and ungainly. He would have been appalled to
know that a movie called *Hester Street* (near Cherry Street) drew
fashionable crowds over fifty years later, that his humiliation
was advertised as art. Now on Cherry Street stand tall buildings, low- and middle-income housing. Hispanic people, Chinese people, artists live there, not in squalor. But when I hear
the words "Cherry Street" I think, squalor, confinement, and I
feel the lust to rise up out of them—as if that had not already
been done for me.

In speech and in everything else he liked boldness and
swiftness and despised timidity or hesitation, and he promulgated these tastes as absolutes. Fortunately my brother and
sister and I came to be loud or swift or bold, most of the time;
we picked it up in the atmosphere or had it in the genes or
learned it for survival. The faint of heart, the slow, sometimes
even the thoughtful, were morally inferior as well as aestheti-
cally displeasing. My father was driving up Utica Avenue in
Brooklyn, a steep hill, when an elderly woman, crossing as the
light was changing, saw our car approach and stopped mid-
street. Then she reconsidered and started to walk again. He
slowed down; she stopped. He accelerated; she trotted. Madly
working the gearshift, he came to a violent halt and rolled down
the window. My innards stiffened at the prospect of what terrible words he would say, how he would mortify her, the epitome
of all he scorned. (Rembrandt, too, was reputed to be "a most
temperamental man" who tended to "disparage everyone" and
make "brusque, ironical remarks.") As she stood in the middle
of the street, thoroughly muddled now, he at last hurled out
sternly, resoundingly, "Don't falter!"

My mother could be loud and bold and swift when necessary, but in a manner different from the rest of us. Softer, with prettiness and diplomacy. She was what men call "emotional"; her words and judgments arose from feeling and intuition rather than reason, a mode of operation inimical to my father. He would ask her a question, did she want to go here or there at such and such a time, and she would reply with a string of conditional sentences. "Give me a yes or no answer!" he would shout. I admired his quest for clarity and definitiveness; I took it as a categorical imperative. If every question had a yes or no answer there would be fewer problems in the world, no shilly-shallying. Later I learned that this tactic came from a legalistic tradition and was used in the courtroom to interrogate witnesses. So he had not invented it—though it might have been invented expressly for him.

It wasn't obscenities that I feared my father would hurl at the faltering woman—I had never heard him use those. "God-damned" was his adjective in moderate anger, and "Goddamn it to hell" his expletive when he was seriously enraged; he was a man inhabited by rage, who seemed most alive, most recognizably himself, when in a verbal tempest. His furies lashed the stupidity or willfulness of those around him, and in them would blaze forth like lightning the word "moron," his worst epithet. In our household, "moron" was a word of such immense power and inclusiveness, so thoroughly condemning, that the filthier words I learned later are mild in comparison. "Moron" was the worst epithet because brains were the most precious possession, without which a person was of little or no worth. "There's no substitute for brains," he liked to say. Brains were demonstrated by articulate speech, such as his own disquisitions on political and economic topics. He would fix the listener with his glittering brown eyes and address him or her as a hypothetical You. The thesis might be abstract, the workings of the laissez-faire economy or the dynamics of imperialism, but it would usually be illustrated by a concrete example. "Let's say You have half a million dollars to invest. Now supposing You happen upon an extremely advantageous . . ." And so on. Then at some point—perhaps You were about to indulge in a shady deal, to act with less than utter probity—he would reassure his listener, "I mean editorial You, of course, you understand." He never failed to make this explanation about editorial You, an odd scruple in a man who was otherwise quite ready to call people morons.

He was generally pleased with his three children because he judged them intelligent, but women, to be worthy, had to be pretty as well. Those who were not he called "dogs" and found it painful to be in their presence. "She's a dog," he would say with revulsion, but a different kind of revulsion than he used for "Moron!"—a sort of regretful revulsion, as if it were not the woman's fault that her presence pained him, whereas in the case of "Moron!" the person was held responsible. Among my friends, who were perpetually crowding into the house, he liked the ones who were bright, pretty, and lively; he asked them questions so he could enjoy their replies and tease them a bit, and he addressed lectures on politics to them, using editorial You; the others he avoided.

When he felt insufficiently appreciated or when my mother disagreed with his views, he would say with rueful conviction, "A man is never a prophet in his own home town," and till I was grown I mistook the key word for "profit," possibly because he was a businessman as well as a lawyer and often spoke of "the profit motive," for example, as the real reason for the United States' hostility to communism ("Markets! Markets! It's all economics! The profit motive!"). Strangely enough, I attributed almost the right meaning to the adage anyway, though I was puzzled by its semantic awkwardness. Then at some point I realized it was "prophet" he had been uttering all those years. So it was not respect and credit and glory that he sought, but spiritual allegiance. Disciples. In a less exalted sense, company.

He loved company, especially on errands or trips to the doctor and dentist. He cajoled me into watching him get haircuts and have his shoes shined, and on a few Saturdays even took me along to see a client upstate, to have company for the drive. He would present me with aplomb to the barber or client, try to get me to say something clever, then proceed with business. I always brought a book. I, who loved the idea of going places alone and thought it the pinnacle of adulthood, would suspect that, like our government in its hostility to communism, he had an ulterior motive—to get me out of the house or tell me a secret—but he didn't. He truly wanted company.

In turn he would offer to drive us—his children—and our friends to places, and given the way he loved to drive, he would want to drive us to places we preferred to walk to, and would feel slighted when his offers were declined. He had little understanding of walking for pleasure, of allowing time to flow unorganized, of not wishing to "make good time." He took walks, as far as I was aware, only during the summers, in the country, when he would often ask me along for company. We would set out down the dirt road and he would commence beating the bushes on either side for a good walking stick. He couldn't amble along without a purpose, so the purpose became finding the walking stick. I would find a few candidates, but they generally didn't meet his standards, which were unclear. At last he would find just the right one—thick, sturdy, a good height; he would rip the twigs and leaves from it and, holding it in his right hand and stomping it on the ground, walk still more purposefully, trying it out. We went along, talking; he explained things to me, not about the natural surroundings we were in, of which he knew nothing, but political and social things; sometimes I even had the pleasure of being editorial You and having my responses solicited in a Socratic way. Before I was ever satisfied with our walk, he would turn around. It seemed the thrill of the walk was over once he had found the stick and tested it. At the end of the walk he would usually toss it back into the woods, and when the next walk came around he regretted it. "I had such a good walking stick last week— what ever happened to it?" He had a nostalgic turn of mind. Nothing today was as good as it had been yesterday, and nothing was ever as good as it could be.

The world in general showed an offensive, needless disorder. At the refusal of people and events in the world of our household to arrange themselves as he wished and knew to be best, he often called, in alarming tones, for "discipline." He was forever "putting his foot down." "Discipline! Discipline!" and when I was quite young it would frighten me to think of what terrible rules might be forthcoming. But it was only the word. The foot never came down. After such scenes my mother, who was intimidated neither by his pronouncements and threats nor by their volume, would tell me that his father, "the old man," had been a stern disciplinarian, and that while his sons forever resented him for it, they kept the notion that it was the way to be a father. I am hard put to remember any rule he actually laid down. No comic books and no reading at the dinner table are all that come to mind, and the latter we—my sister and I, the offenders—often ignored. This is not to say that his bark was worse than his bite. His bark *was* his bite. To know him meant to have been exposed to his fierceness, fiercely articulate. But even then what did you know, really? Only that he had an immense vat of boiling fury inside, in precarious balance, waiting to be tipped over.

Certain times when his anger was provoked, or when he wished to give the impression that it was, he would stand quite still and say he was "counting to ten." He would press his lips into a hard thin line and I would imagine, pounding inside his head, "One, two, three . . ." Then he would speak quietly, in a tight voice. He took pride in these moments of tantrums controlled notwithstanding great provocation, and even seemed to expect admiration from us, his near victims. But no one congratulated him, for we understood he was only pretending: the provocation lacked the mysterious extra grain that rubbed the equally mysterious sore place in his soul and caused the explosive, intolerable pain, sweeping him past the gates of civilized restraint to a far and savage, solitary place. Then there was no counting to ten. Then he would call volcanically for "peace and quiet." "Will you let me have some peace and quiet!"— holding his head as if it might erupt. At the apogee of the tantrum he would yell at my mother, "You make my life miserable!" and would flee, slamming the front door so the house shook. I would hear the engine starting up in the driveway, sputtering as violently as he, then the whiz of the car escaping down the street. I was sure he would never be back. The next hour or two, alone in my room with the door closed, I would try to decide whom to live with after the divorce, and conjure the scene of myself being consulted in the judge's chambers, a dark room with dark drapes and green carpets and oak furniture, the judge in black robes and gray hair, with a somber countenance, feeling sorry for me in my plight—the whole scene something like a Rembrandt painting, murky, a spiritual murk, redolent of profundity and pain. It was a difficult decision; there were significant pros and cons on either side, but I knew how to give a yes or no answer, and most of the time (not always—not when I was too repelled by his noise) I would decide to go with my father, never doubting that he would request me of the judge: he was easier to live with, his arbitrariness congruent with my own; he set fewer rules and left me more to myself. I felt a temperamental affinity, I understood him, or so I believed. And the absence of my mother would not really be an absence, I felt obscurely. A mother is so close, you can carry her around inside wherever you go. But a father can escape. And then who would talk to me? His presence, like that of all men, was exotic. When he came home at night I would ask what he had done out in the world, and he would tell me. I would have a glimpse of what awaited me.

I felt sorry for my mother for the impending loss of us both (and how baffled she would be at my choice!), but after all, she had provoked him, hadn't she? Yet why did his reaction have to be so violent—why the words so torrentially bitter? Why remove a splinter with pliers? The answer was a mystery known as the family temper, spoken of by my aunts and uncles by marriage with a resignation they might have employed for the genealogical shape of a chin or a hand. No one sought its origin, mired in the bogs of history and the tangle of chromosomes. No one had ever gotten anywhere trying to reform it; you lived with it and navigated your way around it, like a neighbor's savage watchdog.

I don't think my father knew what he was so angry about

either. He was not introspective by nature and the habit of introspection had not yet suffused the middle class so that one undertook it as a duty whether or not so inclined. He too must have felt his terrible temper as a hereditary burden no more eradicable than his inherited and tireless heart, which kept cruelly beating when every other organ had failed and when he tried to yank from his chest the patches hooking him to the heart monitoring machine, mistaking them for life-sustaining equipment. And because he was not introspective and his words were spontaneously borne on currents of logic or enthusiasm or impulse or rage, we were not a family who ever "talked things over." When I hear nowadays the psychological language urging family members to settle differences by calm discussion, to reveal their feelings, be "open," when I see snatches of television families "working things through," I get a sense of comic unreality. I try it so that my children do not become thralls to verbal fire and brimstone, but I have a sense of rubbing against the grain, of participating in some faddish, newfangled ritual. I feel like shouting out what I want and hearing others shout back, and slugging it out with ever more pungent insults. . . .

While I drifted in fantasies of our life together, in which I would know instinctively how not to provoke him, the car would pull into the driveway, the door would open and close with a temperate sound. Relief and disappointment: no dramatic change now, no exotic twosome. I never gave a thought to where he might have been during that hour or two. Probably just driving, counting to ten, till the wild sea-green vein in his right temple stopped pulsing.

After these outbursts, my mother could remain cool for days ("belligerent," he would call her; "Why do you walk around with a chip on your shoulder?"), but she sensibly refused to believe she made his life miserable. I, who took all words literally, especially those spoken with passion, still thought it logical and inevitable that one of them should leave. The concept of leaving was not in my mother's repertoire of possibilities, and besides, she regarded the words as no more meaningful than steam or lava. She preferred to give credence to other of his remarks, such as when in company, if she referred to her size—she was a very large woman—and he had had a drink or two, he would say gaily, "I love every inch of it," though most of the time, quite unlike her, he was reserved to the point of prudery about sexual matters. I saw him twist my mother's arm with the playful sadism that was his sign of physical affection, but I never saw a real embrace or a real kiss.

She said too that when they were alone he was another way entirely; he merely had to "show off" in front of others. She was instinctively right about matters of the heart; it was probably this very rightness, those relentless instincts, amiably presented, unsupported by any rational structure, that my father found so exasperating. Also, despite her conventional moral judgments, she had endless sympathy and excuses for wrongdoers. Public Defender, he called her, and this too, I realized only later, was a legal term with a very specific meaning. He might be ready with money, words, car rides, and devotion, but he could not, or would not, comprehend moral ambivalence or extend sympathy for emotional confusion. Once, when I was in my twenties, I tried talking to him about some painful dilemma, which took nerve—we all talked a lot, constantly, but we did not "have talks." As I started to cry he walked out of the room. When he saw it was something no money or car ride could help, that I was not editorial You this time, he was confounded, as confounded as the woman crossing the street.

I never saw but one tear of his: at the funeral of my mother's mother he delicately flicked at his lower lid with his pinkie, smiling cavalierly, pretending it was a speck. My grandmother, she of Williamsburg, was a woman of the sort he loved: feisty, clever, pretty, bold, swift, decisive, and opinionated, and years earlier he had taught her, in Yiddish, to play gin rummy, in which all those qualities could be brought to bear, and had pronounced her an excellent player, which was very unusual, because most of the people he played cards with, including my mother and the five men in his weekly pinochle game, he called morons.

When he was old and sick and I visited him, I brought along many pairs of corduroy pants to hem—I had young children and was busy, I couldn't waste a minute. He wasn't saying much. But sitting on the back porch, watching me pick up one pair of corduroy pants after another, he did say, "You haven't stopped sewing since you got here." I nodded and kept on. Would it not be sufficient, he was asking, simply to keep him company, even if he could no longer offer the flow of words? He may even have been acknowledging—little as I like to think he knew about such matters—that I couldn't sit still and watch him die, I could hardly sit under the best of circumstances, so I let down hems for growing children. At that moment he was undergoing, as Jakob Rosenberg says of Rembrandt's last portrait, "some decline in . . . expressive power." His face showed "a diminished intensity." His spirit, so amply present in the serene and judicious photo, was leaving puff by puff. He was in the process of ceasing to care.

I have had the graduation photo of my father for almost ten years, since he, raging without words, died, and the picture postcards of the Rembrandts for about two years. Only the other day did the fourth one, my father in his sixties, fall into my hands, completing the group, that is, notifying me that they formed a group. My father would find all this silly and suppositious, especially since I clearly live, as he did, by the word. I would not attempt to explain to him, even if I could, that the pictures have been speaking to me in sentence fragments, subjects only, for a very long time, and that the arrival of the fourth picture was the long-awaited predicate. And then they had to be translated.

The Last Frontier

For George Madison it was the final indignity. His wife, Louise, woke first that Sunday morning, to find the two older children in their sleeping bags on the floor but the three-year-old gone. The chair George had placed in front of the door to substitute for the broken lock lay on its side. Louise threw on a robe and ran out into the corridor of the Peter Minuit Hotel, where they had been sent after a fire in their apartment building, shouting the baby's name, Denny, short for Dennis. A torn bag sent a barrage of empty beer and soda cans rolling across the floor. She navigated her way around these and a clump of children huddled over toy soldiers, ignoring the boy from across the hall who proudly waved a plastic bag containing a captured mouse. When she heard an answering, gurgling shout she swept through the partly open door from which it had come. The baby, wearing his terrycloth stretch suit with the padded feet, stood near a rickety bridge table where four big boys clustered. On the table lay a hand mirror and one of the boys bent over it, sniffing something through a straw.

"Denny!" she called sharply. The baby, seemingly unharmed, ran happily to embrace her knees.

"Pigs!" she shouted at the boys. "What do you want with a little baby!"

"No one hurt your precious baby, lady. He walked in just like you. He's cute."

"Trash!" Louise hissed.

"Hey, watch your mouth, girl. Take him, just get out, okay?"

She scooped up the baby and, nearly colliding with a girl on a skateboard, ran back to their room, where she woke George.

"We are not staying in this rathole one more minute," he said when he heard her story.

None of her objections—where would they go, what could they do, with three children and three suitcases?—could shake his will. Within an hour Denny and the others, Ronald, eleven, and Coralie, seven, were dressed and had had their orange juice with doughnuts from the box Louise kept on the windowsill, the suitcases were packed, and the Madisons were downstairs in the mud-colored lobby that smelled of ashes and air spray. George slapped the useless key on the desk before a lean, sleepy-looking man chewing on a toothpick. "This is no place for us," he accused. The clerk adjusted the toothpick and lowered his head over his newspaper.

Outside the Peter Minuit, George felt a surge of relief, like waking from troubled sleep into blessed reality. The life assigned his family had been an error made in some downtown office; now that it was corrected, his body expanded in the open air of midtown Manhattan as if something essential were restored.

"You're a crazy man, you know?" Louise said hours later. "How long you think we can all keep walking?" She was pushing the baby in the stroller luckily salvaged from the fire, with Coralie hanging on to the side. George and Ronald carried the suitcases. All day they had been in and out of apartment buildings. "I can pay rent," George told the doormen. "We're working people. No welfare." His Aunt Matilda had warned him about making that clear, but it did no apparent good. With two exceptions, forlorn sunless places costing more per month than George presently earned, the answer was no. Often rent was not even an issue—you had to buy the little cells for unthinkable sums. A couple of building superintendents, remarking on his accent, had tried to be helpful, suggesting he look around the edges, uptown in Harlem or downtown in Alphabet City. George nodded politely. The city people had tried to lure him there too, but he had not traveled all this way to be worse off than he began, or to raise his children in such unlovely, frankly perilous surroundings. The family had stopped twice to use the bathroom, first in the Cooper Union for the Advancement of Science and Art and then, a few miles north, in the Museum of Natural History, where they had had to pay. "But we'll only be a minute," George protested. The clerk pointed to a sign above his booth: "Pay what you wish but you must pay something." George took a dollar from his pocket. "How many?" the white man said, disdainful. "Five. Family of five." After the museum they stopped to get slices of pizza and Cokes.

"These children can't go on much longer," Louise said. "We better go up to your aunt's."

"Matilda's got no room, you know that. I'll find us something."

They trudged south, and then west, Coralie whining that her feet hurt. "Hush," Louise murmured. "Just hush up now."

The light was fading. Exhausted, Louise began to doubt her own eyes: quite a few people on the street, the children, mostly, seemed to belong to another order of reality. A small antennaed Martian, green from top to toe, pranced by, holding a woman's hand. Behind them, a troop of skeletons. Convicts in their stripes, a mermaid, and a centaur appeared out of nowhere.

Ronald glanced at his mother's gaping face. "Halloween, Ma."

"Trick or treat?" A girl held out her hand. She wore a silver tiara and a long white dress with stars sewn on the skirt and carried a scepter. Her denim jacket was open to show loops of rhinestones around her neck. George passed her by and pressed his family on. Louise had to yank Coralie by the hand; she was walking backwards, gazing after the beggar queen.

Suddenly George came to a halt. They stood in the twilight on a bleak empty street near the land's edge; the river sent its chill through the air and Coralie whimpered that she was cold. Opposite them was a squat, four-story white building with plate-glass doors, a building George had been in half a dozen times over the last few weeks, hunting down mazes of corridors for the secretaries who had ordered lunches. On weekdays men in business suits and women in high-heeled shoes, carrying briefcases, streamed in and out, but today it was deserted.

The baby whined and clutched at his pants.

"Shh, one more minute." George leaned down to pat him. "Just another minute." He rushed them all across.

"Excuse me," he addressed the guard fussing with the locks on the door. He was a young black man in a blue uniform, scarcely older than Ronald, it seemed. "Would you mind—the baby needs to use the bathroom. . . ."

"Uh-uh. You need a pass to get in. Try the coffee shop down the street." He waved east.

"Come on, man." George smiled with a certain charm. "He's just a baby."

"This is not a public building. Anyway, it's closing."

"Which island you from?" asked George. "I can tell the way you speak."

The guard looked astonished and murmured, "Barbados."

"We're from Saint Thomas. Charlotte Amalie, you know? American citizens. You a citizen yet?"

"Look, I don't care what you are—"

"Come on, be a good fellow. It'll take a minute, how about it?"

Evidently the young guard was not yet a thorough New Yorker, for in the end he pointed the way, frowning. Louise and the others waited on the street for what seemed an unduly long time. When George finally returned with Denny, he thanked the guard cordially. "This way," he commanded, back outside. "Walk slow."

"What's in your mind, George? How much longer—"

"Just follow me."

He led them around one corner, then another, till they came to a heavy metal fire door at the rear of the building. A rolled-up handkerchief held it slightly ajar.

"Get in here, hurry."

"Dad, what are you doing?" Ronald said. "You'll get us arrested."

"It's no crime for a man to take care of his family. You all were cold, weren't you? So come along!"

He ran jerkily through a dim corridor, the suitcases bobbing at his sides. When he found the elevator he used on his deliveries, he urged them in and pressed four, the top floor.

"This is no good, George. It's crazy."

"You tell me something better and I'll do it. Wait, you'll see."

More dim corridors brought them to a vast black open space. George found the switches on the walls, and dozens of lights came on. They were square black fixtures, row upon row, high up, imprisoning circles of light like moons dropping from the ceiling.

"What kind of place is this?" Coralie whispered. "A castle?"

It was a twentieth-century castle, cavernous, and divided into sections, rooms without walls, or rather half-finished spaces trying to become rooms. Tables, chairs, and couches stood about in purposeless groups. Household bits, an ironing board, a broom, a lamp, unattached doors and windows, leaned against the far walls. Television sets hung from the ceiling like chandeliers.

Coralie danced away and vanished. As if from a great way off, her voice rang out, "Mama! A regular house!"

Louise ran towards the voice, pushing Denny. Coralie was plunked on a beige couch in an elaborately furnished living room, her feet dangling over a mustard-colored carpet. This room was almost complete: coffee table, a small, elegant desk, a china closet, paintings on the walls, sliding glass doors that led to what resembled, inconceivably, a terrace, and on one wall, shuttered half-doors that opened to a commodious kitchen. The front door opened on an outside hall leading nowhere. The children were rushing here and there, exploring; Denny climbed out of his stroller to trail after them.

"It's missing the last wall," said Coralie. "It's not a regular house."

"It's got a roof," George replied gruffly.

Louise opened the refrigerator. Empty. "It's not cold. Not turned on." She tried the faucets in the sink. No water. But there were a few pots and dishes and glasses in the cabinets.

Off the living room George noticed a master bedroom with an ample double bed. The very sight of it made him want to lie down and never get up, but he needed to fix the lock and the alarm on the fire door downstairs first. When he returned he found Louise trying the knobs of the gas range, to no avail.

"Didn't I tell you I'd find something? What do you think?"

"I think you need to have your head examined." The place looked familiar in an unsettling way; she had the feeling she had seen it before, long ago, somewhere else, and not quite so cluttered.

"Dad," Ronald began gingerly. "Dad, don't get mad, but . . . we can't stay here. You know what this is? It's not real."

"What do you mean, not real!" George stormed into the living room and threw himself on the couch, slapping the cushions with fury. They were soft, unresisting. "This couch is real, ain't it? That big bedroom there is real. You shut up now, about real and not real. I'm deciding what's real."

"George, take it easy," Louise said. "You're wore out. The bed is real, so go lie down on it. You kids help me with the sleeping bags. Then we'll go find where to wash up. You're all grimy."

"I'm starving," Coralie said.

Louise took the doughnuts and a bag of apples from her carryall. "You make do with these for now. I'll get you a good breakfast before school tomorrow." She went to put her bag on the desk and drew back with a start. There was a large framed photograph of a woman, and several smaller photos in a plastic cube. Yes, she knew these people all right. But it had been so long. Ronald would hardly remember, and Coralie was too young. . . . Nevertheless, while the children were busy eating, she placed the photos in the top drawer.

By seven-thirty the next morning they were ready to leave. The men's room near the elevator had been decent enough, although Coralie objected to the liquid soap—she said it looked like pee—and Louise said she was dying for a shower.

"Take your shower at Matilda's," George grumbled. "Or at that Mrs. Axelrod's."

After Louise checked one last time to be sure they hadn't left any traces, and surreptitiously replaced the photos, they tiptoed down three flights of musty stairs, carrying suitcases, stroller, and baby. George adjusted the lock on the fire door before they set off in the hazy sunshine. A cool watery smell rose from the river, and the breeze at their backs was soft, not yet wintry. On the street still lingered a benign aftertaste of dawn.

"I'll meet you later at Matilda's," he said at the subway. "You going to manage all right with those suitcases? Ronald, you help your mother."

"What about tonight? One night, okay, but—"

"Not now, sugar. I'm late." He kissed the four cheeks and dashed. George worked at a delicatessen a few blocks south, unpacking supplies, making deliveries, clearing tables. His fellow workers were much younger or much older men, several of whom didn't speak English; a few in the kitchen displeased him with the seedy demeanor of people who did not lead regular lives. To George it was crucial to lead a regular life to the extent that one was available; overnight he had come to cherish the new found haven for its fluffy bed and its drapes and carpeting, and most of all for its shuttered half-doors between the kitchen and living room, through which food and drinks might be served, a nice touch. Back home they had had a small neat gingerbread house in a pretty part of town and he had been an electrician, doing all right, but he would never do much better. And for five years his Aunt Matilda had been urging them to come. She was lonely for family in New York, she wrote—since her husband had died there was no one of her blood, and George was like her own son. He had a useful trade; he wouldn't lack for work. As for those clever children, why, here they could become anything. Her letters touted the names of black entertainers and athletes and politicians. From the quantity of names, Louise used to say, you would think that black people had taken over, the millennium had come. Matilda was keeping her eye out for an apartment: the building's super owed her a favor for the time she nursed his infant grandchild through a week of projectile vomiting; she had been a practical nurse in her youth. At last there were four vacant rooms on the floor below, and George and Louise made the giant leap. He had taken the first job he saw—a Help Wanted sign in a downtown window one month ago—to get the family started, but he was sure to find work in his own line soon enough. He would be moving on up, and with Louise working too, it would not take long. Their new neighborhood, Washington Heights, was on the drab side, its streets fallen from grandeur, but for all that it was no slum. The bustle of large and noisy families was generous, fluid; it accommodated new arrivals. Naturally they missed the grace of the island, most of all the gaudy splashes of flowers everywhere, but they were prepared for that. There was no preparation for the building's going up in flames two weeks later, wild bursts of color like gorgeous bougainvillea turned treacherous. They had hardly any furniture to lose yet, not even a TV set. The loss was less tangible.

Misfortune deposited them in municipal hands, to dispose of as they would. Men and women with spectacles and clipboards asked intimate questions, then sent them to the Peter Minuit Hotel, which existed, they explained, to provide for the unfortunate. What it provided was deprivation. It dragged George's spirit into foul byways, through smells, dirt, and all the emblems of decay. Seeing his wife and children join its wretched colony was the ultimate mortification.

Meanwhile Matilda moved in with a friend next door to the charred building, the friend being a sister of the same super. Guilt-stricken, she did what she could—took the kids in after school, minded Denny while Louise went out to work, even found work for her. With Matilda's help, Louise soon had her days all organized: Monday, Mrs. Axelrod; Tuesday, Mrs. Butler; Wednesday, off—she tended to errands and looked for an apartment; Thursday, Mr. Vickers, the easiest because she never saw him—he left the key with the doorman and the money on the kitchen table; Friday, Mrs. Takamura, wife of a diplomat, and tennis friend of Mrs. Axelrod. Louise would arrive before nine and clean as fast as she could, discouraging all conversation till the ladies thought her dull-witted or mute, in order to finish in time to pick up Coralie at school. Ronald, who had made friends, might want to stay on and play ball—he should not be always saddled with a little sister. She hoped it was ball he was playing. You could not badger a boy with questions, but she scrutinized him carefully on his return, and when doing the laundry, the heavy jeans, in the basement of Matilda's building, was reassured to find smudges of dirt on the knees or the seat of his pants; that was as it should be when boys played ball. After the day's work she would rest at Matilda's place, in front of the friend's big color TV, holding Denny on her lap. She didn't much care what she looked at and let Coralie fiddle with the dial. Coralie fancied reruns of cheerful families whose problems got solved in half an hour. Their houses or apartments looked alike, all with a big sofa absurdly set in the middle of the living room, but monotonous as they were, Louise would gladly have accepted any one. She lapsed into reveries picturing her family in those places. With the right clothes and TV makeup they could look as fine as any Partridges or Keatons, Cunninghams, Bradys, or Bradfords, Huxtables, Romanos, Evanses, or Thomases—enough to populate a small village back home. Coralie in particular was very pretty, taking after George with her wide face and strong cheekbones, and George was a stocky square-jawed man, even better-looking since he had grown the mustache. She would be more than willing to fret over little mix-ups that seemed intractable but were always cleared up in the end.

Since today was Monday and Mrs. Axelrod watched the clock, she hurried the children down the subway steps, and using the map, she and Ronald figured out the route uptown.

"You said breakfast, Mama," Coralie reminded her when they got out.

"Breakfast, Mama," Denny repeated.

"Breakfast! Good Lord, how could I forget? It's all this moving around. And that place we stayed at."

"Mama, you know what that place was?" Ronald asked.

"Don't tell me, Ronald. I don't want to know no more than I already do. We'll go in here for Eggs McMuffin. Come on."

After she dropped Coralie at school, Ronald insisted on walking her back to Matilda's, where she would leave Denny. It was clear she could never make it alone with the suitcases and stroller.

"You'll be late."

"No I won't. I'll run. I'm trying out for the track team." He got her into the elevator and run he did, through the lobby to the front door in a streak, backpack slapping against his shoulders. A good boy, Louise thought as the door slid shut.

"We moved," Coralie told Matilda after school. "To a castle."

"What kind of castle! Don't you start telling stories, girl."

"Ask my mother when she come back up. I'm not telling stories."

Louise entered with a basket of laundry and sat heavily down. "It's no castle, Matilda. Just some peculiar place George found."

"George found a place? That's real good. Why you so glum, then? How much rent you pay? Where's it at?"

"Downtown."

"Downtown where, Louise?"

"Fifties, maybe?"

"No address?"

"It's temporary. Just till we can find something better."

Wiry and shrewd, Matilda regarded her for a moment. "Comfortable, at least? Furnished, or what?"

"Oh, very comfortable." Louise curled deeper in the soft chair. It was the first night in two weeks she and George had had a room to themselves.

"Why'd you bring these old suitcases, then?"

"Lord, I am so tired. I waxed four floors this morning.

How's my baby doing, eh? Come here, sweet baby. Was he a good boy today, Matilda?"

"Good boy today," Denny echoed.

"You want to be secretive, you go 'head. I'm going to fix dinner."

Louise turned her attention to *Gilligan's Island.* A group of castaways had put together living quarters on their desert island. Simple but adequate. Uninterested in the plot, she studied the various domestic arrangements, but they proved of no help. Manhattan was not a desert island. The story was pure fantasy, fantasy characters living in a further fantasy, like Coralie's plastic nesting boxes, melted in the fire.

George was not so close-mouthed. "You hear we found a place?" he said to his aunt over dinner, lentils and sausages. "I knew I would. Big! You could put twenty more families in the extra space. Just wait till I get working on it, then we—"

"Working on it!" Ronald almost choked. "Dad—"

"Ronald!" His mother nudged his leg.

"Well, I'll be looking forward to an invitation. When you say so, of course." Matilda sounded cool.

"Mind if I leave two suitcases here?" Louise asked.

She stared. "I won't ask you no more questions. Put them in the closet where Delia won't trip on them. She'll be home from work pretty soon, so why don't you go on down to your nice new home so's I can clean up."

George insisted that they stay. There was no reasoning with him—he snapped and sulked if Louise or Ronald protested. Anyway, what could they suggest in its place? It was better than the Peter Minuit, she had to admit. Lonely, yes, after the lushness of home, the warm air sweet and weighty with human life, but loneliness was better than neighbors who terrified you. And George was doing his best. Near the elevator he had discovered a row of well-appointed offices, and in the largest was a bathroom with a tiled shower. By turning a few valves he made water flow in the kitchen sink; he even managed to turn on the gas so they could have coffee in the morning and Louise could fry bread and eggs for the children—with all the fancy shutters and carpeting, there was no toaster. Once he had adjusted some wires behind the refrigerator, she could keep food overnight for the lunches she packed as the sun came up; she even began fixing simple suppers, to avoid imposing on Matilda so often. Evenings, after the homework was done and Denny asleep, they sat in the living room gazing up at the TV suspended in air—George had gotten it to work with extension cords—and displaying the sprightly families in the featureless homes, never a picture crooked on the wall or a newspaper strewn on the floor. Watching, Louise would grow faint with unease. The families on TV lived in no real place, and yet if real people lived there, perhaps it became real. Or could the real people be turned instead into fantasies? The border between those realms, once clear and precise, was stretching open, perhaps to swallow her like a ravine. Luckily fatigue cut short such speculation. It was not simply her days at work. The hardest work was scurrying around after all the eating, sleeping, washing, and dressing, to destroy every trace of human passage.

One night when they finished supper early they heard a familiar blithe tune, buoyant voices singing about moving on up to the East Side, to a deluxe apartment in the sky. The screen showed a black family this time, the father a runty-looking fellow with a mustache, the mother very handsome in an ample, genial way, and a fine-looking son. The kind of young man George would be happy to see Ronald become—he had thought that even years ago, when he first saw this family and Ronald was a mere baby. It might well happen, too—Ronald had grown to be a clever, responsible boy. . . . They were arguing, the father showing himself, as always, to be a loud and silly man. As he strode angrily about, the living room came into view. George's throat stuck and he could not swallow. He disguised a gasp with a cough. A heavy silence shaped itself around him.

It was almost a relief when Coralie shouted, "Daddy, look!" A shriek for the impossible, the sound rimmed with wonder and protest.

George leaped from the couch and bounded off the un-
walled threshold of the apartment, past the lights and gargan-
tuan cameras. As he tore the cord from the wall the faces were
sucked into a tiny white light that died like a vanquished star.
"Daddy, Daddy!" she cried again. "Did you see?"

He took a deep breath. The irascible mustached man on the
screen had looked so foolish in his rage. He swept Coralie up
in his arms and whirled her about. "Hey, big girl with the big
voice! Look how heavy you are now! Are you too big to play
pony like we used to?"

Overjoyed, she swung her legs over his shoulders as Louise
and Ronald watched, stiff and silent. Look-alikes, George often
thought them. Dark full faces, keen orange-tinged eyes. This
very moment those keen glances were shaming him, and un-
justly. Wasn't he doing all a man could possibly do under the
circumstances?

In bed that night Louise felt the misery in his curved back
and put her arms around him. "George, honey, we've been
lucky so far. But you know it can't last. Anyway, it's just not
right. No neighbors, nothing. Like off in outer space, you
know?"

There was only the sound of his breathing.

"And it's getting cold, and no heat at night."

Anger shot to his skin, to be appeased by her hands. "I'll
get us some space heaters." He turned to face her.

"George," she sighed. "Do you even hear me?"

"I'll be your space heater, eh? How's that?"

He kissed her and she sighed again, then put it all aside and
gave in. There were few enough pleasures.

She did not tell him that the night before, while he and
Ronald were out getting Chinese food, an old black woman in
sneakers, dragging a mop and pail, had appeared outside. Outside the apartment, that is, in the spacious darkness Louise
pretended was a forest surrounding them, the cameras bizarre
trees and bushes.

"Hold it," the woman had said, spotting Louise. "I must of

got out at the wrong floor. What's this here?"

"Four."

"Shit. I done pressed the wrong button. I'm supposed to do three on Monday and Wednesday. Who can keep track, I ask you. I thought the one for up here came in the mornings. What you doing here now?"

"They asked me." Louise shrugged. "I guess there's something special going on in the morning."

The woman had already started dragging her mop towards the elevator. She looked back over her shoulder. "You bring your kids with you? Jeez, what you young girls won't think of."

Louise breathed again when the woman disappeared. From then on she spent every spare moment searching for a place to live, sometimes alone, sometimes with Coralie and Denny. She didn't like leaving them with Matilda all the time, hearing her pained questions and telling pained lies. When Denny got chilly or cranky they resorted to what shelter was at hand. She tested the beds in the furniture department of Macy's, sat at the dining room tables and imagined her family seated around her, each one before an impeccable, tasteful place setting, with Denny in a high chair. They might just as easily have ended up here. But Denny got restless in department stores. His favorite place was the Museum of Natural History ("Pay what you wish but you must pay something"): behind glass loomed dioramas of exotic dwellings, igloos, Indian villages, even the lairs of wild animals. It was cozy and soothing in the dusky rooms encircled by glaring beasts, so real and menacing, yet utterly harmless. And downstairs was a fully equipped cafeteria where they stopped for snacks. It might be spooky at night, though, sleeping in the shadow of dinosaur bones. . . . Coralie wanted to live next door in the Planetarium, under the stars, but Louise explained that the stars in the Planetarium came out only at show times. "Aren't they the real stars?" she wanted to know. "They're the real stars, but in a sort of picture. You can't see them unless they turn on the machine." Coralie was not satisfied with this explanation. Louise was puzzled herself.

Over on Fifth Avenue stood a stately mansion through

whose doors passed beautifully dressed people surrounded by an aura—what was it? Ownership, she decided. If only she could enter, she too might move in that aura, where nothing could be denied her. She would care for it well, leaving not a trace in the morning—she knew how. But the man at the entrance said children under ten were not permitted. That would never do.

In the big museum farther up the avenue everyone was permitted (again, "Pay what you wish but you must pay something"). Whole classes of children, shepherded by their teachers, stampeded up its imposing front stairs. Indeed, the crowd packing its lobby was huger than the crowd at the airport six weeks ago that seemed like six years, and more avid than the shoppers who streamed off the ships each afternoon to fill the streets of Charlotte Amalie. The room Louise loved best, perhaps because it reminded her a little of home, looked like a greenhouse, huge and light, sun streaming in the slanted glass walls. They could eat here in its waning rays, and the children could play beneath the immense potted plants. They would sleep on the long leather benches in the adjacent rooms or even, she thought in a moment of despair, across the lobby on the old stone tombs of kings and queens.

She finished early on a Thursday, Mr. Vickers's day, and after an hour of apartment hunting in a shabby district, wandered into the YMHA—there was no hurry; Coralie was visiting a friend from school. The guards on each floor were friendly, and one showed her the heated swimming pool. The children would love that; they hadn't had a chance to go swimming since they got here. There were showers galore, and a lounge with soft couches, and surely somewhere a kitchen. She studied the catalogue; you could learn to do just about anything, it seemed. She could take up the guitar, or photography, or ballet—she used to be a good dancer before Ronald was born, when she and George had gone dancing every Saturday night. Coralie could learn arts and crafts, and Ronald and George could shoot baskets in the gym. There was even day care. Actually, the catalogue explained, the day care was for the babies of teen-aged girls who needed to finish high school, hardly her case, yet they might make an exception. . . .

But always there came the hour to return from these excursions to real life, either to meet the children at Matilda's or to go home. She was coming to think of it as home; day by day it housed a life with emerging outlines, and the pattern frightened her. She might be sitting in front of Matilda's friend's TV one afternoon and see herself. Ronald would rush in with a few of his ballplaying friends, sweaty, robust, energetic boys, worried over some little problem involving a lost bat or a failed exam, which she would set about solving only to complicate matters, but in the end all would be well, only a web of misunderstandings, nothing real.

She dragged herself reluctantly from the Y, and when she arrived at Matilda's, fell into a chair and shut her eyes.

"You that tired, child?"

"I sure am."

"When you go home tonight you get yourself a good rest. Don't do no more fixing up or whatever you do, just get yourself to sleep."

"I want to go home now!" Coralie clamored.

"We can't, honey. Not yet." It was only five-fifteen. George had said six was safe, but Louise didn't feel safe till six-thirty or seven, and even then, never quite safe.

"Why?"

"Oh, stop whining. Did you have a nice time with your friend? What's her name again?"

"Cindy. She wants to come to my house. Can she come to my house tomorrow?"

"No, not tomorrow."

"Why not?"

"Why not?" Denny echoed. Louise took him on her lap. He was too docile for a three-year-old. And she didn't recall the other two constantly echoing things. This life was taking its toll even on him. "Because I said so, that's why. Because we live too far downtown. Too long a trip for her mama to pick her up."

"She could sleep over. She could get in my sleeping bag."

"Coralie, we'll talk about it later—"

"What's this sleeping bag business? Ain't you all got beds yet?"

"Ronald and me, we sleep on the floor—"

"The beds are coming this weekend," she told Matilda.

"Huh! Well, stop your bickering. My program's coming on—they done give it a new time."

Coralie pouted and slunk away to the kitchen, and Louise bounced Denny absently as the theme song began. The family that was moving on up. There was the heavy, handsome woman with the deep voice, talking to another black woman. Louise couldn't remember seeing her before—it had been so long . . . From the way the lady of the house was giving instructions, friendly and specific, like Mrs. Butler, the other must be her maid. She answered back sassily, though, very familiar for a maid. Suddenly Denny catapulted from her lap to the screen, his index finger jabbing.

"Our living room! Our couch!" he cried. "The lady be sitting on our couch!"

"Stop poking that screen, Denny," said Matilda. "What's he saying?"

"Look, the mirror! Look, now our kitchen! There's things on the table."

"Denny!" Louise grabbed him. "Stop it!" Just when she was thinking maybe he was a little slow. "It's nothing. We have a couch something like that, that's all."

Denny struggled to get free. "Our house! Why are they in our house?"

"Louise, honey." Matilda turned to her. "What kind of place you living in? You got an East Side apartment like that?"

"Of course we don't."

Matilda sat up very straight. "That's why you never ask me over. You don't want no one there seeing who your family is."

"Matilda, you're talking crazy! How could we pay for a place like that? And you know I'd ask you if I could. It's just not fixed up yet."

"I want to go on TV too," Denny was hollering. "Mama, can I go on TV next time? Please?"

Coralie ran in from the kitchen, shouting, "Who's going on TV? Who?"

"I better go. George'll be home soon. Coralie, get your jacket. Ronald can come on down by himself. I'll leave a subway token."

"Yes, maybe it's time you went."

"Matilda, please. You just don't know. . . . Sometimes I fear I'm coming unstitched."

George arrived home slightly later than usual that night—he too had stopped to see a few cheap apartments advertised in the paper. But there was no point in looking, the supers had said: already taken. He was shoving despair to one side like a rampant undergrowth as he stepped out of the elevator, to find the place blazing with light. George had grown used to imagining, at this point each evening, that he was walking home through the amiable streets of his neighborhood, and he peopled them with faces from home. There, people in town had known him and greeted him, returning from work. Here it was like living on a desert island, or being the last family on a dark earth after they dropped the bomb. No dark earth tonight, though, but eerily bright, like coming home sick in the middle of the day.

He found Louise in the kitchen. "Why all the lights?" He kissed the children, picked Denny up and tossed him about.

"It was like this when we got here. Something's funny, George. I don't know. . . . The things outside are different too."

He saw from the kitchen window that the cameras had been rearranged. And out the sliding glass doors, behind the terrace, stood two enormous pieces of Masonite painted to show a city skyline by night. "Nah, it's nothing. I'll go turn them out. What's for dinner?"

"Hot dogs, potato salad, baked beans."

"Okay. I'll be right back. Don't none of you worry."

He found the switches and restored the safe darkness. No sooner had he settled on the couch with his newspaper than from the distance there came voices and heavy footsteps. The space outside flared up anew, showing George two tall, young-ish white men clumping through his neighborhood towards his house. He stood up quickly. In an instant Louise and the children were at his side.

"Hey," one of the strangers called, "what's going on here? What are you people doing?"

"Living," George said. "My wife's fixing dinner. My children are doing their homework. The baby don't do much of anything yet, you know how it is."

The intruders, holding cardboard coffee cups, stared at each other for a long moment. "Look, I don't know what you're talking about," said the same man, "but if you go quietly now you won't get into trouble."

"You're at my door, but you're not saying who you are."

"Your door! For Chrissake . . . Okay, okay, I'm the assistant producer and this is the cameraman. We're shooting an hour-long special in the morning and we need to set up the apartment upstairs. You get it? This is no real place to live."

"*It* may not be real," Louise said, surprising George, "but *we* are real."

"I'm real," said Ronald.

"I'm real too," said Coralie, and the baby echoed it, as he always did.

"You're real, sure!" exclaimed the assistant producer. "I'm not quarreling with that. I can also see you're new here, the way you talk. But the fact is, this is not meant for living in."

"But I've seen people living in it," said Louise. "And we're realer than they are."

"Well, that's just the point!" he blurted. But then he stopped short.

"Don't you see, man," said George equably, "if we're real and we live here, that makes it a real place to live."

"Listen. Listen!" The assistant producer began pacing and waving his arms distractedly, like a character in a TV family.

"I am not going to stand here having this . . . this ridiculous discussion. You don't belong here and I'm asking you politely to leave. Will you leave now?"

"I'm willing to pay rent," George said. "Nobody ask me before. Maybe I can't pay all you want, but I can pay something. We're both working people." An image flashed by him— his ordinary family of five, earning their keep by doing their natural living on TV, in front of the cameras. They could speak up loud and clear, act out little scenes, whatever was required. Ronald could be pretty funny when he was in the mood, and the baby was certainly as cute as any TV baby.

"It's not a question of paying rent! It's just not the way things work here! Now, for the last time, if you don't leave I'll have to call the police and we'll all waste a lot of time."

"You going to have the whole family arrested?" George let out a short laugh. "The baby too? What for? My wife for boiling hot dogs? My little girl for doing her spelling? Who are we hurting? What kind of city is this, anyway? No, man. You carry on with your stuff out there, we carry on with our living. We don't bother you none, you don't bother us." He would yield no more. The swift image had evaporated. In truth, he did not wish to live on TV, to make a ranting clown of himself like the small mustached man who lived on the screen, nor to have Louise show herself off like the spunky, long-suffering wife. He wanted his real life in the real world, though it appeared to have no place for him.

"This is too weird," groaned the cameraman to the other in disgust. "I'm getting to work. I don't know about you, but I want to get home before midnight." He tossed his jacket onto a stool and began wheeling one of the cameras to a nearby set.

"Thanks a lot," the assistant producer called out. All in a row, the family faced him, proclaiming their existence, occupying the space as if it would take heavy machinery to dislodge them. "What are you people planning to do? Stay here all night?"

"First we'll have our dinner," George replied, "sit around with the kids, maybe watch some TV. You know."

"Goddamn!" The assistant producer made fists and struck his own forehead. "Goddamn! What the fuck am I supposed to do?"

"These are young children," George warned. "They don't hear that kind of talk in the home."

"Sorry," the man muttered. "Sorry."

Killing the Bees

After Ilse and Mitch had both been stung twice, Mitch sprayed insecticide around the flower beds at the side of the house, where the bees seemed to congregate. But the very next day Cathy, their youngest child, got stung on the back of the neck. It was a bright May afternoon, the three of them out on the lawn with the Sunday papers, Cathy plugged into her Walkman. Quiet Ilse made a great fuss, jumped up and grabbed a handful of damp soil from the flower bed to slap on the bite, then crooned soothing words—as if, Cathy said with a brave patronizing smile, she were an infant and not almost fifteen.

"But doesn't it hurt a lot?"

"It hurts, Mom, but I'll live."

"What's the matter?" Mitch must have been dozing behind the travel section. He rearranged his body in the lawn chair and blinked, trying to look alert. He was a graying man of fifty-three, handsome in a ruddy, solid, ex-athlete's way, with strikingly pale blue eyes. He owned a chain of hardware stores. A safe man, Ilse thought each evening when he returned from work. And decent, competent, sexy: mornings, watching him dress—the ritual bending, reaching, zipping, and buttoning—she felt a reflexive pleasure, compounded with satisfaction, like the interest on capital, at how durable this pleasure had proved. If that was love, then she loved him well enough.

"It's those bees again. We really must do something about them. Poor baby. Come, let me wash it and put on some ointment."

"God, what would you do if I had rabies?"

Ilse knew why she was making a fuss: the one time she herself had been stung as a child—at four years old—her usually attentive mother hardly seemed to care. That baffling lapse, the utter failure to respond properly, even more than the throng at the airport or the loudspeaker barking, the pinched, scared faces and the forest of gleaming tall boots, told Ilse something portentous was happening. Her father had already kissed them goodbye and disappeared, leaving her mother teary, and she was close to tears again five minutes later, showing some papers to a mustached, uniformed man at a desk, who waved his clipboard in the air and called them to a halt in a gritty voice. Soon, like a little firecracker fizzling out, he spat a bad name at them and sent them on. Her mother was tugging her by the hand, rushing towards the stairs at the plane, when Ilse let out a howl.

"Shh! Don't make noise. What is it?"

"Something is in my dress! In back!"

Her mother yanked at the dress and slapped her back hard—to kill the bee, she said later—but that only made the sting worse.

"Be still now, Ilse!" she ordered. "I'll take care of it afterwards."

But Ilse wailed running up the stairs, and as they entered the plane people looked up disapprovingly. Her mother kept her head bowed. Only when they were above the clouds did she become herself again, rubbing spit on the sting till Ilse calmed down.

"When we meet our cousins," she said, belatedly kissing the sore spot, "can you say 'How do you do,' in English? How do you do?" She exaggerated the shape of the words on her lips and Ilse repeated. How do you do. But for long after, she felt betrayed in her moment of need.

In England, when she asked for her father, her mother said, "He's coming. He'll come as soon as he can." In time she understood there was a war going on: the children at school wouldn't let her play and made fun of the way she spoke. Her mother couldn't get a job and often they were hungry. Just as the

hunger was becoming unbearable, food would appear, Ilse
never knew how. If she complained, her mother said crypti-
cally, "Still, we're lucky. Lucky." She stopped asking about her
father and eventually the war was over. When they went looking for a flat in London she heard her mother tell the landladies
he was killed in the war. Then her mother would murmur some
words very low, as if she were embarrassed, and the landladies'
granite faces would loosen a bit, and a Mrs. Soloway finally let
them have a room.

In bed with Mitch that night, Ilse heard a humming noise,
muffled, but rhythmic and relentless like the plangent moan of
an infirmary.

"Listen. Do you hear anything?" she whispered.

"Only you breathing." Mitch lay with his head on her
stomach, his arms locked around her hips. Always, after they
made love, his voice was heavy and sweet with a childlike
contentment. "You sound sensational, Ilse. Do it a little
harder." He began kissing her belly again.

She smiled even though the noise agitated her. "Not that,
silly. Listen. It sounds like something in the wall."

He groaned and sat up, businesslike, turning on the lamp
as if that could make the noise clearer. They stared at each
other, concentrating, and indeed enlightenment came. "I bet it's
those fucking bees. They've managed to get into the wall now.
Jesus Christ!" He turned away to roll himself in the sheets.

"Hey, I didn't put them there," Ilse said softly. "Come on
back."

"You know what I'll have to do now? Make a hole in the
goddamn wall and spray inside. Just what we needed. A bee
colony."

"My sweet baby," she said, stroking him. "My prince to the
rescue. My Saint George killing the dragon."

"It's going to stink to high heaven," he said.

Mitch slept, but hours later Ilse was still trapped in wake-
fulness by the humming noise. She pictured a gigantic swarm
of bees fluttering their wings together in the dark, a shuddering

jellylike mass. It was an unbearable sound, ominous, droning. Of course, she thought. Drones.

The next two evenings Mitch forgot to bring the extra-strength spray home from the store. On the third day Ilse phoned to remind him. "Look, I hate to keep nagging, but I've hardly slept."

"They can't come out, Ilse."

"I know. I'm not afraid of bees anyway. It's the noise. Just bring it, will you please?"

After dinner he listened with his ear to the wall for the place where the noise was loudest, then chipped with a screwdriver until a tiny hole appeared. Quickly he shoved a small rectangle of shirt cardboard over the hole, and using that as a shield, made the hole bigger. When it was about a half inch in diameter, he told Ilse to go out of the room and close the door. She closed the door but stayed, standing back. It didn't seem fair to protect herself while he was in danger. Besides, she felt an eerie fascination. Mitch moved the cardboard aside and inserted the nozzle of the spray can. The smell was nasty and stinging, but not as bad as she had imagined. Then he covered the hole again and they fixed the cardboard to the wall with thumbtacks. Ilse heard a sharp crackling like the sound of damp twigs catching a flame.

"What's that?"

"It's them. That's what you wanted, isn't it? Let's just hope it gets them all."

A wave of nausea and dizziness assaulted her, and she lay down till it passed. That night she slept well, in blissful silence.

The following morning, one of her days off—she worked as a part-time secretary at a law firm in town—she was outside, kneeling to put in the marigolds, when she noticed a patch a few feet off that looked like speckled black velvet. She crawled closer. The corpses of bees, hundreds, thousands, the obscene remains of a massacre. She had never thought about where they would go, never thought further than getting rid of them. Why hadn't they simply rotted in the wall unseen? Peering up, she spied a dark mass the size of a cantaloupe, attached like a tumor to the outside wall not far from their bedroom window, and almost hidden by the thick leaves of the maple. Somehow they had never thought to look for a hive, but now it seemed obvious.

Ilse was not squeamish. She had disposed of dead ants and flies and even mice, but the sight of the slaughtered bees paralyzed her. She knelt in the garden for a long time, then dragged herself inside and phoned Mitch, but when he answered she found she couldn't tell him right away.

"This must be our lucky day," she said instead. "Both wanderers heard from." There had been a postcard from their son, Brian, who was working on a cattle ranch in Wyoming, and another from Melissa, who had just completed her second year of law school and, with three girlfriends, was recuperating for a week in Jamaica before starting her summer job.

"That's great." He sounded distracted.

Stammering a bit, Ilse mentioned the dead bees and the hive near the bedroom window.

"A hive, eh? I should have known. Well, just sweep them up, Ilse, okay? I'll have a look when I get home."

"Yes, well—you can't imagine how hideous . . . These are enormous bees. It's like a battlefield. . . . What should I do with them?"

"Do with them? Put them in the garbage, sweetheart. Unless you want to hold a mass funeral."

"I see I shouldn't have bothered you."

"Ilse, it's just that I've got a store full of customers. Leave it if you can't do it. Or have Cathy do it. It's not worth bickering over."

She tried sweeping them into a dustpan, but as she watched the bodies roll and tumble, the wings and feelers lacing and tangling, she felt faint. Finally she abandoned the task and left the marigolds, too, for another day. When Cathy came home from school she asked her to do it and Cathy obliged, with pungent expressions of disgust but no apparent difficulty.

Mitch got on a ladder and sprayed the hive. There was silence for several nights and they thought it was over. Then

Ilse woke before dawn and heard the humming in the wall, fainter, but still insistent. She began to weep, very quietly, so as not to wake Mitch.

After the war her mother got a clerical job at the National Gallery in London, where she met an American tour guide and married him.

"We're going to have a new life, darling," she told Ilse excitedly. Mostly they spoke German when they were alone, but her mother said this in English. "We're going to America with Robbie. Denver. You'll love it, I know." Ilse nodded. She was a silent child, the kind who seems full of secrets. At school she had few friends, was politely enigmatic, and did her work adequately, but the teachers nonetheless accused her of dreaming. In America she changed. Robbie was all right; he looked like a cowboy and sounded like Gary Cooper, and Ilse treated him as a casual friend of the family. But she did love America. No one shunned her. They liked her British accent and were eager to hear stories of life in London. I can be a normal girl, she whispered to herself one morning in the mirror. From now on. And she behaved as she perceived other normal girls to behave, a tactic which worked so well that she adopted it for the rest of her life. Meanwhile, when she was old enough to understand, around Cathy's age, she went on a binge of reading books about the war, till she was satisfied that she comprehended what had happened to her father, what his final years or months had been like, and had lived them in her bones up to the point where his own bones lay in a ditch, indistinguishable from the millions of others.

"You never talk about him." She expected her mother would hedge and say, About who? but she was mistaken.

"What can I say? He died in the war."

"But I mean, about how."

"Do you know how?" her mother asked.

"Yes."

"Well, so do I. So . . ."

She was craving a significant scene, tears and embraces, or

lies and shouting, culminating in cloak-and-dagger truths, secret horrors not included in any books, and above all in profun-
dities vast enough to connect the past to the present, but her
mother offered nothing.

"Did you cry?"

"What a question, Ilse. I cried plenty, yes."

But she was not about to cry anew for Ilse. They were
lucky, her mother repeated with lips stiff and quaking. "Remember all your life what a lucky person you are."

Ilse fled from the room. Now she had long forgiven her
mother. At the time they boarded the plane for London, she
realized, the day she got stung, her mother was twenty-four
years old. A girl the age of Melissa, who was swimming and
dancing in the Caribbean moonlight and about to earn extravagant sums of money. And at the time of their talk, her mother
had known Robbie for as long as she had known Ilse's father.
Her mother was truly lucky. In compassion, Ilse stopped pester-
ing her and let her live her lucky life.

Twice more Mitch moved aside the cardboard and sprayed
into the hole. Twice more the bees crackled, the room smelled,
and the nights were silent, then the noise returned.

"It's no use. We need an exterminator." And he sighed a
husbandly sigh of overwork.

"I'll take care of that." Ilse was expert at arranging for
services and dealing with repairmen. In the yellow pages she
found just what was needed: Ban-the-Bug, which promised to
rid your home of pests for good. Ban-the-Bug's logo was a
familiar black-bordered circle with a black line running diagon-
ally through the center. Three times a week Ilse saw that same
symbol, but in red, on the door of Ban-the-Bomb, a local group
with a small office opposite her own. Except instead of the
mushroom cloud in the center, Ban-the-Bug's circle displayed
a repulsive insect suggesting a cross between a winged cock-
roach and a centipede. The black line was firm and categorical:
it meant, Ilse knew, No More, Get Rid Of, *Verboten.*

On the telephone, she did not even have to supply details.

Ban-the-Bug understood all about the problem and would send a man over late that afternoon.

"Don't worry, you'll never have to hear that sound again," a reassuring, motherly voice told Ilse.

Never again. She would sleep in peace. The soothing promise echoed as she shopped and chatted in the market and set out on the kitchen counter all the ingredients for a Chinese dinner. With another secretary from the law firm she was taking a course in Chinese cooking, and Mitch and Cathy had been teasing her for a demonstration. Cathy had brought a friend home from school, and both girls volunteered to help. As Ilse sautéed garlic and ginger, the kitchen filled with a luxurious, tangy odor. She chopped the pork and set the girls to work on the peppers and scallions and cabbage.

The smell made her hungry, and as usual, hunger made her think of being hungry in London, such a different kind of hunger, long-lasting and tedious, like a sickness, and panicky, with no hope of ever being fully eased.

That was far away now, though. Her present hunger is the good kind, the hunger of anticipation.

The girls are jabbering across the large kitchen. Having raised two children to adulthood, Ilse is not passionately interested in the jabbering of teen-agers. But this conversation is special. It snares her. Evidently they are learning about World War II in history class, and Mary Beth, a thin, still flat-chested girl with straight blonde hair, is a Quaker, Ilse gathers. She is explaining to Cathy the principles of nonviolence.

"But there must be limits," Cathy says. "Like supposing it was during the war and you saw Hitler lying in the road, half dead and begging for water. You wouldn't have to actually kill him, just . . . sort of leave him there."

"If a dying person asks me for water I would have to give it," says Mary Beth.

"Even Hitler?"

Mary Beth doesn't hesitate. "He's a human being." Ilse chops pork steadily with her cleaver. She rarely mixes in.

"But my God! Well, supposing he asks you to take him to a hospital?"

"I guess I would. If it was to save his life."

"You'd probably nurse him and help him get back to work, right?" Cathy is irate, Ilse notes with a keen stab of pleasure in her gut.

"No, you don't understand. I'd never help him make war. But see, if I let him die it would be basically the same as killing him, and then I would become like him, a killer."

"So big deal. You'd also be saving a lot of people."

"I'd rather try to save them by talking to him, explaining what—"

"Oh, come on, Mary Beth. What horseshit."

Ilse accidentally grazes her finger with the cleaver and bleeds onto the pork. She sucks, tasting the warm blood with surprising glee. It has just left her heart, which strains toward her daughter with a weight of love.

"Look, Cathy," replies Mary Beth, "the real issue is what do I want to be? Do I want to be a truly good person or do I want to spend the next fifty years knowing I could have saved a life and didn't? How could I face myself in the mirror? I'd be, like, tainted."

This Mary Beth is a lunatic, that much is clear, thinks Ilse. Get rid of her this instant. Out, out of the house! But of course she cannot do that. The girl is Cathy's blameless little friend, invited for a Chinese dinner.

"Who gives a damn about your one soul!" exclaims Cathy. "What about all the other souls who'll die?"

Enough already, please! moans Ilse silently, watching her blood ooze through a paper napkin. What kind of people could teach their children such purity? They should teach her instead about the generous concealments of mirrors. Taste every impurity, she would like to tell Mary Beth, swallow them and assimilate them and carry them inside. When you're starving you'll eat anything. Ilse has. And none of it shows in any mirror.

"I'm sorry for those people. I mean it. I'd try to help them too. But I can't become a killer for them."

"That's the most selfish, dumbest thing I ever heard."

It begins to appear the friends will have a real falling-out. Not worth it, in the scheme of things. "How're you girls doing with the chopping?" Ilse breaks in. "Oh, that looks fine. Mary Beth, do the cabbage a little bit smaller, okay? Cathy, would you get me a Band-Aid? I cut my finger."

As soon as she gets the Band-Aid on, she hears a van pull into the driveway. Ban-the-Bug. The symbol with the grotesque insect is painted on the van. In her torment she has forgotten the appointment. She greets the smiling young man at the kitchen door and takes him around to the side of the house where the hive is. Behind her she can hear the girls tittering over how good-looking he is. Well, fine, that will reunite them. And indeed he is, a dazzling Hollywood specimen, tall, narrow-hipped, and rangy, with golden hair and tanned skin. Blue eyes, but duller than Mitch's. Wonderful golden-haired wrists and big hands. He is holding a clipboard with some papers, like a functionary, and *Ban-the-Bug* is written in red script just above the pocket of his sky blue shirt, whose sleeves are rolled up to the shoulders, revealing noteworthy muscles. Ilse points out the hive and he nods, unamazed.

"I would judge from the size," he says, "you've got about forty thousand bees in there."

Ilse gasps.

"Yup, that's right." His tone is cheerfully sympathetic. Really a charming young man. Perhaps attended the local community college for two years, like Brian, Ilse thinks, found he was not academically inclined, though bright enough, and looked for any old job till he could decide what he wanted. He would make a nice tennis instructor. "They're honeybees. There's most likely a lot of honey in the wall."

"Oh, can we get it out?" Ilse loves honey.

"Well, once we spray, it won't be good anymore." He sounds genuinely regretful. "You see, the bees take turns fanning the honey with their wings to keep it at sixty-five degrees.

But now with the warm weather it'll melt pretty fast. You might even have to break though the wall and get rid of it. It could smell or stain, it's hard to say."

She envisions forty thousand bees frantically fanning, protecting their product and livelihood, their treasure and birthright. That is the terrifying, demented noise she hears at night.

"Will you get them all?"

"Oh sure." He laughs. "No problem. We guarantee. Any that don't die just fly away—with the hive gone, you won't be seeing them around. Except if you have holes in the wall some might try to get back in and start all over."

"I don't think there are any holes."

"Could you just sign this paper, please?" He holds out the clipboard.

Ilse is always careful about what she signs. Robbie taught her that when she first came to America. "What is it?"

"Just routine. That we're not responsible for any damage to property, the terms of payment, the guarantee, and so on. Go ahead, read it. Take your time."

Feeling rather foolish, she scans the document. It is merely what he said, as far as she can see, and seems excessively formal for so simple a transaction. The undersigned is to pay half now and half on completion of the service, but since this case will probably require only one visit, the young man says, she can pay all at once. A hundred dollars for forty thousand bees. A quarter of a cent per bee, Ilse rapidly calculates, though it is a meaningless statistic. She signs and hands the document back.

"How long will it take?"

"Ten, fifteen minutes at the most."

"No, I mean before they're all gone."

"Oh." He chuckles at his little error. "The stuff works gradually, like, in stages. You might still hear something this evening, but then, during the night"—and he grins so ingenuously that she realizes he is just a boy, after all—"*baaad* things will happen to them."

He pauses, but Ilse has no ready response.

"Okay, I'll do the inside first." He fetches several cans and a small toolbox from the van and follows her up to the bedroom, where she shows him the makeshift cardboard patch. He nods as if he has seen it all before, and asks her to leave the room and close the door. Although she again has a secret hankering to stay and watch, Ilse obeys. So she never gets to see exactly what is done, but sits at the kitchen table, writes out a check, and waits. The girls have vanished for the moment, leaving their assigned vegetables ably chopped. In a few minutes the Ban-the-Bug man reappears and goes outside to do the hive. After she thanks him and watches him drive away, Ilse scrubs her hands at the sink before returning to the food—why, she does not know, for she has touched nothing alien except his pen and paper.

Mitch, when he comes home, is pleased at what she has accomplished, and listens respectfully as she relates all the pertinent facts. The dinner is excellent and lavishly praised, and the girls seem to be reconciled. Mary Beth is not such a thoroughgoing prig, as it turns out—she can be highly amusing on the subject of her family's foibles and idiosyncrasies. Later, in bed, Mitch wants to make love, but Ilse cannot summon the spirit to do it. He is disappointed, even a trifle irked, but it will pass. There will be other nights. She lies awake listening. The sound is feebler, and intermittent. She trusts it will stop for good very soon, as she was promised.

The next day, after work, she returns home and finds Cathy stretched out on a lawn chair, Walkman on, eyes closed. She calls to get her attention and Cathy unplugs. Ilse asks her to gather up and dispose of the corpses, which are so numerous they look like a thick, lush black and gold carpet. Shaking her head morosely at her fate, Cathy fetches a broom and dustpan. Ilse remains there as if turned to a salt block, watching her daughter work.

"Do we really need to go to all this trouble?" Cathy grumbles. "I mean, maybe you could use them for fertilizer or something."

She darts two giant steps to Cathy, grabs her shoulder, and

shakes her hard. "How dare you say such a thing!" Her other hand is lifted, in a fist, as if to deliver a killing blow. "How dare you!"

Cathy, pale, shrinks back from her mother. "What did I say? Just tell me, what on God's green earth did I say?"

What I Did for Love

Together with Carl I used to dream of changing the power structure and making the world a better place. Never that I could end up watching the ten o'clock news with a small rodent on my lap.

He was the fourth. Percy, the first, was a bullet-shaped, dark brown guinea pig, short-haired as distinct from the long-haired kind, and from the moment he arrived he tried to hide, making tunnels out of the newspapers in his cage until Martine, who was just eight then, cut the narrow ends off a shoebox and made him a real tunnel, where he stayed except when food appeared. I guess she would have preferred a more sociable pet, but Carl and I couldn't walk a dog four times a day, and the cat we tried chewed at the plants and watched us in bed, which made us self-conscious, and finally got locked in the refrigerator as the magnetic door was closing, so after we found it chilled and traumatized we gave it to a friend who appreciated cats.

Percy had been living his hermit life for about a year when Martine noticed he was hardly eating and being unusually quiet, no rustling of paper in the tunnel. I made an appointment with a vet someone recommended. On the morning of the appointment, after I got Martine on the school bus, I saw Percy lying very still outside the tunnel. I called the vet before I left for work to say I thought his patient might be dead.

"Might be?"

"Well . . . how can I tell for sure?"

He clears his throat and with this patronizing air doctors

have, even vets, says, "Why not go and flick your finger near the animal's neck and see if he responds?"

Since I work for a doctor I'm not intimidated by this attitude, it just rolls off me. "Okay, hold on a minute. . . ." I went and flicked. "He doesn't seem to respond, but still . . . I just don't feel sure."

"Raise one of his legs," he says slowly, as if he's talking to a severely retarded person, "wiggle it around and see if it feels stiff." He never heard of denial, this guy. What am I going to tell Martine?

"Hang on. . . ." I wiggled the leg. "It feels stiff," I had to admit.

"I think it's safe to assume," he says, "that the animal is dead."

"I guess we won't be keeping the appointment, then?" I'm not retarded. I said it on purpose, to kind of rile him and see what he'd say.

"That will hardly be necessary."

To get ready for the burial, I put Percy in a shoebox (a new one, not the tunnel one), wrapped the tissue paper from the shoes around him, and added some flowers I bought on the way home from work, then sealed it up with masking tape. Carl and I kept the coffin in our room that night so Martine wouldn't have to be alone in the dark with it. She didn't cry much, at least in front of us. She keeps her feelings to herself, more like me in that way than Carl. But I knew she was very attached to Percy, hermit that he was. The next morning, a Saturday, the three of us set out carrying the box and a spade and shovel we borrowed from the super of the building. Carl's plan was to bury him in the park, but it was the dead of winter, February, and the ground was so frozen the spade could barely break it.

"This isn't going to work," he said.

Martine looked tragic. She's always been a very beautiful child, with a creamy-skinned face and an expression of serene tragic beauty that, depending on the situation, can make you want to laugh or cry. At that moment I could have done either.

We were huddled together, our eyes and noses running from the cold, Martine clutching the shoebox in her blue down mittens.

"I know what," Carl said. "We'll bury him at sea."

Martine's face got even more tragic, and I gave him a funny look too. What sea? It was more than an hour's drive to Coney Island and I had a million things to do that day.

"The river. It's a very old and dignified tradition," he told her. "For people who die on ships, when it would take too long to reach land. In a way it's nicer than an earth burial—in the course of time Percy's body will drift to the depths and mingle with coral and anemone instead of being confined in—"

"Okay," she said.

So we walked up to the 125th Street pier on the Hudson River. This is a desolate place just off an exit of the West Side Highway, where the only buildings are meat-processing plants and where in the daytime a few lone people come to wash their cars, hauling water up in buckets, and even to fish, believe it or not, and at night people come to buy and sell drugs. I looked at Martine. She handed me the box like she couldn't bear to do it herself, so I knelt down and placed it in the river as gently as I could. I was hoping it would float for a while, at least till we could get her away, but my romantic Carl was saying something poetic and sentimental about death and it began to sink, about four feet from where we stood. It was headed south, though, towards the Statue of Liberty and the open sea, I pointed out to her. Free at last.

We got her another guinea pig, a chubby buff-colored one who did not hide and was intelligent and interested in its surroundings, as much as a guinea pig can be. We must have had it—Mooney, it was called—for around a year and a half when Carl began talking about changing his life, finding a new direction. He was one of those people—we both were—who had dropped out of school because it seemed there was so much we should be doing in the world. I was afraid he would be drafted, and we had long searching talks, the way you do when you're twenty, about whether he should be a conscientious objector, but at the last minute the army didn't want him because he had flat feet and was partially deaf in one ear. Those same flat feet led all those marches and demonstrations. Anyhow, he never managed to drop back in later on when things changed. Not that there was any less to do, but somehow no way of doing it anymore and hardly anyone left to do it with, not to mention money. You have to take care of your own life, we discovered. And if you have a kid . . . You find yourself doing things you never planned on.

He started driving a cab when Martine was born and had been ever since. It's exhausting, driving a cab. He spent less and less time organizing demonstrations and drawing maps of the locations of nuclear stockpiles. Now he spent his spare time playing ball with the guys he used to go to meetings with, or reading, or puttering with his plants, which after me, he used to say, were his great passion. It was not a terrible life, he was not harming anyone, and as I often told him, driving a cab where you come in contact with people who are going places was more varied than what I do all day as an X-ray technician, which you could hardly call upbeat. Most of the time, you find the patients either have cancer or not, and while you naturally hope for the best each time, you can't help getting to feel less and less, because a certain percentage are always doomed regardless of your feelings. Well, Carl was not satisfied, he was bored, so I said, "Okay, what would you do if you had a totally free choice?"

"I would like to practice the art of topiary."

"What's that?"

"Topiary is the shaping of shrubberies and trees into certain forms. You know, when you drive past rich towns in Westchester, you sometimes see bushes on the lawns trimmed to spell a word or the initials of a corporation? You can make all sorts of shapes—animals, statues. Have you ever seen it?"

"Yes." I was a little surprised by this. You think you know all about a person and then, topiary. "Well, maybe there's someplace you can learn. Take a course in, what is it, landscape gardening?"

"It's not very practical. You said totally free choice. I don't think there could be much of a demand for it in Manhattan."

"We could move."

"Where, Chris?" He smiled, sad and sweet and sexy. That was his kind of appeal. "Beverly Hills?"

"Well, maybe there's something related that you can do. You know those men who drive around in green trucks and get hoisted into the trees in little metal seats? I think they trim branches off the ones with Dutch elm disease. Or a tree surgeon?"

This didn't grab him. We talked about plants and trees, and ambition, and doing something you cared about that also provided a living. Finally he said it was a little embarrassing, but what he really might like, in practical terms, was to have a plant store, a big one, like the ones he browsed in down in the Twenties.

"Why should that be embarrassing?"

"When you first met me I was going to alter the power structure of society and now I'm telling you I want to have a plant store. Are you laughing at me, Chris? Tell the truth."

"I haven't heard you say anything laughable yet. I didn't really expect you to change the world, Carl."

"No?"

"I mean, I believed you meant it, and I believed in you, but that's not why I married you." Lord no. I married him for his touch, it struck me, and the sound of his voice, and a thousand other of those things I thought I couldn't exist without. It also struck me that I had never truly expected to change the power structure but that I had liked hanging out with people who thought they could. It was, I would have to say, inspiring.

"Do you think I'm having a mid-life crisis?"

"No. You're only thirty-three. I think you want to change jobs."

So we decided he should try it. He could start by getting a job in a plant store to learn about it, and drive the cab at night. That way we could save some money for a small store to begin with. He would have less time with me and Martine, but it would be worth it in the long run. Except he didn't do it right away. He liked to sit on things for a while, like a hen.

That summer we scraped together the money to send Martine to a camp run by some people we used to hang out with in the old days, and since it was a camp with animals, sort of a farm camp, she took Mooney along. Her third night away she called collect from Vermont and said she had something very sad to tell us. From her tragic voice, for an instant I thought they might have discovered she had a terminal disease like leukemia, and how could they be so stupid as to tell her—they were progressive types, maybe they thought it was therapeutic to confront your own mortality—but the news was that Mooney was dead. Someone had left the door of the guinea pigs' cage open the night before and he got out and was discovered in the morning in a nearby field, most likely mauled by a larger animal. I sounded relieved and not tragic enough, but fortunately Carl had the right tone throughout. At the age of eleven she understood a little about the brutalities of nature and the survival of the fittest and so on, but it was still hard for her to accept.

Martine is a peacefully inclined, intuitive type. She would have felt at home in our day, when peace and love were respectable attitudes. We named her after Martin Luther King, which nowadays seems a far-out thing to have done. Not that my estimation of him has changed or that I don't like the name, only it isn't the sort of thing people do anymore. Just as, once we stayed up nights thinking of how to transform the world and now I'm glad I have a job, no matter how boring, and can send her to camp for a few weeks.

Anyway, the people running the camp being the way they were, they immediately bought her a new guinea pig. Aside from her tragedy she had a terrific time, and she came home with a female pig named Elf, who strangely enough looked exactly like Mooney, in fact if I hadn't known Mooney was dead I would have taken Elf for Mooney. I remember remarking to Carl that if things were reversed, if Mooney had been left at home with us and died and we had managed to find an identical bullet-shaped replacement, I might have tried to pass it off as Mooney, in the way mothers instinctively try to protect their children from the harsher facts of life. But Carl said he wouldn't have, he would have told her the truth, not to make her confront harsh reality but because Martine would be able to tell the difference, as mothers can with twins, and he wouldn't want her catching him in a lie. "You know she has such high standards," he said.

In the dead of winter, even colder than in Percy's era, Martine told us Elf wasn't eating. Oh no, I thought. *Déjà vu.* The stillness, then the stiffness, wrapping it in the shoebox, burial at sea . . . Nevertheless, what can you do, so I made an appointment with the vet, the same old arrogant vet—I didn't have the energy to look for a new one. I was feeling sick when the day arrived, so Carl took off from work and went with Martine and Elf.

"There's good news and bad news," he said when they got home. "The good news is that she doesn't have a dread disease. What's wrong with her is her teeth."

I was lying in bed, trying to sleep. "Her teeth?"

"You've got it. Her top and bottom teeth are growing together so she can't eat. She can't separate them to chew." He gave me a demonstration of Elf's problem, stretching his lips and straining his molars.

"Please, this is no time to make me laugh. My stomach is killing me."

"What is it? Your period?"

"No. I don't know what."

"Well, listen—the bad news is that she needs surgery. Oral surgery. It's a hundred twenty-five including the anesthetic."

"This is not the least bit funny. What are we going to do?" Martine was putting Elf back in her cage, otherwise we would have discussed this with more sensitivity.

"Is there a choice? You know how Martine feels—Albert Schweitzer Junior. I made an appointment for tomorrow. She'll have to stay overnight."

"I presume you mean Elf, not Martine."

"Of course I mean Elf. Maybe I should call a doctor for you too."

"No, I'll be okay. What's a stomachache compared to oral surgery?"

"I don't want you getting all worked up over this, Chris." He joined me on the bed and started fooling around. "Thousands of people each year have successful oral surgery. It's nothing to be alarmed about."

"I'll try to deal with it. Ow, you're leaning right where it hurts." Martine came into the room and Carl sat up quickly.

"She's looking very wan," she said.

"Two days from now she'll be a new person," Carl said.

"She's never been a person before. How could she be one in two days?"

"Medical science is amazing."

"I have no luck with guinea pigs." She plopped into a chair, stretched out her legs, and sat gazing at her sneakers. I noticed how tall she was growing. She was nearly twelve and beginning to get breasts. But she wasn't awkward like most girls at that stage; she was stunning, willowy and auburn-haired, with green eyes. There was sometimes a faint emerald light in the whites of her eyes that would take me by surprise, and I would stare and think, What a lucky accident.

"Maybe none of them live long," I said. "I doubt if yours are being singled out."

"They have a four-to-six-year life span. I looked it up in the encyclopedia. But in four years I've gone through almost three."

That night I had such terrible pains in my stomach that Carl took me to the emergency room, where after a lot of fussing around—they tried to send me home, they tried to get me to sleep—they found it was my appendix and it had to come out right away. It was quite a few days before I felt like anything resembling normal, and I forgot completely about Elf's oral surgery.

"Chris, before we go inside, I'd better tell you something."
Carl switched off the engine and reached into the back seat for
my overnight bag. He was avoiding my eyes.

"What happened? I spoke to her on the phone just last
night!" I was about to leap out of the car, but he grabbed my
arm.

"Hold it a minute, will you? You're supposed to take it
easy."

"Well what's wrong, for Chrissake?"

He looked at me. "Not Martine. Jesus! Elf."

"Elf." I thought I would pass out. I was still pretty drugged.

"She got through the surgery all right. We brought her
home the next day. But . . . I don't know whether she was too
weak from not eating or what, but she never started eating
again. And so . . ."

"I never liked that doctor. How did Martine take it this
time?"

"Sad but philosophical. I think she's used to it by now.
Besides, she was more concerned about you."

"I'm glad to hear that. So where is the corpse? At sea
again?"

"Well, no, actually. That's why I wanted to tell you before
you went in the apartment. The temperature has been near zero.
The river is frozen."

"Just give it to me straight, Carl."

"She's wrapped in some plastic bags on the bathroom windowsill. Outside. The iron grating is holding her in place. I was
going to put her in the freezer with the meat, but I thought you
might not care for that."

"Couldn't you find a shoebox?"

"No. I guess nobody's gotten new shoes lately."

"And how long is she going to stay there?"

"They're predicting a thaw. It's supposed to get warm, un-
seasonably warm, so in a few days we'll take her out to the park.
Anyway, welcome home. Oh, there's another thing."

"I hope this is good."

It was. He had found a job working in the greenhouse at the Botanical Garden.

Since Martine never brought the subject up again after the thaw and the park burial, I assumed the guinea pig phase of her life was over. Two weeks after she returned from camp that summer, the super who had loaned us the spade and shovel for Percy came up to say there was a family in the next building with a new guinea pig, but their baby was allergic to it and couldn't stop sneezing. Maybe we wanted to do them a favor and take it off their hands?

Martine and I turned to each other. "What do you think?" I said.

"I'm not sure. They're a lot of expense, aren't they?"

"Not so bad. I mean, what's a little lettuce, carrots . . ."

"The medical expenses. And you don't like them too much, do you, Mom?"

I tried to shrug it off with a blank smile. I looked at Mr. Coates—what I expected I'll never know, since he stood there as if he had seen and heard everything in his lifetime and was content to wait for this discussion to be over. I wondered how much of a tip he would get for the deal. Nothing from us, I vowed.

"I've noticed," Martine said. "You don't like to handle them. You don't like small rodents."

"Not a whole lot, frankly." They looked to me like rats, fat tailless rats. For Martine's sake I had wished them good health and long life, but I tried not to get too close. When she was out with her friends and I had to feed them, I used to toss the lettuce in and step back as they lunged for it. I didn't like the eager squeaks they let out when they smelled the food coming, or the crunching sounds they made eating it. And when I held them —at the beginning, when she would offer them to me to stroke, before she noticed how I felt about small rodents—I didn't like the nervous fluttery softness of them, their darting squirmy little movements, the sniffing and nipping and the beat of the fragile heart so close to the surface I could feel it in my palms.

"But they don't bother me so long as they're in the cage in your room." Which was true.

"You could go over and take a look," said Mr. Coates finally. "I'll take you over there if you want."

"Maybe I'll do that, Mom. Do you want to come too?"

"No. I know what guinea pigs look like by now."

"What color is it?" Martine was asking him on the way out.

"I don't know the color. I ain't seen it myself yet."

I didn't pay any more attention to Rusty, named for his color, than I had to the others. I made sure to be in another room while Martine and Carl cut his nails, one holding him down, the other clipping—they took turns. Martine started junior high and got even more beautiful, breasts, hips, the works, with a kind of slow way of turning her head and moving her eyes. She also started expressing intelligent opinions on every subject in the news, test tube babies, airplane hijackings, chemicals in packaged foods, while Carl and I listened and marveled, with this peculiar guilty relief that she was turning out so well—I guess because we were not living out our former ideals, not changing the world or on the other hand being particularly upwardly mobile either. Carl was happier working in the greenhouse, but we still hadn't managed to save enough to rent a store or qualify for a bank loan.

At Martine's thirteenth birthday party in May, we got to talking in the kitchen with one of the mothers who came to pick up her kid. I liked her. She was about our age, small and blonde, and she had dropped out of school too but had gone back to finish and was even doing graduate work.

"What field?" I asked. I was scraping pizza crusts into the garbage while Carl washed out soda cans—he was very big on recycling. In the living room the kids were dancing to a reggae song called "Free Nelson Mandela," and the three of us had been remarking, first of all, that Nelson Mandela had been in prison since we were about their age and in the meantime we had grown up and were raising children and feeling vaguely disappointed with ourselves, and secondly, that dancing to a record like that wouldn't have been our style even if there had been one back then, which was unlikely. Singing was more our style. And the fact that teen-agers today were dancing to this "Free Nelson Mandela" record at parties made their generation seem less serious, yet at this point who were we to judge styles of being serious? The man was still in prison, after all.

"Romance languages," she said. She was playing with the plastic magnetic letters on the refrigerator. They had been there since Martine was two. Sometimes we would use them to write things like Merry Xmas or, as tonight, Happy Birthday, and sometimes to leave real messages, like Skating Back at 7 M. The messages would stay up for the longest time, eroding little by little because we knocked the letters off accidentally and stuck them back any old place, or because we needed a letter for a new message, so that Happy Birthday could come to read Hapy Birda, and at some point they would lose their meaning altogether, like Hay irda, which amused Martine no end. This woman wrote, "Nel mezzo del cammin di nostra vita."

"What does that mean?" Carl asked her.

" 'In the middle of the journey of our life.' It's the opening of *The Divine Comedy*. What it means is, here I am thirty-five years old and I'm a graduate student."

"There's nothing wrong with that," said Carl. "I admire your determination. I'm driving a cab, but one day before I die I'm going to learn to do topiary, for the simple reason that I want to."

She said what I knew she would. "What's topiary?"

He stopped rinsing cans to tell her.

I never read *The Divine Comedy*, but I do know Dante goes through Hell and Purgatory and eventually gets to Paradise. All the parts you ever hear about, though, seem to take place in Hell, and so a small shiver ran up my spine, seeing that message on the refrigerator above Happy Birthday. Then I forgot about it.

In bed that night I asked Carl if he was serious about learning topiary. He said he had been thinking it over again. Since he had gotten a raise at the greenhouse, maybe he might give up the cab altogether, he was so sick of it, and use the money we'd saved for the store to study landscape gardening.

"Well, okay. That sounds good. I can work a half day Saturdays, maybe."

"No, I don't want you to lose the little free time you have. We'll manage. Maybe there's something you want to go back and study too."

"I'm not ambitious. Why, would I be more attractive, like, if I went to graduate school?"

"Ha! Did I hear you right?" He let out a comic whoop. "I don't even remember her name, Chris. Listen, you want me to prove my love?"

That was the last time. The next day he came down with the flu, then Martine and I got it, and just when we were beginning to come back to life he had a heart attack driving the cab. He might have made it, the doctor said, except he was alone and lost control of the wheel. They told me more details about it, just like a news report, more than I could bear to listen to, in fact. I tried to forget the words the minute I heard them, but no amount of trying could make me stop seeing the scene in my mind. They offered me pills, all through those next insane days, but I wasn't interested in feeling better. Anyhow, what kind of goddamn pill could cure this? I asked them. I also kept seeing in my mind a scene on the Long Island Expressway when Martine was a baby and we were going to Jones Beach. About three cars ahead of us over in the right lane, a car started to veer, and as we got closer we could see the driver slumping down in his seat. Before we could even think what to do, a state trooper appeared out of nowhere and jumped in on the driver's side to grab the wheel. Sirens started up, I guess they took him to the hospital, and a huge pile-up was averted. Watching it, I felt bad about how we used to call cops pigs. That sounds a little simpleminded, I know, but so was calling them pigs. And now I wondered how come a miracle in the form of a cop happened for that person and not for Carl, which is a question a retarded person might ask—I mean, an out-of-the-way street in Queens at eleven at night . . . It happened the way it happened, that's all. A loss to all those who might have enjoyed his topiary. I do think he would have done it in his own good time. If only we had had a little more time, I could have taken care of him. I wouldn't have been a miracle, but I would have done a good job. The way he vanished, though, I couldn't do a thing, not even say goodbye or hold his hand in the hospital or whatever it is old couples do—maybe the wife whispers that she'll be joining him soon, but I have no illusions that I'll ever be joining him, soon or late. I just got a lot less of him than I expected. Another thing is that the last time we made love I was slightly distracted because of the graduate student he admired for her determination, not that anything transpired between them except some ordinary conversation, but it started me wondering in general. Stupid, because I know very well how he felt, he told me every night. Those words I don't forget. I let them put me to sleep. I lie there remembering how it felt with his arms and legs flung over me and can't believe I'm expected to get through decades without ever feeling that again.

So I did end up working half days on Saturdays. In July Martine was supposed to go back to the camp run by the progressives and pacifists, where she had always had such a great time except for her tragedy with Mooney, and I didn't want to begin my life alone by asking for help.

"I don't have to go," she said. "If we don't have the money it's all right. I don't think I even feel like going anymore." My beautiful child with the tragic face. Now she had something worthy of that face.

"You should go, however you feel. When you get there you'll be glad."

"Except there's a slight problem," she said.

"What's that?"

"Rusty. I'm not taking him. Not after what happened to Mooney."

"No," I agreed.

"Which means . . ."

"Oh God! All right, I can do it. How bad can it be? A little lettuce, cabbage, right? A few handfuls of pellets . . ."

"There's the cage to clean too."

"The cage. Okay."

It was hard, her going off on the bus, with the typical scene of cheery mothers and fathers crowding around waving brown lunch bags, but I forced myself through it and so did she. I would force myself through the rest of my life if I had to.

First thing every morning and before I went to bed I put a handful of pellets in Rusty's bowl and fresh water in his bottle, and when I left for work and came home I dropped a few leaves of something green into the cage. Since I never really looked at him I was shocked, the fourth night after Martine left, when Mr. Coates, who had come up to fix the window lock in her room, said in his usual unexcited way, "Your pig's eye's popping out."

The right eye was protruding half an inch out of the socket and the cylindrical part behind it was yellow with gummy pus, a disgusting sight. "Jesus F. Christ," I said.

"He won't be no help to you. You need a vet."

The thought of going back to that arrogant vet who I always suspected had screwed up with Elf was more than I could take, so I searched the yellow pages till I found a woman vet in the neighborhood. When I walked in the next day carrying Rusty in a carton, I knew I had lucked out. She had curly hair like a mop, she wore jeans and a white sweatshirt, and she seemed young, maybe twenty-nine or thirty. Her name was Doctor Dunn. Very good, Doctor Dunn, so there won't be all that other shit to cope with.

To get him on the examining table I had to lift him up by his middle and feel all the squirminess and the beat of the scared delicate heart between my palms.

"It looks like either a growth of some kind pushing it forward, or maybe an abscess. But in either case I'm afraid the eye will have to go. It's badly infected and unless it's removed it'll dry up and the infection will spread and . . . uh . . ."

"He'll die?"

"Right."

Seventy-five dollars, she said, including his overnight stay, plus twenty-five for the biopsy. Terrific, I thought, just what I need. It was lower than the other vet's rates, though.

"I want to explain something about the surgery. He's a very small animal, two pounds or so, and any prolonged anesthesia is going to be risky. What this means is, I can't make any guarantees. I'd say his chances are . . . seventy–thirty, depending on his general condition. Of course, we'll do everything we can. . . ."

"And if I don't do it he'll die anyhow?"

"Right."

Squirming there on the table was this orange rat whose fate I was deciding. I felt very out of sync with reality, as if I was in a science fiction movie and how did I ever arrive at this place. "Okay. I guess we'd better do it."

The receptionist I left him with told me to call around four the next day to see how he came through the surgery. *If* was what she meant. That evening out of habit I almost went in to toss him some celery, then I remembered the cage was empty. There was no reason to go into Martine's room. But I decided to take the opportunity to clean the cage and the room both. I had found that the more I moved around the more numb I felt, which was what I wanted.

On the dot of four, I called from work. Doctor Dunn answered herself.

"He's fine! What a trouper, that Rusty! We had him hooked up to the EKG the whole time and monitored him, and he was terrific. I'm really pleased."

"Thank you," I managed to say. "Thank you very much." In one day she had established a closer relationship with him than I had in a year. That was an interesting thought. I mean, it didn't make me feel emotionally inadequate; I simply realized that's why she went through years of veterinary school, because she really cared, the way Carl could have about topiary, I guess.

"Can you come in and pick him up before seven? Then I can tell you about the post-op care."

Post-op care? I had never thought of that. I had never even thought of how the eye would look. Would it be a hole, or just a blank patch of fur? Would there be a bandage on it, or maybe she could fix him up with a special little eye patch?

I found Rusty in his carton on the front desk, with the receptionist petting him and calling him a good boy. "We're all crazy about him," she said. "He's quite a fella, aren't you, Rusty-baby?"

Where his right eye used to be, there was a row of five black stitches, and the area around it was shaved. Below the bottom stitch, a plastic tube the diameter of a straw and about an inch long stuck out. That was a drain for the wound, Doctor Dunn explained. He had a black plastic collar around his neck that looked like a ruff, the kind you see in old portraits of royalty. To keep him from poking himself, she said.

"Was he in good condition otherwise?" I thought I should sound concerned, in this world of animal-lovers.

"Oh, fine. Now . . . The post-operative care is a little complicated, so I wrote it down." She handed me a list of instructions:

1. Cold compresses tonight, 5–10 minutes.
2. Oral antibiotics, 3× a day for at least 7 days.
3. Keep collar on at all times.
4. Feed as usual.
5. Call if any excessive redness, swelling, or discharge develops.
6. Come in 3–4 days from now to have drain pulled.
7. Call early next week for biopsy results.
8. Make appointment for suture removal, 10–14 days.
9. Starting tomorrow, apply warm compresses 5–10 minutes, 2× a day for 10 days.

"Here's a sample bottle of antibiotics. Maybe I'd better do the first dose to show you how." She held him to her chest with one hand, while with the other she nudged his mouth open using the medicine dropper and squeezed the drops in, murmuring, "Come on now, that's a good boy, there you go." As she wiped the drips off his face and her sweatshirt with a tissue, I thought, Never. This is not happening to me. But I knew it was, and that I would have to go through with it.

When I went to get some ice water for the cold compress that night, I saw the message the graduate student mother had left on the refrigerator near Happy Birthday, which was now Happ Brhday. "Ne mezz l camn di nstr vita," it read. I knew some letters were missing though not which ones, and those that were left were crooked, but I remembered well enough what it meant. I sat down to watch the ten o'clock news with Rusty on my lap and put the compress on his eye, or the place where his eye used to be, but he squirmed around wildly, clawing at my pants. Ice water oozed onto my legs. I told him to cut it out, he had no choice. Finally I tried patting him and talking to him like a baby, to quiet him. Don't worry, kiddo, you're going to be all right—stuff like that, the way Carl would have done without feeling idiotic. It worked. Only hearing those words loosened me a little out of my numbness and I had this terrible sensation of walking a tightrope in pitch darkness, though in fact I was whispering sweet nothings to a guinea pig. I even thought of telling him what I'd been through with my appendix, a fellow sufferer, and God knows what next, but I controlled myself. If I freaked out, who would take care of Martine?

I figured seven and a half minutes for the compress was fair enough—Doctor Dunn had written down 5–10. Then I changed my mind and held it there for another minute so if anything happened I would have a clear conscience when I told Martine. I held him to my chest with a towel over my shirt, feeling the heart pulsing against me, and squirted in the antibiotic. I lost a good bit, but I'd have plenty of chances to improve.

In the morning I found the collar lying in the mess of shit and cedar chips in his cage. I washed it and tried to get it back on him, but he fought back with his whole body—each time I fitted it around his neck he managed to squirm and jerk his way out, till beyond being repelled I was practically weeping with frustration. Two people could have done it easily. Carl, I thought, if ever I needed you . . . Finally after a great struggle I got it fastened in back with masking tape so he wouldn't undo it. But when I came home from work it was off again and we wrestled again. The next morning I rebelled. The drops, the compresses, okay, but there was no way I was going to literally collar a rodent morning and night for ten days. There are limits to everything, especially on a tightrope in the dark. I called Doctor Dunn from work.

"Is he poking himself around the eye?" she asked. "Any bleeding or discharge? Good. Then forget it. You can throw the collar away."

I was so relieved.

"How is he otherwise? Is he eating?"

"Yes. He seems okay. Except he's shedding." I told her how when I lifted him up, orange hairs fluttered down into his cage like leaves from a tree. When leaves fell off Carl's plants, which I was also trying to keep alive though that project wasn't as dramatic, it usually meant they were on their way out. I had already lost three—I didn't have his green thumb. It seemed my life had become one huge effort to keep things alive, with death hot on my trail. I even had nightmares about what could be happening to Martine at camp. When I wrote to her, though, I tried to sound casual, as if I was fine, and I wrote that Rusty was fine too. Maybe Carl would have given her all the gory details, but I didn't mind lying. He was going to be fine. I was determined that pig would live even if it was over my dead body. Luckily I wasn't so far gone as to say all this to Doctor Dunn. "Is that a bad sign?"

"Shedding doesn't mean anything," she said. "He doesn't feel well, so he's not grooming himself as usual. It'll stop as he gets better."

I also noticed, those first few days, he would do this weird dance when I put the food in his cage. It dawned on me that he could smell it but not see it. While he scurried around in circles, I kept trying to shove it towards his good side—kind of a Bugs Bunny routine. Then after a while he developed a funny motion, turning his head to spot it, and soon he was finding it pretty well with his one eye. I told Doctor Dunn when I brought him in to have the drain removed. She said yes, they adapt quickly. They compensate. She talked about evolution and why eyes were located where they were. Predators, she said, have close-set eyes in the front of their heads to see the prey, and the prey have eyes at the sides, to watch out for the predators. How clever, I thought, the way nature matched up the teams. You couldn't change your destiny, but you had certain traits that kept the game going and gave you the illusion of having a fighting chance. We talked about it for a good while. She was interesting, that Doctor Dunn.

A few days later she plucked out the stitches with tweezers while I held him down.

"I have to tell you," she said, "not many people would take such pains with a guinea pig. Some people don't even bother with dogs and cats, you'd be amazed. They'd rather have them put away. You did a terrific job. You must really love animals."

I didn't have the heart to tell her that although it didn't turn my stomach anymore to hold him on my lap and stroke him for the compresses, he was still just a fat rat as far as I was concerned, but a fat rat which fate had arranged I had to keep alive. So I did.

"Well, you could say I did it for love."

She laughed. "Keep applying the warm compresses for another day or two, to be on the safe side. Then that's it. Case closed."

"What about the biopsy?"

"Oh yes, the lab report. It's not in yet, but I have a feeling it wasn't malignant. He doesn't look sick to me. Call me on it next week."

In eleven days Martine will be back. Beautiful Martine, with her suntan making her almost the color of Rusty. I'll warn her about the eye before she sees him. It doesn't look too gruesome now, with the stitches out and the hair growing back—soon it'll be a smooth blank space. In fact, if not for the missing eye she would never have to know what he went through. The house will feel strange to her all over again without Carl, because whenever you're away for a while you expect to come home to some pure and perfect condition. She'll be daydreaming on the bus that maybe it was all a nightmare and the both of us are here waiting for her. But it'll be an altogether different life, and the worst thing is—knowing us, sensible, adaptable types—that one remote day we'll wake up and it'll seem normal this way, and in years to come Carl will turn into the man I had in my youth instead of what he is now, my life. I even envy her—he'll always be her one father.

So I'm applying the warm compresses for the last time, sitting here with a one-eyed guinea pig who is going to live out his four-to-six-year life span no matter what it takes, in the middle of the journey of my life, stroking him as if I really loved animals.

The Sound of Velcro

He woke, as always, to the sound of her sneakers opening, six little rips, swift and searing like Band-Aids ripped away to expose the raw, crimson day. Shudders crossed his spine. He pictured her roughly parting the lips of each sneaker, lifting the tongue to remove her long, smooth foot. Opening his eyes, he watched her place the sneakers side by side to air on the windowsill, toes pointing outdoors. He knew her movements by heart, the way small children learn their mothers' rituals and cling to them for safety. Off with the sweaty headband, shake out the hair with two fine tosses of her head, cross arms to peel up the shirt. Then she kissed him quickly on the lips, blocking the light as she bent over, the heels of her hands pressed into his shoulders, and he smelled the dissonant sweetnesses of sweat and toothpaste. Her yellow hair was warm and glinting. Softness fell over him like a net.

"You should try it sometime, Joe," and she poked him gently in the stomach before striding to the shower. "You're getting soft." The other day, she had teased, "You'll lose your looks."

He granted himself five more minutes. This was the most arduous task of the day—forcing his body to get started. Lately when he stood up he felt a faint stiffness, a numbing disorientation. It must be the change in weather, summer announcing itself so abruptly. He was thirty-three years old and not heavy, but he felt ponderous and old as he prodded himself from bed part by part, like Cro-Magnon man rising to face the puzzle of civilization.

He had never known Van other than taut and muscular and civilized, except when she was pregnant. Her face was drawn then, her hair drab, but he had preferred her lapsed from perfection. Physical perfection was more than intimidating; there was something unmistakably crude about it, as if the body were aspiring to a condition beyond itself, to spirit, as absurd and slightly titillating as apes dressed up as humans. The baby died at three months, one of those unaccountable deaths, asleep. Joe tried to imagine the instant of passage from sleep to death: what was it like, did the baby know, feel a shiver or a catch of the breath? But no one could ever know what a baby knew. Simply overnight, where there had been life there was a void. He felt it defied natural law, the conservation of matter. He had tried to puzzle it out with Van, but she disliked anything with the aroma, however slight, of mysticism. She was not one to lie in the dark and speculate. He wanted to talk, too, about what the child might have been like, whether it would have had her swiftness and energy, or his dreamy temperament and drowsy eyes. At first she wouldn't answer, then one night she put her hand over his lips softly and said, "I can't. Don't you see? I just can't." And then she curled in a ball and wept into the pillow, and Joe felt helpless beside her, afraid she would melt away and leave him alone with his sorrow. The next morning Van was running again, returning streaked and sweaty, gasping with sobs. He urged her to stop pushing herself, at least to cry in the comfort of bed, but she said why waste time and get fat besides? A while later, she had a miscarriage.

"It usually means something was wrong to begin with," she said, crisp and dry-eyed this time. "It's not meant to be." She spoke more fervently than ever about her career, interior design, and the need for contacts and networking. She drew up a schedule of household chores, presenting it to Joe like a challenge. He accepted it calmly, more calmly than she expected, he noted with a boy's twinge of satisfaction. Compared to the advertising agency, where he managed half a dozen accounts with the deftness of a juggler, domestic work was easy and familiar. He didn't mind helping out—along with his brother, Hughie, he used to help his mother too, if asked.

Walking to work through the park on this pale, hot June morning, he heard a sound uncannily like Vanessa's tearing open her sneakers, the sound of Velcro, only louder and angrier, and again the chill ran down his spine. How out of place it was, in the greenery. The sound repeated two, three more times, with a harsh caw at the end. Alive. A bird, or some monstrous cricket? It left him bemused. As he slogged his way through the day, struggling to be diplomatic with his most demanding account, a cosmetics firm, the echo remained. Who, or what, could produce a sound like the most advanced of plastics?

That evening he found a letter from Hughie. It was as if a nugget of Joe's boyhood had waited patiently all day in the mailbox: there was the familiar vertical, plump script on the small white envelope, the words "Street" and "New York" and "Denver, Colorado" meticulously spelled out. It was months since he had called Hughie. He would call immediately, tonight, maybe even ask him to visit. . . .

He tore the letter open in the elevator. It was typed, which was vaguely disappointing. He might have basked in that placid writing as in an embrace.

> Dear Hooch,
> It is a long time since we were in touch and I hope you and your wife Vannesa are doing okay. I am fine exept I have a little problem Hoochie if you could help me out. The place where I am working the magazine place is laying off workers. But I was hired from the program from the Guild so they are finding me another job guess where, New York City. The shipping department in Long Island City.

Joe turned the key in the lock without looking, his eyes fixed on the letter, and dropped into a chair. His heart was pounding with a fearful eagerness.

> Hooch I am coming to New York anyway so do you think you could put me up for a while. Till I get myself setled

not for long. It would be very nice to see you brother and
I am easy to live with you know. Please let me know and
my love to you and your lovely wife.

Love,
Hughie.

His brother was four years older and mildly retarded, so mildly
that it was not apparent right away. People soon caught on,
though, mostly because of Hughie's slow way of speaking, like
talk near the edge of sleep, from a hazier plane of consciousness.
Their mother used to say he was searching for the proper words,
and Joe would imagine him rummaging, as in a dark closet, for
words he had stored for later use but forgotten exactly where.
In their Ohio town Hughie had suffered a minimum of mock-
ery. Their parents strove with near-saintly patience to encourage his dignity; people felt it, and liked him. Joe relished Hughie's slowness, a relief from the world hastening by, pressing its
demands. When they were together he could feel the rhythms
of Hughie's sweetly monotonous voice, reflecting that curious
inner apparatus, seep through his blood. The rhythms seemed
to rise from a different order of time, like the slow rhythms of
the earth creeping through its geological cycles while the first
fish found its way to land and drew the first breath. At the age
of nine, Hughie was sent away to a special school; the gap
between him and the others was widening, and he would be
better off, their mother said, among his own kind. Joe missed
his presence—large, strong, tractable. Power and mildness
united.

Van first met Hughie at their wedding eight years ago. Joe
could read the relief in her eyes—thank God, not some monster!
Even rather handsome. People used to remark that they looked
alike, except for their coloring—Joe was the darker one. Tall and
benevolently hulking in a light gray suit—a trifle snug; he must
have bought it himself—Hughie had hugged her impulsively.
Too tight. For an instant she looked scared. Trapped. Even at
twenty-four, she was disturbed by anything flawed. In his excitement, Hughie grinned too broadly and kept the grin too

long; like a captive mirror image, her smile stayed fixed. He wanted to dance with her—a crashing rock song where it didn't matter what you did. When it was over she rolled her eyes and exhaled in a rush. Joe had to turn away, because there appeared before him, unsought, a glimpse of an entirely different kind of wife, maybe not so palely and delicately beautiful, but one who could hug Hughie after his clumsy dancing and even hold his hand walking from the dance floor. But that was not to be. He had hardly had time to know other women. It was Vanessa whom he loved and who had claimed him from the start. It had been she who spoke to him at the college dance where they met, and she who moved close to him in the car so that their legs were touching. He found her alarmingly bold, even wild, one of those unattainable girls who look demure in public and then in private reveal their voracious ardor coming from God knows where. Joe was modest, had never dreamed of such luck. "Why me?" he would joke as they lay tangled on the rug in her dormitory room. "An innocent boy from Ohio?" "Maybe it's your innocence," she would say, laughing. "Or maybe your legs. Or this. Or this." She was commanding, he was her docile follower. His fraternity brothers envied him, and he felt chosen. He couldn't even remember their deciding to marry—one summer day it was happening. Van arranged everything, and she glowed with pleasure and authority. Her light reflected on Joe and he glowed too, in his vague way. "We're going to have such good times," she whispered in his ear right in front of the minister and all the guests, as they performed the ritual kiss. She even slid her tongue in his mouth for an instant, and he could hear a low laugh in her throat. How could he not have been bewitched? Later he understood how, more than his looks, it was his docility that drew her, but by then the reason hardly mattered. They were together, embarked on their good times.

The sound, the strained day at the office, the letter: Joe was confused. Another wave of numbness assaulted him. The room seemed to be rocking like a giant cradle, with him helpless inside. He blinked to clear his vision and tried to think what his next move should be. Have a glass of water. Take it slow. Put away the briefcase. Get out of the business suit.

They were invited to a dinner party in Chelsea, Vanessa reminded him when she got home. Joe didn't even know the people, he grumbled.

Clients. She shrugged, as if that were their sole identity. "I have to, Joe. I'm just getting somewhere."

As her clientele grew, there were more and more dinner parties, to exhibit her work and to entice. The guests were all great talkers. Joe would heave himself into bed with his head pounding and his tongue groggy, to fall asleep to the sound of Vanessa, wound up like a mechanical doll, analyzing the social intricacies of the evening. Nor would the summer be any respite. The gatherings would move to the beach, where fashionable clothes would drop away to reveal splendidly bronzed and polished bodies uttering the same urbanities against a backdrop of sea, sand, and sky.

"When I was growing up," he said, tearing the laundry paper from a clean shirt, "business was during the day and friends were for pleasure."

"Times have changed." So had she. She even made love with a new, efficient zeal; ready anytime, barely speaking, quickly aroused and quickly satisfied, she could leap with dispatch to the next project—the way after running she leaped in and out of the shower, into her clothes and out the door—while he lay abandoned, flesh still buzzing.

From across the room he watched her dress for dinner, her body flashing by in parts, a machine programmed with strategies to achieve goals. Lately he had wayward visions of leaving her for another life, in which tableaux of hiking and going to ball games drifted alluringly, but as soon as he tried to envision anything specific, the images slipped from his grasp like live fish snatched from a stream. The notion of life without her frightened him. It seemed almost physically impossible, as though he had given his soul to her in trust and could carry only his body away. Alone, he would be a shell, a zombie. He imagined her carrying his essential self within, a homunculus, as she had carried the ill-fated babies, and shook his head to cast out the horror of the image. Be realistic, he told himself, just as she would. Even in purely practical terms, a new life was an immense undertaking. He could hardly retrace how they had arrived at this complex one; it seemed to have pulled them in like a hidden magnet. The struggle was in hanging on.

"I got a letter from my brother today."

"Hughie?"

"That's my only brother."

A pause as she inserted an enormous copper earring. It gave a lambent, coppery tinge to her hair. "And how is he?"

"Fine. He's got a new job in New York. He wants to stay here for a while, till he finds a place."

Another hesitation for the other earring. He thought he saw a shadow of distaste flicker over her lips, twitching the corners. "I don't know, Joe. Do you think it would work out? We're so overextended as it is. . . ." She dabbed perfume in the hollow of her collarbone and rubbed it in, drawing slow, thoughtful circles with two fingers. "And then we have the house in Amagansett for August."

Already dressed, he sat on the bed and waited. He felt he was seeing through her skull: the clever little cells whirring and dancing a labyrinthine reel, calculating the strength of her position.

"Well, how long do you think it would be?"

"A few weeks, maybe. He likes to be independent."

Now it was she who waited, but he would not plead. "Okay, let's give it a try. That's all anyone can do, right?" she said with a bright look. "Would you zip me up?"

He zipped her dress and rested his cheek on her hair. Up close she was not a machine at all. The fabric of the loose gray dress was so soft it seemed to melt in his fingers. Her perfume was all around him, a scent like dew, something expensive that he received every Christmas from his cosmetics account. He put his face in her neck, his hands on her breasts. She leaned back into him.

"Why can't you be as beautiful inside as out?" he asked.

She jerked away. "What is that supposed to mean?"

"You know very well what it means. You don't really want him. You don't want anyone, do you?"

She turned. He was shocked to see her eyes fill with tears. "That's not true. I've always wanted you."

The power of it made him step back, alarmed. "Well, Hughie, for instance."

"Look, I'm not going to lie and tell you I'm overjoyed. But I'll do it, since it's so important to you."

"You won't mean it, though. You won't do it from the heart."

"Oh, the heart. Oh, Joe. Does it really matter? I'll be the good hostess. . . . Why, don't you think I can do it?"

"I'm quite sure you can do it. You can do anything."

"And why is that bad?" she asked him. He found he couldn't say.

All the way to the dinner party, in the cab, they were silent.

The guests were ecstatic at Vanessa's handiwork. For the wealthy middle-aged clients she had produced a setting just short of opulent, with a minimum of colors, but bold ones—red and gold. There were potted plants the size of small trees, Oriental rugs, and swaths of drapery. Totally unlike her own tastes, Joe marveled—muted grays and mauves in plain lines, with choice touches of extravagance like the copper earrings, or the playful green silk kite she had hung in their bedroom. He recalled only dimly, with nostalgia, the secret place in her that germinated the extravagance; he hardly glimpsed it anymore.

The meal featured vegetables so fashionable they did not yet have English names. The rich cappuccino, steamed in an Italian machine Vanessa had ordered, made Joe slightly sick. He went to the window for air but could find no way to open it. The place was an air-conditioned cage. His blood lurched down to his feet, making his head spin. In the bathroom, surrounded by a geometric design of Mexican tiles, he doused cold water on his face and lay on the marble floor till he revived.

There was a naturalist at the party. Joe told him about the sounds in the park that had sounded like Velcro.

"Katydids. Or possibly grackles. Quite a few people have noticed it. They make a similar sound, only louder and harsher, of course. I guess I should say the Velcro makes the same sound as the katydids. The odd thing is that the little buggers themselves are fooled. When they hear the Velcro they respond."

It would be idiotic to show his distress. "What is the world coming to?" he quipped instead.

"Oh, but Velcro," a woman dressed in a tuxedo put in, "is the greatest invention since the zipper. For certain things. I guess you wouldn't want it on your pants. That would be a bit blatant, wouldn't it?"

"A zipper engages," said Joe. "It's satisfying to see the two sides mesh."

The woman eyed him with new interest and moved her chair closer, smiling. "Oh, you like that, do you? Teeth gripping, merging? How do you feel about snaps, or thongs and loops?" She crossed her legs and let her heel slide out of her pump. As he performed his expected part—for in this life flirtation was a social task he had had to learn like all the others—Joe thought of Hughie. What would Hughie do at a party like this, what could he say? What would this bow tied woman do with him?

He was among the first of the airline passengers to appear. Joe hung back in the crowd to stare for a moment. Hughie's short wheaty hair was combed boyishly over his forehead, his face was ruddy and candid like the faces in beer commercials, and he had put on some weight. The beginnings of middle age, yet a middle-aged Hughie was incongruous. He wore a light, creased summer suit with loafers and carried a garment bag. His patterned green tie, which would horrify Vanessa, was loosened and hung askew. Among his own kind, Joe thought. Yes, many of the arriving passengers had that puzzled look. Suddenly he found himself running. In the enclosure of Hughie's arms, tears rose to his throat. He felt like an exile touching the soil of his native land, feeling for his buried self: a prodigal son.

Hughie stroked Joe's car with admiration. "This is a real nice car, Hooch. Italian, right?" To Joe's surprise he named the model and the year. "I know because it's my hobby. I keep a scrapbook of the different cars and models. You must be doing real well."

All at once, as if the journeying universe were shifting gears, things were nearly at a standstill. Even the traffic buzzing around them was held in a trancelike stillness. No reason in the world to hurry, with Hughie beside him. The point was being with him, not getting anywhere. Driving slowly home, Joe felt supernaturally privileged, savoring a pure sensation of life unshackled by time.

"You know, what I think I'll do," he told Hughie dreamily, "is take some time off to show you around. I have a lot of sick leave piled up."

On Saturdays Van was out visiting showrooms. Joe fixed sandwiches and helped his brother unpack. While Hughie took a shower he lay on the couch in a reverie soon broken by the firm click of the door.

"What a day!" She kicked off her high-heeled shoes. "All the taxis seem to have gone into exile. Or maybe the drivers returned to their native lands. Did he get here okay?"

Just then Hughie entered, wearing jeans and a fresh sport shirt with blue and white checks. His hair was damp and noticeably thinning on top and his eyes were slightly narrowed— unsure what he might find but ready staunchly to confront it.

"So nice to see you again, Hughie." She went to kiss him on the cheek. "How was your trip?"

They had started out on time, he reported, and quickly reached a very high altitude, he didn't know exactly how high, but then they had gone lower to avoid some air pockets, according to the captain. His voice, Joe was thinking, sounded like an old phonograph record dragging at the start; you expected it at

any instant to pick up the proper speed. There were three ste-
wardesses, one really cute who gave him a free ginger ale; he
turned down the lunch, though, because it didn't look too good.
There was no movie, but he had listened to a comedian on the
earphones. Vanessa at this point settled on the couch and rested
her head on a pillow. Joe felt strangely awed by Hughie. Meals
on planes were hard to resist, the way they were thrust at you
by swift, official hands. He himself habitually ate whatever was
put in front of him. Hughie's seat companion was a very nice
woman, he was saying, who told him all about her grandchildren, every one a musical prodigy. Finally, after a half hour of
circling Kennedy Airport, they landed with a big bump.

"Well," said Vanessa limply, "so you got here all right.
Look, it's my night to cook, but I'm exhausted. Why don't we
go out? Did you ever try Japanese food, Hughie? Or there's a
seafood place—"

"Hughie, if you'd rather stay home your first night—"

"Oh no, I love to eat in restaurants. Remember, Hooch, I
always loved when Dad took us to that chicken-in-the-basket
place? I like Italian."

At the restaurant Vanessa's face and voice were set in the
bright impassivity Joe knew well, used for certain trying clients
and dealers. She could maintain it for about forty-five minutes
before the effort showed. At dinner parties he would stop in and
help her out; here, he thought bitterly, she could fend for herself. When they were handed menus she telegraphed Joe a look
which meant, Can he read? But of course he can read, Joe tried
to telegraph back, though his face was less adept. He wrote me
the letter, don't you remember? As though it were yesterday,
he recalled Hughie coming home the summer he was eleven,
proudly bearing a first-grade book, *Little Bear's Visit,* which he
insisted on reading aloud several times a day. Joe could read it
too, and faster, but he understood enough not to compete. By
eighteen, when he finished at school, Hughie was able to pass
the written part of the driving test. "My boy's a real worker,"
their father said, his arm around Hughie's shoulder, and their

mother had baked a cake reading Happy Graduation, Son. How could he telegraph all this across a white tablecloth on which a single yellow rose in a bud vase wafted imperially between them?

Hughie studied the menu for a long time. "I don't see spaghetti and meatballs," he said at last.

Before Vanessa could comment, Joe led him to the lasagna, and in a rush of loyalty, ordered lasagna too. Hughie observed curiously as they dismantled artichokes, but refused to try one.

As with prospective clients, Van tried to draw him out. Yes, Hughie said, his eyes fixed on the yellow rose, he would sure miss Denver. "I had a lot of friends from the Guild. We did a lot of things, I was telling Hooch before. Joey, I mean. Hikes and swimming and movies. I worked out at the Y. Lifting weights." He showed a bicep. "Maybe I can find a Y here."

"We belong to a health club," Joe said. "You could come for a while as my guest." Hughie would do fine there. Uniformed in shorts and sneakers, the young executives were reduced to a common denominator of muscle and sweat; their talk about weight lifting always sounded simpleminded anyway.

"Okay." He lit a menthol cigarette and Vanessa gave a slight cough. "I had this special friend, Marie. We were very good friends."

"Yes? Well, maybe she'll come to visit when you have your own place."

"I don't think her parents would let her. I wanted to marry Marie, but they didn't want to let us. We used to go out every Friday and Saturday. I took her places. Dancing." Jerking his head up, he looked straight at Vanessa. "Do you remember we danced at your wedding?"

"Certainly."

"I'm a much better dancer now. Marie taught me. But her parents, you know what I mean?"

"What was it? Did they think she needed a . . . a more protected environment?"

Joe winced. It was the same chill as when she ripped open her sneakers.

"I think they thought I couldn't take good care of her. I would. But they were scared, so they made her scared."

"Maybe you'll meet someone else here," Joe said.

Hughie gave him a glance that made him feel shamefully naive. "Marie was so pretty. She had hair like yours," he told Vanessa, "but . . ." He grinned and winked. "There was more to her. Upstairs, if you get what I mean."

"Hughie, do you know how unhealthy it is for you to smoke?" Van asked.

"Oh, I'm sorry. I didn't know you didn't like it." He stubbed out the cigarette.

They didn't linger over dinner because Vanessa wanted to see *Zelig*, which she had missed the first time around. Joe and Hughie laughed all the way through, but she found it disappointing. A one-gag film, she said in the cab going home. Diluted philosophy. "So people assume the characteristics of those around them. So identity is more fluid than we realize. Well, and what else is new?"

Hughie stared, then closed his mouth with deliberation. Years ago, Joe knew, he would have asked guileless questions. Life had done this to him, made him circumspect, and Joe felt a pang for whatever humiliations had taught his brother discretion. But life does that to everyone, he could imagine Van saying dispassionately, the clever along with the simple.

He was still an early riser. From bed, Joe heard him greet Vanessa the next morning and ask where the instant coffee was.

"We don't have instant coffee. Look, I've got to run. Literally," and she gave a short laugh. "But I'll stop for some on the way back, all right?"

"I don't want to be any trouble."

"It's no trouble. If you're desperate here's the espresso machine." Scrupulously, she explained how to work it. "Or else plug this one in. Here's a fresh filter."

Hughie sounded as he had when Joe first explained about stealing bases and double plays. But eventually he had learned.

"Vanessa," he said. "That's a nice name. It sounds like that word, what's the word, when you pat someone?"

"Caress?"

"Right, caress. Vanessa. Caressa."

"Most people call me Van."

"That sounds like a man's name. Van Johnson. Van Halen. He's a rock star."

"Hughie, I've got to go or I'll be late for an auction."

The door closed sharply and Joe got up to make a pot of coffee.

"I think she was mad at me."

"No, she's always in a hurry in the morning. Her work is very pressured."

She was meeting with a client that evening. Joe was glad— after a day of seeing the sights of New York he wanted to watch the Mets game uninterrupted. Whenever he had a rare free evening to watch baseball she hovered around making coy remarks about the way the players' uniforms fit or asked mock-ignorant questions. To satisfy her, he would pretend to be amused. Now he fetched two beers and a bowl of macadamia nuts and stretched out alongside Hughie. As if the Guatemalan hemp rug were a magic carpet, Joe was transported to a simpler age. If he looked only at the screen, the green of the ball field aglow like the grass of Eden, and ignored the sleek furnishings and Picasso prints and circles of soft light set in the ceiling, it could be a June of twenty-odd years ago; he would be interpreting the plays, but in black and white, for an eager Hughie, while their mother did something feminine and provident in the kitchen and their father read his newspaper, from time to time—when the boys whooped—raising his eyes to the game.

On Friday Vanessa canceled a dinner date and got into bed early with a magazine. "Just a little tired," she told Joe. She was rarely tired. Tiredness was his preserve. "Doing it," as she had promised, doing Hughie, must be wearing her out. He realized they had not been out with friends or clients all week. Nor had they talked very much or made love—he had been staying up late, sitting with Hughie or staring alone into the night, then tiptoeing to bed in the dark. If she stirred or put her arms around him he pretended to have fallen asleep. He felt almost an aversion to her body alongside his, as though Hughie's in the next room, was tugging him away. How could he give himself to both?

She looked up from her magazine and asked whether Hughie was having any luck finding an apartment.

"I've taken him around to a few brokers. But you know how it is. Everything's sky-high. He'll probably have to look in Brooklyn or Queens, but I don't want to rush him. He's enjoying the sights."

"Queens is a good idea." She yawned. "You're getting to sound a little like him, do you know? Sort of slow. Short sentences. Repeating."

"Maybe I'm meant to be slow. Maybe I'm not meant for this kind of life."

"What kind of life?"

"This." He gestured vaguely around the bedroom, everything in it carefully chosen, in irreproachable taste. The brilliant silk kite on the wall seemed an emblem of cheer, but failed to cheer him. Again he felt a numbness in his legs, maybe the onset of arthritis. She had said he was getting soft, but he was actually stiffening, like clothes left out on a line in freezing weather. "What kind of life are you meant for, then?"

"I don't know."

"Not a shipping clerk, I'm sure."

"It's more useful than what I do. He wraps magazines. People read them." He waved at the one she was holding. "What do I do besides make money?"

"Money means you can have the kind of life you want."

"You make it sound so simple. Maybe I don't want . . ." He stopped because it was a useless conversation. He didn't know what he wanted. "It's odd, you know, seeing him after so long. I don't know why I didn't stay more in touch these last few years."

"People go off on different paths. It's not as if you have a lot in common."

"But we do! We have everything in common. Sometimes I wonder what it's like to be retarded. I mean, what it feels like inside his head."

She looked at him curiously. "How come he still calls you Hooch?"

"They tell me it was what I called him as a baby, and he started saying it back."

"I know, you once told me. I mean, why does he still call you it now?"

"Well, why not? I guess to him that's my name."

She gazed at him for a moment, then suddenly smiled and stretched her arms wide. "Come here then, Hooch. I've been missing you."

The name on her lips was like trespassing. But he obeyed, went over and took her in his arms. When she started to unbuckle his belt he drew back. "I can't now, Van. I promised to take him out for ice cream."

In truth, they were spending far more time sightseeing than in brokers' offices. They had ridden on the Staten Island Ferry, where Joe pointed out Ellis Island and the Statue of Liberty, caged for refurbishing like so much of the city; had gazed out from the top of the Empire State Building, no longer the tallest in the world, Hughie remarked; bought trinkets in Chinatown—for Hughie, facsimiles of the Brooklyn Bridge and the Chrysler Building, and for Vanessa, embroidered blue velvet slippers; and even rented roller skates in Central Park: when they stood upright they began stumbling and guffawing like boys. But like school vacations, such fun could not last forever. After two weeks it was time for Hughie to start his job. The day before, Joe took him shopping for shoes and the Polaroid camera he had been longing for, then stopped to get a supply of subway tokens and a map. In the evening he wrote down Hughie's route in a series of steps. "Now don't lose this paper."

"I'll put it in my wallet."

"And keep an eye on your wallet in the subways. There are pickpockets." He advised him to get to bed early, to be fresh in the morning.

Hughie laughed. "I've been working for a long time, Hooch. I know what to do."

"He's quite able to be independent," Van said when they were alone. "He's managed without you for years."

"I know, but I feel responsible. It's a new place."

"You want him to be our baby, Joe. But he isn't. At least not mine."

That was not quite it, he thought. What he needed of Hughie was larger and more complex. In Hughie's bulk rested his own past, his other selves, lives he might have led if only he had had the chance. She managed to reduce every subtlety, and he looked at her with something like loathing. Then, frightened at his feelings, he went to sit in the dark kitchen with his head in his hands.

Mornings, now, each set off in a separate direction. Joe brought home a backlog of work piled up during his absence and Vanessa began going to dinner parties alone. Late in the evening he and Hughie would take walks, stopping for ice cream cones. They had become the couple, their roots twined too deep to be understood by an outsider. Vanessa said nothing. Clearly her strategy was to wait it out. Joe almost wished for jealous scenes, tears of exclusion and neglect—something specifically nasty to charge her with. But she was consummately civilized. And she was stronger, he knew; she would never break first. Meanwhile, strolling down the humid streets, he and Hughie talked about old times and how all had changed, about their father, who had died of a stroke four years ago, and their mother, who had moved to a retirement community in San Diego, where she sounded content and, to their common dismay, somewhat remote when they telephoned.

"It's usually the opposite," said Joe. "Parents get older and you worry about them and take care of them. She doesn't want to be taken care of or to take care either. I guess she had enough in her time."

"Mm," said Hughie.

Sometimes they didn't talk at all. Hughie would gaze enthralled at the crowded summer avenue pulsing like a carnival, while Joe walked alongside wondering what it was like inside his mind. Was it a poorly lit landscape, drab and ill-defined, with some familiar shapes looming more clearly than others out of the haze? Or a schematic map, like the subway map Hughie had learned to read, major stops color-coded and living undulations forced into straight lines and angles? Perhaps an old-fashioned file from before the days of computer storage: folders labeled in block letters, heaps of unscrutinized, misplaced data devoid of the shadings of attitude or opinion. No. Hughie thought. Joe knew that. But in pictures? In a voice speaking words? Could memories spring to the surface as needed, or were they dredged up by ponderous machinery? How were the connections made, what were the contours of the path between observation and judgment? Did he refer to fixed and reliable standards? Then what happened when spontaneity was in order? How did he judge when to use the standards and when to proceed on instinct? Or maybe such distinctions were meaningless—Joe himself didn't know for sure anymore. If only he might be retarded—just for a little while, of course, to see what it was like. Life would be so much easier, so many expectations could be ignored. Gauntlets tossed down on every side and you wouldn't have to pick up a single one.

On one of their walks Hughie said shyly that he had made a friend at work. "A girl."

"Hey, you didn't waste much time. What's her name?"

"Carol. She's younger than Marie, but she doesn't live with her parents. She lives in a big house with six other people and a couple who help them. I'm going to take her out one of these days, maybe to an Italian restaurant." He stopped walking as if he needed all his resources to speak. "Hooch, I have to find a place. I mean it. It's nice at your house, but I need somewhere of my own."

Joe had been dreading this moment. He explained about the lower rents in Brooklyn and Queens.

"Would it be far? Could I get to work from there?"

"Sure. In Queens you'd be even closer to your job."

They found a furnished two-bedroom apartment in Queens, the ground floor of a three-family house. The furnishings were decent but barren of governing design: the colors and shapes did not complement each other, the things were not placed in conscious relation to the path of light. He was looking through Vanessa's eyes, Joe realized. He must uproot them and replace them with Hughie's. And gradually the rooms relaxed into a nonchalant welcome, imposing nothing and indifferent to the choice of life lived within them. While the landlord showed Hughie the tiny garden in back, Joe went into the smaller bedroom and lay down. The bed was covered by a white chenille spread like the bed of his boyhood. There was an elm tree out the window. How tired he was, suddenly, and numb. The thought of returning home to the nineteenth floor to be encircled by fine objects was more than he could bear. How nice it would be to lie here like this, on the familiar, nubby spread, for a long time. He let himself drift to the fragile stage before true sleep, when dreams are drifting bubbles of sight and sound and smell, and visions come as beckoned. Soon he was smelling his mother's Sunday dinners, leg of lamb and roast potatoes, and the heavy aroma of peach pie in the oven. It lasted no more than a few seconds. He heard Hughie's footsteps and jumped up.

"It's good, but what about the lease and the money and everything? I mean, I can't figure all that stuff out that he said." Hughie was cranky and shook his head from side to side. To get the machinery going, Joe thought.

"You can definitely swing it. Don't worry, I'll work it all out for you. The point is whether you like it, if you'd be happy living here."

"I want to be able to take Carol out sometimes."

"You'll have plenty left to take Carol out. If you like it, I think it's a terrific deal. Do you think you'll be too lonesome, though, all by yourself?"

"Well, I have to, don't I? You just have to get used to things."

"I don't know," Joe said. "Maybe . . . Lately I've been thinking . . . But we can talk about it later, I guess."

"Furnished?" Vanessa frowned. "I said I'd help you pick things out."

"Thanks, but it's okay." Hughie didn't look at her. "Not as nice as you could make it, but okay." He said he needed to take a walk to think things over, and Joe stepped forward.

"No! I want to go myself for once!"

They had never heard him shout before. A moment later, they heard him fumbling outside with his keys, which always annoyed Van.

"I've told him to get those colored rings to tell them apart. What's wrong? Do you think he's having second thoughts?"

Joe shouted at her for the first time since the baby died. "Why don't you shut up for once? What does it matter how long it takes him to lock a door?"

She paled, then got very red.

"I'm going to go with him," said Joe.

"He said he wanted to take a walk by himself."

"I'm not talking about any walk." He hadn't planned to tell her till the lease was signed, he hadn't even been absolutely sure, but the words erupted. "I'm going with him."

She stared, as she would at a stranger who had done something unforgivably gauche. "Your idea of humor must have regressed lately. I don't find that funny."

He dashed into the bedroom, grabbed a suitcase down from the top of the closet, and began tossing socks and underwear into it.

"Have you lost your wits or something, Joe? I feel like I'm watching a nineteen forties movie."

"Keep talking, go on. It won't change anything."

"I don't understand! I thought when he left, everything would be the same as before. We'd have the house at the beach next month, we'd . . . Joe, I've tried to be patient, really, I haven't said—"

"You don't understand anything, that's right. You don't understand how to live."

"How to live? Watching baseball games and going to the zoo on weekends—is that how to live? Do you mean to tell me you're leaving me—me!—for a retard?"

"I'm going to live with my brother. I hate . . . I hate . . ." Again he couldn't say what, except that nothing in his line of vision seemed to belong to him, especially not the kite, which shouldn't be pinned on a wall anyway, but aloft. "All of this!"

"All of *what?*" she wailed.

"This! Us! Everything!"

She knocked the suitcase to the floor and the clothes spilled out. "I'll tell you what's going on. You're tired of doing your share and living with a woman who's your equal. And you're jealous of my work. You'd like to come home and find me in an apron, baking you a pie."

"You've got it all wrong. I'd like to come home and not find you at all. I'd like to have someone to bake a pie *for.*" He bent to pick up his things, but she grabbed them and hurled them around the room. She threw a shoe at him. She snatched a painted hand mirror from her dresser, resplendent, elaborately carved, something she had found in Acapulco last winter, and threw it at his head. Joe ducked. A sharp edge grazed his temple and he felt an ooze of blood. He went to the bathroom to wash it, and when he returned she was on the floor sobbing, holding the pieces of broken glass and the empty frame.

"I can't believe this is happening! Over Hughie! It's ridiculous. What am I supposed to do? I need you!"

Joe knelt to take the glass from her hands. They were cut in several places, not deeply. Thin streams of blood showed in the lines of her palms. "You'll do fine," he said gently. Now that it was done, his anger evaporated and he was sorry for her, bleeding on the floor. "You'll get further. We'll work everything out fairly."

"Oh, please," she wept. "Please! You're mixed up. This is not really what you want. You're just confused. . . ."

The word pitched him back into rage. "I'm not confused! I'm not! What do you care, anyway? You don't need me, you don't even know who I am. You just need someone to fit into your scheme. You can replace me in a week."

Her face was quiet and stunned. "Is that what you think? Is that really what you think? God!"

"Well, isn't it true?"

Her body gave a furious shudder and she punched him hard in the leg. "You'll be back! You won't last a week with him. I can just hear your dinner-table conversation. 'Guess what I saw today, Hooch!' " Her voice slowed and thickened like a record at the wrong speed. She had it perfectly.

"Don't do that!" He held a shard of glass at her cheek. "Do you hear? Don't ever do that."

Later, when he and Hughie left, she had only one parting word: "Queens," drawn out in a long tittering laugh. Her head was tossed back and the dazzling white throat arched like a bow, the word its arrow.

Hughie still couldn't face her. He hung his head and mumbled his thanks. "It's all because of me," he said in the elevator.

"No, I should have done it long ago. You were only the . . ." "Catalyst" was the word he meant, but he didn't feel up to explaining.

The apartment would not be ready for several days, so Joe took a double room at a hotel downtown. While Hughie studied the various signs regarding fire exits and checkout time and room service, Joe imagined them talking when the lights were out, as they used to. There were things that must be brought out, amorphous, churning parts of himself like muck stirred up from the bottom of a pond. They could surface only for his brother, in the dark. He would place them in Hughie's keeping, where they would be safe.

"Hughie," he said after they had been in bed for five minutes. "Hughie?"

"Mm."

Joe spoke very slowly. "I've lost the way. I have to get back to a more simple way. Get away from . . . how I've been living." There was no response except a deep snore.

The next day, a Sunday, Hughie had a date to take Carol to the aquarium at Coney Island and invited Joe along. It would cheer him up, he said.

Carol was a robust girl with spectacular red hair tied in a ponytail and smooth straight bangs. Hughie had said she was twenty-five, but in her white culottes and yellow tank top and sneakers she looked like a high school cheerleader. All through the roar of the subway she chattered good-naturedly; they had to bend close to hear. If she had known Joe was coming, she said, she would have brought along one of her housemates, but this way she had two dates at once.

Joe had not ridden the subway for some time. It was steamy and dirty, and he wondered how people tolerated it. At the aquarium he was pressed into service by Carol—she was too impatient to read the signs posted on each tank but wanted to know everything. Then she would dash away before he was finished. Fondly, she held Hughie's arm and pulled him along, peering and pointing into the blue-green waters. Joe trailed numbly after, unable to summon any interest in the fish. This was how it must be, he thought, taking children on instructive outings.

After the aquarium they walked on the boardwalk, eating hot dogs and ice cream. Carol said she loved amusement park rides—she recounted a school trip to Rockaway's Playland years ago—and finally induced Hughie to ride the Ferris wheel. He seemed a happy captive, but Joe, waiting below, couldn't help wishing they were alone, dawdling at the water's edge, watching the eternal waves roll in. While Hughie took Carol home, he went back to the hotel and lay half-mesmerized by the hum of the air conditioner, dreaming of how much better things would be just two days from now, when they set up house together. There was no escaping the frenzy of the working day, but he would have the evenings to rediscover the simple pleasures. Somewhere amid that oceanic blandness he would find what he had lost, the self everyone was alleged to possess, but which had slid through his fingers like a fish. His body was stiffening in the cold, but he hadn't the will to rise and turn off the air conditioner.

The first few nights in the new apartment, he fell asleep cocooned in peace. When he missed a body at his side, he curled his arms around a pillow. Mornings he woke to silence, or to the sounds of Hughie moving about serenely in the kitchen. Evenings they took walks, but here the streets possessed no carnival excitement, so they would return early and a bit dejected. Hughie would want to play checkers or watch over Joe's shoulder as he reviewed copy and layouts—usually of glamorous women luring men by their perfumes or the smoothness of their skin. He was full of questions, but by now Joe thoroughly loathed talking or even thinking about the cosmetics account—he saved this routine work for late at night, when his mind was dull. Before he went to bed Hughie liked to watch the eleven o'clock news, sighing and fretting over sensational local crimes. This had irritated Vanessa, who would launch into sermons about the warped priorities of television news while Joe tried to telegraph that it was no use. Now he felt the same sermons itching on his tongue.

One evening around nine, Hughie surprised Joe by bringing Carol home after a movie. She carried a pizza, which she set down on the table where he had spread out his papers—a promotional brochure for a brokerage firm, suggesting real estate investments. He moved them aside.

"Anyone mind if I take my shoes off?" said Carol. "My tootsies are on fire." She bent down to undo her sneakers, fastened with Velcro. Joe winced.

They wanted to know what he was working on.

"How the very rich can keep a step ahead of the taxman. What I'd really love to do is 'Gimme Shelter' in green boldface caps, with a cartoon of Mick Jagger astride the Trump Tower."

He looked up at their baffled faces. He had forgotten. He was so disoriented, so mired in confusion, that he had utterly forgotten whom he was talking to. "Taxes and business," he amended. "Nothing very interesting."

They opened the pizza. Joe listened as they enumerated all the places they had eaten pizza in their lives and compared the quality. Again he wondered what it was like inside Hughie's head, but now the prospect was terrifying. A funhouse maze where everything changed shape and position with no warning and no reason, where reason itself was one more imponderable to be accepted on faith. No. Hughie was clear about the important things, love and death, trust and devotion, loneliness and fear. That was why Joe had left to go with him. But it was also why even with Hughie there would be no escape, he saw, not ever. Like everyone else, Hughie suffered in darkness. Joe had seen him mortified, had seen on his face and still saw the blunt awareness of all he was unaware of, the world rising, monolithic and impenetrable, before him. Hughie could see its vastness, the dimensions of all he would never know; what he did not see were its intricacies. How did he see the circumstantial fact of his own life and death, then? How could he live, or know what he wanted or how to choose? To Joe, every choice seemed impossible, right down to the choice now at hand, a slice from the plain half or the half with anchovies. How could you ever choose, without knowing much more, or much less?

After the pizza they watched a situation comedy on television. There appeared to be a household of only women and children, and a good deal of bickering. Joe was lost, his mind veering in a mist, now and then colliding with the plot, which he found incomprehensible, a surreal barrage of non sequiturs. But Hughie and Carol were following, laughing at the same places as the canned laughter. Velcro laughter. They were holding hands on the couch. The mists in his head parted and Joe saw the future. Hughie and Carol would want to marry, eventually. Then where would he go? They might have babies, why not? They would be following the paths of ageless generations before them, being fruitful and multiplying, earning their bread in pain and joy. And if the babies turned out like their parents, so what? They too would live and love and suffer and die like everyone else. While he would be the uncle. Uncle Joe, who had never managed to find his own life. The children would grasp that, retarded or not. He would be invited for birthdays and Thanksgiving dinner and would bring expensive gifts. He would be consulted on many matters—balancing the checkbook, taxes, insurance, vacations. Maybe Hughie and Carol would buy a modest house someday; he would go along to make sure they got a fair deal. But after such excursions they would go home, and where would he be?

He had to escape. If only he could rip his skin off like Velcro, in one huge resounding tear, and beneath would be the true man, fresh and eager as a newborn, who would know what to do and how to be, free of doubt and torment. The pure inner man revealed, ready to begin. Indeed, sitting quite still, he could almost feel it starting. His body seemed to fill with air like a balloon stretched to the bursting point. The tension was unbearable but necessary. It was important to sit utterly still to contain the tremendous pressure. Only his eyes moved, settling on Hughie and Carol, who seemed very far away, at the end of a telescope, cheerfully eating ice cream and never suspecting what momentous change was about to occur. Of course it would be painful like any metamorphosis, but he was not afraid, no more than his mother had been afraid the first time. His fists clenched and his teeth clamped together as his body grew rigid.

"Hooch, what's the matter? Do you feel okay?" Hughie got up from the couch and stared.

Joe heard his brother's voice from far off but couldn't respond. He tried to draw himself inward. No one must touch him right now.

"Hooch! Say something! Come on!" Hughie stood before him, arms hanging at his sides.

"Should I get him an aspirin or something?" he heard Carol say. "What should we do?"

He wished they would stop their talking and leave him be.

No one had ever told him it would be so painful, this waiting to be born. He was almost losing consciousness, yet he was intensely conscious too, of all the earth's matter, inside and outside, pressing on his skin. He heard a faint, familiar noise like something being ripped apart. Yes, soon all the katydids and grackles in the park would be singing, heralding his transformation with their screeching caws.

"Hughie, do something," Carol shrieked. "Do something! Look at him shake!"

The Painters

The pair of children looked Asian, two or three years old, their glossy heads like lacquered bowls bobbing in the sunlight. Kneeling at the wide-open window, they pulled white tissues from a box and sent them wafting down on the breeze. A flimsy-looking iron gate reached to their stomachs, but every few seconds they popped up to lean out over it, clapping their hands as the tissues caught on the branches of trees, wrapped around a lamppost, and fluttered leisurely to the concrete below like great snowflakes.

Not a soul in sight. Della watched from across the street, a floor above them—the fifth; they would not see her if she waved. If she called out, the sound could startle them, make them lose their balance. She shut her eyes and curled her hands into fists as one child leaned way out, the tops of the bars pressing into his legs. The police? It was her first day here; she didn't even know the opposite building's address. And the time it would take, the heavy footsteps clattering up the stairs . . . Meanwhile they would fall and she would relive this moment all the years to come, remembering herself watching at the window of the empty bedroom in her new apartment, her new life, thinking about how she would remember herself at the window, watching. . . .

Just then a dark-haired woman appeared from the invisible spaces of the apartment across the street, plucked each child from the windowsill, and snatched up the box of tissues. Shut the window, thought Della, but the woman receded into the invisible spaces.

Della turned to savor the emptiness that surrounded her, mute and undemanding. The apartment was a stroke of luck, found quickly by an acquaintance who was adept at such things—inexpensive, airy, and in good shape, apart from dark walls enclosing an aura of shabbiness. Devoid of identity, but not for long. The moving truck would be arriving any minute, bearing half the contents of her former home. Once Ezra had told her, those rooms had felt like the scene of something unsavory, a parody of the life she thought she was living. Della had packed feverishly, all thought suffocated by the radio tuned to the most raucous station she could find. This irritated Ezra, who was an announcer for a classical music station, but in his guilt and confusion he had dared not complain, only hovered nearby looking pained, clearly uncertain whether it was more urbane to offer help or not. Are you sure you don't want to keep it? he had urged. It would give you some stability. It doesn't seem fair for you to be the one moving out. Della had answered, No, you keep it. Live in it with her. Look where stability has gotten me.

Numbed by the heat, Della sank down to the floor, leaning against a mud-colored wall, and ran her fingers along the floorboards: good hardwood floors, and recently scraped. She ran her fingers down her bare leg: good long legs, recently suntanned over the July 4 weekend, before Ezra told her. In her youth she had been a ballet dancer—faceless in the corps but swift and exhilarated, fulfilled; her enduring fringe benefits were a litheness of movement and a knack for twisting up her hair in sleek knots. Good legs, she thought, yet they hadn't counted in the long run. For all she knew, the new woman was drab and stumpy.

When the movers left hours later, it was as if Della stepped out of a dream. With the old chest of drawers, the washing machine (Ezra had insisted), the armchairs, desk, and stereo surrounding her, it was plain to see that she would have to live here. Her life, whatever that meant, her flesh's short span of animation, would trudge forward in time, in the unending cycles of light and darkness, its own cycles and wants felt within these walls.

She slipped the new keys in her pocket and walked out onto the hushed and darkening street. Perhaps she would be mugged, even killed. Only the first moments would be dreadful, and then the rest of her life effortlessly taken from her. But she passed no one menacing, only a heavy old woman in Bermuda shorts inching her way forward with a walker. On the lively avenue she sat at a small plastic table and ate two slices of pizza, and on her way home took note of a Chinese restaurant, a delicatessen, and a barbecued ribs place.

She felt very little conviction about trudging forward. Nevertheless tomorrow, once her telephone was installed, she would find painters; the landlord, snarling, had refused any repairs—"You're getting a bargain as it is!"—but it was not possible to live, with convictions or not, between those dark green and mud-colored walls. She unrolled a narrow futon—bought to replace the double bed where she had slept in an illusion—stretched out on her stomach, and fell into a deep sleep.

Three days later the painters appeared promptly at nine, recommended by the same able acquaintance who had found the apartment. They were not really painters, she had told Della, but artists. Of course they were as good as or better than real painters, but cheaper. And they spoke English, they could understand instructions, which many real painters didn't these days, and in addition could do carpentry and practically anything else Della might want done. In short, a find.

Della was accustomed to painters in white overalls arriving with surly mumbles, laden with supplies. These painters, in jeans and navy blue T-shirts and backpacks, arrived empty-handed, greeted her, and introduced themselves as if it were a social occasion. The man's name was Paolo and he looked intimidating: stocky, strong, and dark, with longish straight black hair, sharp assessing eyes, and a cigarette drooping from his lips. The woman, Margie, who did more of the talking, had an efficient, calming manner, something like a neophyte nurse or a schoolteacher. She was an inch or two taller than Paolo and was fresh-faced and blue-eyed, with very white teeth and hair

so blonde it was almost white, cut like a man's except for wisps
of bangs brushing her eyelids. At once Della wondered whether
they were a couple, if they lived and slept together as well as
painted together. Probably not. Paolo, whose few words were
spoken in a slight Spanish accent, was too forbidding for Margie, and she seemed too ingenuous for him.

"Okay, where is the paint?" he said after a tour of the four
large rooms.

"Oh, I didn't know—I guess I thought you would take care
of all that." She felt foolish—had she expected an ambulance
corps, a vehicle equipped for any contingency?

Paolo shrugged. "We'll go out for the paint. Do you have
brushes, rollers, a ladder?"

Della shook her head. No expression altered his face—only
a formidable neutrality.

"No problem," Margie said cheerily. "We'll put it all in the
truck."

"Oh, do you have a truck?"

"Brand-new. Our pride and joy." Margie darted to the
window to point out a dilapidated maroon pickup parked across
the street, its back piled with an assortment of wood and metal.
"Now we don't have to lug our stuff through the streets. Paolo
does very large pieces."

Della glanced up at the building opposite. The babies,
thank goodness, were sitting sedately at the windowsill, dip-
ping wands into a bowl set between them and blowing bubbles
through the iron bars. The bubbles caught the summer sunlight
in patches as they drifted radiantly upwards.

"This job could take a while," Paolo said. "It's going to need
a lot of plastering. Whoever did it last time painted right over
the cracks." He came to the window to crush his cigarette on
the bricks outside, glanced below at the small flower garden,
and put the butt in his pocket. "It could be slapped on in three
days, but we don't do that kind of work."

"You also may need two or even three coats to cover up
these weird colors," said Margie. "What colors did you have in
mind?"

"White. All white. As much as it takes." Suddenly she felt light and happy and protected in their presence. Even Paolo's gruffness was soothing: no smooth promises. "I've got the time. I took a month off from work to move in and fix the place up." Della worked for a publishing firm, designing book jackets. Her vacation money would pay these strange painters who fit in no ready category. In her old life, the painters sent by the landlord had been gray-haired men or teen-agers who spoke Greek and nodded enigmatically to whatever she said and left their cigarette butts on the floor.

"Are you going to be here the whole time, then?" asked Margie.

"Yes, I'm going to paint with you."

The first morning, after they all changed into shorts, Della painted a closet in the room where Paolo was scraping and plastering the ceiling. It was a room she intended to use as a studio in case she did any free-lance work, or as an extra bedroom in case her son, Frank, came to stay. Frank was in the Peace Corps in Costa Rica, building a school or a hospital, she had forgotten which, but that would not last forever. Paolo worked in silence, standing bare-chested on the ladder he had borrowed from the super, a cigarette pasted to his bottom lip. Della had given him a saucer for an ashtray, which was balanced on the top rung.

His voice startled her. "Are you going to live here alone?"

"Yes."

"It's a nice place. Light."

That seemed to be all. From the living room came pounding music. Margie, pulling a radio from her backpack, had asked if Della would object to the rock music of WAPP. Della would object to nothing except Ezra's creamy tones.

"Where do you live?" she ventured from the closet, in Paolo's direction.

"We have a loft in SoHo. Ancient, but big enough so we can both work. My work needs a lot of space."

"I used to live not far from there, on Bleecker Street. Then we lived in Chelsea, but I moved here because my husband took

up with a younger woman." She shocked herself a bit, with
that. But why not? She no longer had a rooted social position,
she could say anything she pleased. Even "took up with."

"That's too bad. How young?"

"Thirty-three. Precisely ten years younger than I am."

"That's the age Margie is. I'm thirty-five."

"Really? I thought you were both younger. I thought you
were kids."

Paolo smiled, making the cigarette tremble precariously.
"We thought you were younger too. These things are rough, I
know. Margie's husband left her for a man. They were married
five years and he discovered, or decided, he was gay."

"She seems very innocent, for that." Paolo said nothing,
kept plastering. "Where are you from?"

"Argentina."

"But Paolo is Italian, isn't it?"

He gave her a sideways glance. "There are many Italians in
Argentina. Some less now, in my family."

"Do you mean . . . ?" For her work Della had read a book
about the military regime in Argentina, she told him. She had
designed the jacket. "Is that why you came?"

"I had to. First they killed my father. My uncle and my
brother-in-law disappeared—my sister was left with two babies. I was next. I got here nine years ago, practically crawling
up two continents."

"That's terrible. Did you have anybody here, family,
friends?"

"A friend of my father's, yes, otherwise I'd still be living
underground. After I got the green card I worked in the flower
market. That's where I met Margie—she came in to buy a plant.
She helped me get back to making sculptures." He stopped
abruptly and climbed down from the ladder. "Time for lunch."

"I wish I had something to offer you, but—" She waved
vaguely at the emptiness and suddenly felt very hungry herself.

"Margie brought sandwiches. She made a ham last night.
There's plenty for you too. Anything around to drink, though?
Beer, maybe?"

Della flushed with pleasure at the invitation. Stepping out of the closet, she took off her painter's hat and shook out her hair. "I'll run around the corner and get some. It'll just take a minute."

He peered past her. "Beautiful closet, Della. High-class work. If you keep this up we'll let you prime the bathroom."

They settled on the floor in the living room, where the two chairs and the stereo were shrouded in plastic drop cloths. Margie, snapping open a can of beer, said, "Paolo told me what happened. For what it's worth, it gets better in time. I thought I would never recover, but I did, pretty much." With the white painter's hat hiding her cropped hair, with her paint-spattered shorts and bare feet, Margie looked like a twelve-year-old boy.

"This is a wonderful sandwich," said Della gravely. "It may be the best sandwich I've ever had. I'm not trying to recover. I'm just trying to get the apartment painted. I may keep painting it over and over, even after you both leave. I'll get fired from my job and go on unemployment and just stay home and paint, till the walls meet each other."

"Please don't paint over our work, Della," said Paolo. "Who knows, someday you may be able to say, These walls are the work of Paolo and Margie."

Della laughed faintly and sipped some beer. She had never been a beer drinker, but it seemed suitable now, in her new life, sharing an indoor picnic with strangers after working and sweating in the heat.

"I know how you're feeling, to talk that way. Can you imagine how I felt, with Bill, when I realized that for five years, every time we were together, my body was not . . . that maybe he was wishing or imagining I was something else? God knows what went through his head. And I thought he liked it. I thought that was how men acted when they were liking it. You know?"

"Please," said Della, hugging her knees tight. "I do know. But I don't want to think about any of that. Maybe ever again."

"Margie has learned to say everything aloud for her health. Her shrink taught her. She wants me to go too, for my anger."

Paolo gave a grunting laugh. "Maybe to have it removed, like a wart."

Margie moved closer to him, till their shoulders were touching. "I wish I could make you see," she said softly. Then to Della, "Paolo is an extraordinary artist. Everything he does is huge and powerful and . . . larger than life. But there are still some things he refuses to understand. I grew up on a farm in Montana. I drove a tractor and pulled turkeys in out of the rain. I hardly knew, when I got married, about people like Bill. But how could I go so long and not see what was right in front of me? I have to understand."

"But I understand perfectly what happened to me," Paolo said sullenly. "Only I don't make peace with it, like you do. It's not a private thing. I don't want to make peace with it."

She had been right at the start, Della thought. They were too different, and the difference made her uneasy. She wanted the new apartment pure and free of conflict. "How about another beer?" They sat silent, like petulant children. "Does either of you know anything about wiring? I have a lamp I'd like to hang in that spare room."

"Why not?" Paolo shrugged again. "I'll bring the manual along tomorrow, just in case. I can also hook up the washing machine that sits there idle."

The telephone woke Della out of thick sleep the next morning. She reached out but found nothing; when she reached to nudge Ezra there was only a grainy wall. She opened her eyes: new apartment, new life. Telephone on the floor, six feet away.

"Hi. I want to know what's going on. You haven't written in weeks and Dad said you moved out."

She had forgotten all about Frank, or at least about telling Frank. On the day Ezra pronounced their marriage over, Della had said he didn't have to know yet, far off as he was in Costa Rica. On that day Costa Rica had seemed an imaginary place and Frank an imaginary son. Now his voice restored him to physical existence. She recalled stuffing his body into snowsuits and grabbing him away from open windows, but with more alacrity than the woman across the street.

"Don't worry, we're both fine. We're living separately, that's all."

In his relentless way, Frank questioned her until she told him how Ezra had decided that their marriage was stunting his personal growth, whereas with his new woman he explored undreamed-of depths and heights. There was a silence; she wondered if they had been disconnected.

"I don't know what to say. Maybe it's just a phase."

"I doubt it. For me it's no phase. I have a wonderful new apartment"—and new painters, she almost added. "Never mind. Tell me how you're doing. How is the hospital coming along?"

It was a school, after all. "I have some good news, at least I hope you'll think so. I'm going to bring Milagros back with me at the end of the two years. We're going to get married. We've been—"

"Milagros?" It sounded like a man's name.

"I wrote you about her in my last two letters, remember? She's one of the architectural students assigned to our project." He paused and Della scanned her memory. "Don't you read my letters?"

"I'm sorry. It's just that I was sleeping soundly. That's . . . wonderful."

"You're not bothered that she's Costa Rican, I hope. Part Indian, actually. I mean, people can think they're very sophisticated, but when—"

"Oh, she's Costa Rican?"

"I wrote you! She speaks very good English, though."

"No, why should that bother me? Only a Nazi would bother me. But they've mostly gone to Argentina, haven't they?"

"Mom, go back to sleep. I've got to go anyway, they're calling me. Give me your new address. But I won't be able to write for a while—we're going on a field trip. I wish you and Dad could work things out. That's really some shock."

Milagros, thought Della as she hung up. She remembered

dimly the lightweight air letters lying on the hall table. Yes, two had arrived after the day Ezra came into the kitchen, where she was measuring out coffee, and told her that their marriage had been a gross érror of long duration, that he needed an entirely different kind of woman, only he hadn't known it till a few months ago, when she materialized in the studio. Della tried to remember what she had done about the coffee. She tried to remember reading Frank's letters, but could retrieve nothing at all since that day except finding the apartment and packing. Not even a movie, though she had liked movies, in her old life. Nor could she recall anything happening in the world. No information from the past three weeks seemed to have adhered, except for the facts about Paolo and Margie: Argentina, the sister left with two children, crawling up two continents, the flower market; Montana, turkeys in the rain, Bill the homosexual.

With those exceptions, thought Della, she had become like H.M. She had read about the case of H.M. a while ago at work, in a book about brain malfunctioning for which she had designed the jacket. H.M. had undergone brain surgery to control epilepsy and afterwards was incapable of learning anything new. Whatever part of him kept new information had been sliced out. H.M. could remember everything he had known before his lobotomy, and he could still understand what was said to him but could not retain it for more than a minute. He was told that his father had died, but immediately forgot it. Well, there was no danger of that happening to her; her father had been dead for many years and she knew it. H.M. had to be reminded again and again. And so it was with every single thing. He could not remember a new face, a new room, a new tune, a movie, or even what had occurred in the movie five minutes earlier. He could not grow past the moment when they cut out parts of his brain. That was quite different from Ezra's lamenting his stunted growth—Ezra was capable of learning new things, he was learning them right now, every day and every night. Only she was stuck in the moment when he told her their long mistake was ending, the nerves linking them were being snipped. Della had designed a very successful jacket for that book: a pane of shattered glass against the bars of a luminous rainbow. Every crack and filigree in the shattered pane was clearly delineated. Light from the colors behind the glass bled through in glimmers. The border of the design was black as night.

She rose and walked to the window. Ah yes, the babies—that she remembered well. They were at it again, stretching their bodies over the iron bars and opening their hands to send tissues skimming on the wind. The tissues looked like a regatta of sailboats seen from far off. Della shielded her eyes and shivered in the heat. She felt she could not bear her life or the terror that the babies would fall to their death as she watched. When she looked again the dark-haired woman appeared, pulled them from the windowsill, and lowered the window halfway. The doorbell rang—Paolo and Margie, come to continue painting.

While Margie finished the ceiling in the spare room, Paolo hooked up the washing machine and Della did a load of wash. Paolo hung the lamp: they all exclaimed on how sinister the color of the walls—gun metal—seemed in the artificial light, then cheered as Della applied the first stroke of chastening white. Paolo scraped and plastered in the bedroom and Margie began spraying the metal kitchen cabinets white. They worked steadily till almost three o'clock, when Della went out for barbecued ribs which they gnawed lazily on the living room floor, listening to the rock music on Margie's radio, punctuated by weather reports. Ninety-six degrees.

"Too hot to work," said Della. "Let's call it a day."

"I want to be air-conditioned," Margie said, rolling a beer can on her forehead. "Let's go to a movie."

They took turns in the shower, where Della had not yet hung a shower curtain. As Paolo emerged with his hair slicked back, apologizing for taking so long—he had had to mop up the whole floor—Della was reminded of the men in her life, Ezra and Frank, her former life, who also flung themselves about in the shower. Neither she nor Margie had that problem, but Margie emerged saying she would be glad to install a new shower head; a sharper, more tingly flow would do wonders for

Della's skin and spirit. They laughed at two Marx Brothers films at a revival house, then Paolo and Margie drove Della home in the pickup and she fell quickly into a deep, long sleep.

Painting in the kitchen the next day, while Paolo was out at the hardware store, Della said, "You always talk about Paolo's work, how big and powerful it is, what wonderful compositions he makes out of junk. What about yours? What's it like?"

"Well, it's small and I guess you would say delicate, in comparison to Paolo's. But then most things are. I work with light. How light hits surfaces and refracts. I build things, little models, and when they're set in various kinds of light, the light and shadows become part of the piece. It changes according to where it's put."

"But when do you get a chance to do it, if you do this kind of work all day?"

"We only do this about half the year, the warm months usually, because, you know, people like to keep the windows open. The rest of the year we mostly do our own work. Sometimes we hang shows for galleries downtown, for extra money. Paolo can work at night, but I'm too tired after a day of this, and anyway, I need daylight. I work on Sundays. That's when he sleeps."

"Do you think you'll go on this way indefinitely, or—" Della didn't know what she wanted to say after "or." Simply, the life Margie described did not sound like a life she could imagine living except for a short period, before embarking on "real" life. Like Frank in the Peace Corps, or herself dancing in the corps of the Joffrey at nineteen. Yet why on earth not? Thousands lived such lives, and no doubt had done so all the years she spent with Ezra.

"Well, I know what you mean, sure. I think I'd like to be married again, even after what happened with Bill. Maybe have a baby. More than maybe. I mean, I'm not going to be able to do that forever. And we've been together four years. But Paolo's not ready, he says. You've heard about the new man, afraid of commitment and all that garbage."

"He seems already committed."

"That's exactly what I tell him, but . . ."

"Isn't that a very American syndrome?"

"He picks things up fast."

They heard the key in the door. Paolo returned with magnets so the kitchen cabinet doors would close properly, and a special bit for his drill so that he could put up standards for bookshelves. Margie, turning on her radio, suggested that when Della finished the kitchen door she might prepare all the windows to be painted. Mesmerized by the heat and a remote blank contentment, Della moved slowly from room to room, dusting the window frames and sills and sticking masking tape around the edges of every pane, until Paolo shouted to them with excitement—come see what he had unearthed in the bathroom. She had to laugh as she confronted the bizarre mottled walls. Dismally faded browns and blues and grays lay bared: bulbous masses assembling for a thunderstorm, strata of history in the form of successive paint jobs.

"Found art!" he cried. "This should be preserved for posterity. It's almost like a de Kooning, if only the colors would be brighter."

Margie gave her clever chuckle. "Beyond New Wave. But you didn't have to scrape down that far. I mean, Della is paying for this."

"I wouldn't charge for anything in the service of art! Even the degree of scraping is a creative act. You should put it under glass, Della. It's a statement about the past, the juxtaposition of eras, like archaeology. You could charge admission. One wall at least."

"Come off it. It's so ugly it hurts," said Della.

"So straight! Where's your nerve? Wait—we have to add something contemporary." He grabbed the can of white spray paint from Margie's hand and sprayed a small heart on the wall above the bathtub. Inside the heart he sprayed the letters *P* and *M,* linked by curlicues. "There!"

"Don't mind him," said Margie. "It must be the heat."

Della went back to taping windowpanes, grateful that the

babies across the street were nowhere in sight. Dreamily she mused about the near future, when Paolo would outgrow this childish phase and marry Margie and they would have the baby she craved. Margie would stay home and not work so hard, and Paolo would . . . Get a job, she almost continued. But that was absurd—she was molding them into something other than they were. Paolo would be discovered and sell his work to rich collectors. Margie would work too, when she wasn't taking care of the baby, and maybe she too would be famous, with her smaller and more delicate pieces. It was a naive fantasy, Della knew; it might even be objectionable. Yet it made her happy.

Later that afternoon Margie went out for pizza and beer, and as they ate on the living room floor Della asked Paolo to tell her something about Costa Rica.

"What does that mean, 'something' about Costa Rica? It's an entire country. What parts do you want to know about?"

"I'm not sure. You could start with the government, like they used to do in school, then the products and resources, the mountains and rivers, remember? Well, maybe you didn't do that. Anyway, start. I'll remember what's important to me."

With a mild jab at the insularity of North Americans, Paolo obliged, and what Della remembered mostly, after he and Margie left for the weekend, was that Costa Rica was one of the few Latin American countries with a democratic government and not under the rule of the military. Actually, Frank must have mentioned that; the fact did not strike her as entirely new. Costa Rica did not even possess a standing army, Paolo said. The United States, however, considered Costa Rica little more than a satellite and had recently proposed to send military advisers there as part of the effort to aid Nicaraguan contras. Paolo was surprised Della knew nothing about this, or about Costa Rica's enormous national debt, since both had been in the papers, but she explained she had not been reading the papers much lately, and even if she had been, she would probably have forgotten what she'd read. Paolo had looked confused by her explanation, but Margie understood and said all of that would pass in time.

*   *   *

Della spent the weekend sleeping and wandering dazedly through the baking streets. On Monday morning, Margie carried in a large shopping bag packed with mounds of tissue paper. "I brought one of my pieces to show you. But we have to be very careful with it. It's fragile." She and Paolo unwrapped it on the washing machine. It was a construction of wood and Masonite about a foot and a half high, finished in gradations of white and gray and suggesting an architect's miniature model. Yet not quite a building; rather, a mélange of possible parts of buildings, a structure of fable. Looking closely, Della saw that Margie had painted a range of shadows here and there, making it tricky to tell which grays were painted and which were a response to the light. Studying the piece was almost like a game, a brainteaser.

"How wonderful. So complex." Indeed, it was more subtle than she had expected, its profusion of planes and angles and crannies, all neatly trimmed and lucid, giving the illusion of a simplicity just out of reach.

"Let me take it over to the light," Paolo said. "You can't really appreciate it here." He brought it into the bedroom, where the morning sun beamed in. Standing at the window, he held it high and revolved it in his hands. As light struck the piece, its patterns shifted; flashes of rainbow appeared, shadows disappeared. *"Ay, Dios mio,* those babies! They'll fall out! Where is their mother?"

"Hey, don't drop it!" Margie took the piece from him and set it down in a corner.

"Oh, not again," moaned Della. "Every other day I think they're about to die."

"One day they will. *Oyé, chiquillos!"* he called loudly.

"No, no!" Della grabbed his arm. "Don't shout! They could lose their balance. Just do nothing. Don't look."

"I can't not look. Let's call the police."

The woman appeared from the invisible spaces of the apartment and pulled the children off the windowsill. She left the window open.

"Señora, por favor!" Paolo shouted something in Spanish. "But they're Chinese. Or Korean," said Della. "She wouldn't understand Spanish."

Paolo called again, but the woman had vanished. "They looked like Latinos to me."

Della's shoulders sagged in exhaustion. She saw Margie, pale and still, sitting on the floor next to her sculpture. In the shadowy corner it had lost its verve; its interest had become purely geometrical and barren. Again Della praised it, but the moment was spoiled. Margie said she would go wrap it up so no one tripped over it.

"Oh, Della, I forgot to mention on Friday . . ." Paolo said. "I pulled up a piece of that ridiculous wavy linoleum—behind the stove, don't worry—and there's a good surface underneath. I could put down tiles if you like—the kitchen would look a lot better. A domestic metamorphosis."

"Ha! I'm not sure I want to go that far. Is the linoleum so bad?"

He gave a loud laugh. "Well, it's not that I'm dying to rip up a floor in this heat."

"Let me think about it." Climbing up the ladder in the bathtub to paint the ceiling, Della began figuring rapidly. The plastering was all done. The spare room was finished, the living room and bedroom close to it. It might be only a few days till . . . The telephone rang rooms away, its first ring since Frank's call from Costa Rica. "Paolo, Margie, would someone get it, please?"

Paolo, who had been painting the bedroom window frame, handed her the receiver with a comic flourish, whispering, *"Un hombre."*

"Della? Hello, Della?"

"Who is this?"

"It's me—Ezra. What's the matter?"

"Nothing."

"Didn't you recognize my voice?"

"What do you want?"

"I had to get your number from Information."

"Well?"

"Who was that answering the phone?"

"The painter."

"He didn't sound like a painter."

"How should a painter sound?"

"I meant he sounded too educated to be a painter. All the painters we've ever had didn't speak much English."

"Well, this one speaks excellent English." She turned towards Paolo and grinned. He grinned back.

"Okay, it's not my business, I realize. I was calling about Frank. This girl he says he wants to marry, Della, may be a very nice girl, but he's far too young for such a big commitment. I don't think it's something we ought to encourage. He may come to regret it."

"You mean marry in haste, repent at leisure?" Della had been pregnant when she and Ezra married. They had also been in love.

"You could put it that way. Then, of course, Costa Rica. It's quite a different culture."

"Are you familiar with Costa Rica? Costa Rica may be the only nation in the Americas without a standing army. One of the few, certainly. And yet now our government—"

"I don't see what that . . . Della, is everything all right? Are you managing?"

"Fine. I have to go now, the painter needs me."

"That's not very funny. I'm writing to Frank to try to explain things. Would you write too?"

"This place is so upside down at the moment, I don't even think I could find a piece of paper." Della hung up.

"The husband?" Paolo asked.

She nodded.

"He has a voice like a radio announcer."

"That's because he is one."

"Maybe he is one because he has that voice."

"You have a point there."

"He's getting lonely, eh? Wants to reconsider?"

"Nope, nothing like that. By the way, you might as well rip up that kitchen floor."

"Are you sure? Do you want to price some tiles first?"

"No, that's okay. Also, about the bookshelves—if I got the wood this week could you help me sand and stain it?"

Paolo gave his usual neutral shrug. "All right, why not?"

She drifted into the living room, where the ceiling and two walls already gleamed white against the old forest green color. Margie's roller was attached to a long stick. As she saw Della she smiled and jiggled it in time to the music, doing a bouncy little dance. Della envisioned the entire room white and glistening, its accumulated gloom sealed into oblivion, with sunlight filtering in through pale wooden slatted shades. "That looks great, Margie. Do you think, if I bought some window shades for the whole place—you know, the Japanese kind—you might put them up?"

"No problem. I'll check out the window frames and see what kind of brackets you'll need."

Late in the afternoon Paolo went out for Chinese food and beer. When all the containers were empty, Margie reached across the living room floor for her huge shopping bag and pulled out a game, Trivial Pursuit, which she announced would distract Della from her troubles and prove that her memory was basically intact. Oh no, Della said, she had lost the competitive instinct. Paolo resisted too, groaning with disdain. But in the end they gave in.

The game turned out to be like Go to the Head of the Class, which Della had played as a girl and also played with Frank when he was small. She was soon winning, for many of the questions were about people and events in the news before Paolo's and Margie's era: FDR, Neville Chamberlain, Billie Holiday, the Lindbergh kidnapping, Jesse Owens, the abdication of Edward VIII. They were before her own era as well, she realized, yet she knew about them. Paolo and Margie could answer questions about Greek and Roman mythology, about the Medici popes, and about the French Revolution, but didn't seem to know much that had happened in the twentieth century before 1960. On the other hand, Margie was very good with questions about art and music and, unexpectedly, baseball. Paolo was better than either of them at geography—he was spectacular at geography, Della noted—but his downfall was questions about American popular culture, particularly that segment of it promulgated on television: he did not know the name of Fred Flintstone's wife, or what *Bonanza* was, or how many children were in the Brady bunch. he was reduced to muttering curses in Spanish, or possibly Italian, when asked the name of Perry Mason's secretary and loyal sidekick.

Della laughed. "I could never forget that—Della Street. My parents were apparently great Perry Mason fans." She had to explain the curious mass appeal of Perry Mason; they had neither read the books nor seen the television series. "I always wondered why. There was nothing memorable about her. She just filled a necessary role. Maybe they liked the sound of it."

"Why didn't you ask them?" said Paolo.

"Well . . . they were drowned in a sailing accident when I was four."

Margie gasped. "You never told us!"

"It never came up. I've only known you less than two weeks."

"Still. So who took care of you? Did you grow up in an orphanage?"

"No. I stayed with an aunt and uncle. I was lucky. To have them, I mean."

"But do you still remember your parents? Can you see them in your mind?" Margie seemed intrigued by the news.

"Oh yes. My father more than my mother, strangely enough. He was a very big man, with very big gestures. He didn't know his own strength, my aunt used to say. I think she blamed him for the accident. I remember this game we used to play. He would sit in a certain chair with his arms outstretched and I would run to him. He caught me and locked me in with his legs—I was his prisoner—then he pushed me away and I ran backwards, then back to him again, over and over, and laughing all the way through. One time he pushed me away so hard I toppled backwards right into the French windows and cut my arm on the broken glass." Della paused. She felt a bit light-headed. "I can still feel the thrill of that game, being captured and enfolded, all warm and safe, and then pushed away. It was only pretend, the pushing away part. It never really felt danger-ous. I still have the scar." The memory was pulsing in her brain like a blip on a radar screen. She held out her arm to show them the small white circle near her wrist.

"My father never went in much for games. He has Alz-heimer's now," Margie said. "Last time I saw him, when my mother died, I had to keep introducing myself. He couldn't keep it in his head from one minute to the next." She poured a long swig of beer down her throat. "I almost think I'd rather be an orphan like you two."

"Orphan! I think at a certain age, my age anyway, it no longer applies. Though maybe it should. Was your mother also . . . political?" she asked Paolo.

"My mother died of a cerebral hemorrhage. Even under a junta some people manage to die of natural causes. It's much less glamorous, I know."

"Okay! You don't have to make it an international incident. What ever happened to your sister? The one who was left with the two small children."

"Ah, my sister. A few years after her husband disappeared, my sister met a man, very nice, very decent. Also a radio an-nouncer, it happens. But she keeps thinking maybe her hus-band is still alive somewhere. She won't get married—she is afraid of being a bigamist."

"But they emptied the prisons long ago, I read. Surely he's not going to turn up after all this time?"

"No. But she's a religious woman. God could send him back. I'm not sure if it would be a reward or a punishment at this point."

Margie finished her third can of beer. She grazed Paolo's bare foot with her own, then crossed her ankle over his. "She should see my therapist. She's terrific with endings. I mean, like a special talent. Scrapes you up off the floor and puts you back into shape for the next bout."

"Maybe you should find someone who does middles," Della suggested.

"There never seem to be any middles, just beginnings and endings. And everyone can handle beginnings. They're the fun part. Endings are the real challenge, don't you think? I mean, they're costing me a fortune. That's money I ought to be using to visit my father in Butte."

Paolo turned to Della, his eyes large with injury, entreating. "But I'm not ending anything! I'm right here with her. I don't know why she keeps talking that way. Too much beer, that's what."

"You're right. I'm talking nonsense." Margie put the beer down. She squeezed Paolo's hand, then kissed it. "Let's get it together here. Your turn, champ."

A week later the apartment was finished. Like new, Della thought. Light filtered through the slatted shades, striping the fresh walls. The kitchen was metamorphosed by a white tile floor. Paolo had hung a pegboard for pots and pans, and screwed the magnets into the latches of the cabinets. The bookshelves, stained and in place, awaited their books, still packed in cartons. In the bedroom, Margie had hung a full-length mirror Della got at the Salvation Army store, and in the bathroom, once Della put up a shower curtain, she had installed a more invigorating shower head. As a final touch, she hooked up the stereo system and speakers. Then they had cleaned up the debris and left. But they must get together very soon, they all vowed. Della must come down to the studio to see their work, and they would go to dinner in Little Italy or in Chinatown. And Paolo and Margie must come back for a real dinner, sitting around a table, as soon as Della got her dishes unpacked and got a table.

She returned to work. It took enormous effort to get herself dressed and presentable for the office each day and do the projects assigned her. She tried to reestablish a routine of shopping on the way home and preparing dinner, as she had done for most of her adult life—programmed like a machine, she had often thought. But she couldn't seem to break the newer habit of dropping in at the pizzeria, the Chinese restaurant, or the delicatessen. Unlike H.M., she had succeeded in learning something new—not to cook dinner. In the evenings she listened to records on the stereo and sent change of address cards to magazines, to her bank and her credit card accounts. When writing to Frank, she remembered to ask how Milagros was, and remembered it was a school he was building, not a hospital. She unpacked dishes and books, and bought items like wastebaskets and ice cube trays, which she had forgotten to take from the old apartment.

Out all day, she naturally didn't see the babies at the window across the street. But when they didn't appear over the weekend, she decided the family must have gone away on vacation. To the country or the seashore, where the buildings were low.

Often she thought about calling Paolo and Margie, but a cloud of uncertainties, like gnats, surrounded her. Perhaps they had only felt sorry for her. Perhaps it was the custom in their generation or in their circles for people thrown together by circumstance to become intimate at first sight, then to forget each other as easily when circumstances changed. But could an instinct like friendship change from one generation to the next, or in different circles? Surely not, yet customs could be more powerful than feelings, and among these new new customs Della was at a loss, like a foreigner, or Rip Van Winkle.

Perhaps Paolo and Margie made friends with all their employers, for fun and profit. Yet hadn't Margie confided that they had never had such a good time on any job? Often they couldn't wait to leave. Paolo, she said, usually felt uncomfortable with new people. Constrained. Why, at their previous job he hadn't even been permitted to smoke indoors and had to go out on the fire escape. Literally fuming, she recalled, with her chuckle. Neither had they been taking advantage of her, Della knew, for their meticulous records of hours worked and expenses at the hardware store tallied with her own: they had not charged for the many hours spent sitting on the floor eating and playing games or telling stories, nor for the whimsical excavation of the bathroom walls. Still . . .

Della tried to brush doubt from her mind, tried to trust. She would call at precisely the right moment—too soon would appear dependent and clinging, too late could find her drifted to the gray recesses of memory. She chose one early evening twelve days after they had left. The sunlight in the apartment was declining, but still rich and gold. Paolo answered on the first ring.

"Della! It's good to hear you! How're you doing?" He sounded truly pleased. With an awkward haste, Della invited him and Margie to come for dinner on Friday or Saturday night.

"I hate to tell you this, but . . ."

Her chest felt rammed in. Don't say it, she thought. But he already had. She was gone. "But why? What happened?"

"I don't understand it myself. One of those things."

"Of course you understand. She wanted to get married and have a baby."

"That was part of it. But there were other things too. She's . . . Oh, it's too involved. We wanted to call you, Della, but things were really rough for a while. I'm okay now. I'll come Friday, or would you rather go out somewhere? Or else come down here and I'll show you my stuff."

"Oh no," whispered Della. Her heart was racing, she was feeling sick, she wanted only not to talk anymore. "No. I couldn't do that."

"I don't get it. Why not?"

"I wanted to see the both of you."

"But . . . You sound like a child, Della."

"I can't help it."

"Oh. Was it just that we were a cute couple? Was that all? The hired help? The spic and his chick?"

"No, no, stop. You don't understand at all. Please, just forget it. I'm sorry."

"Do you want the number where Margie's staying?" he asked coldly.

"Another time, maybe."

She knew they would be there, even before she looked. They were leaning far out, waving at a flock of birds overhead. Back from vacation, or perhaps they had never gone; yes, that was another fantasy. The babies flung their arms about and shouted, so for the first time Della could hear their voices. The syllables were foreign, though at this distance she couldn't tell whether they were Chinese or Spanish or baby talk. As always, they looked about to topple out—she should be used to it by now. But she would never be used to it. It took only one time. She wished they would fall right away, if they were going to, and get it over with. Where was their mother? Where was their father, for that matter? How would she live the rest of her life here?

She turned and walked slowly through the fresh, chaste rooms. Soon the weather would change; the windows would be closed. They would get older, they would grow up. She could only wait.

The Thousand Islands

Somewhere in the drift between sleep and waking, night and light, I heard a man call my name from far away, in a voice that meant I should come join him. It couldn't be my husband—he was lying beside me. I thought it sounded like my father, long dead. And I was afraid, because I can rarely resist the lure of a trip.

My mother used to tell me it was not good to ride the down escalator. She kept the reason mysterious—whether a superstition, or maybe a bizarre moral stricture, or a past disaster, I could never quite make out. In any event, we shouldn't take the risk. So in department stores we rode the escalator up and walked or took the elevator down. Later I learned it was something very personal she drew me into: simply that the down escalator made her dizzy and sick to her stomach. I never felt leery of escalators, nor of elevators in any ordinary, claustrophobic sense, but when I lived alone on the top floor of a tall building I feared, while going down to the basement, that the elevator would not stop there but continue down, down to a subterranean region of eerie, phantasmagoric happenings, just as when Don Quixote is lowered into the Cave of Montesinos and falls asleep, to meet long-dead creatures dwelling in "enchanted solitudes" and enacting floridly romantic adventures. Even going back up, in the instant's pause between pushing the button and the elevator's ascent, my heart and breath again hung suspended as I waited to be transported to the earth's secret, exotic core, from which I too might wish never to return and might chide friends who hauled me up with ropes, for "robbing me of the sweetest existence and most delightful vision any human being ever enjoyed or beheld." The car always went up. Gasping in relief, I would shift my visions accordingly, and imagine that instead of stopping at the top floor it would continue on through the roof and sail aloft like a balloon, past this world in which every single thing was a boundary, to a region of open, dazzling spaces without logic or limits.

*   *   *

My mother never wearied of telling the story of her trip to Watertown, New York, before I was born. She had a seductive way of telling a story, a way that ensnared me in the filaments of her emotions and made me impatient for the time when such worldly adventures would happen to me. It was towards the end of the Depression, on the eve of war in Europe. My father had been fortunate enough to find a government job in Watertown, something to do with taxes. She stayed behind with my sister in her parents' house in Brooklyn, a brownstone with each floor given over to a daughter and her family. She seems to have considered it perfectly natural to stay behind with her parents, which is odd since in another part of her mind she believes a woman should go wherever her husband goes. Except, perhaps, to Watertown. My father would come into town every second or third weekend and on one of these visits he persuaded my mother to ride back part of the way with him, half an hour or so, no great risk, then he would drop her at a bus stop where she could catch a ride home. She gets into the car, leaving my sister in the care of the extended family, and after a time notices that they are out of the city, speeding along a highway. When she remarks on this, my father says he'll let her out in a while. Pretty soon she realizes they are far from the safety of Brooklyn, headed for Watertown.

"He kidnapped me," she would declare with pride and delight.

On the way to his rooming house, my father waved from the car window to a couple of his office mates passing on the street, and called out happily that his wife was paying him a visit. My mother found his landlady courteous enough, though a type she was not accustomed to—tight-lipped, chalky-faced, austere in a particular small-town fashion. While my father was off at work they chatted. Towards the close of the chat the landlady told my mother that she seemed to be a nice woman but that in Watertown nice women, though they might wear rouge and powder, did not wear lipstick. This amused my mother as a lesson in provinciality. Especially since as everyone in Brooklyn knew, lipstick was the most modest form of makeup, powder next, rouge next, mascara next, and eye shadow the ultimate. Eyeliner was not yet used.

On the second day in Watertown, it was arranged that my mother would go downtown to meet my father for lunch. She started walking along the road he had indicated. Soon a car slowed alongside her; the driver honked and called to her to get in. She ignored him. For quite a while he tracked her, occasionally blowing the horn, but, a city girl, she steadfastly ignored him.

When she got to the office she told my father about the man who had tried to pick her up, then they went to lunch. In the restaurant my father greeted some people and introduced her. Imagine her surprise when one, looking puzzled, said, "I saw your wife walking to town. I figured she was coming to meet you and I wanted to give her a lift, but she wouldn't turn around." One of the very men they had passed on the street the day before!

Of course my mother was embarrassed. He had meant well, but how was she to have known? How to explain that in New York City a sensible woman never gets into a passing car with a stranger?

I was conceived, legend has it, on the Watertown trip. Then my father brought her home to her parents' house.

There was another trip my parents made early in their married life, before I was born, that my mother liked to tell about. The Thousand Islands, in Canada. Even though my mother described the Thousand Islands in vague terms—peaceful, small old-fashioned houses, lots of water—she managed, with her talent for narrative and her candid face and expressive voice, to make them sound highly exotic, and thus they remain, the very name thrilling in its magnificent profusion. There too she met a landlady, who told her—my mother is sociable with strangers—that she had never seen Jews before and always believed, as she had been taught, that Jews had horns. My mother informed her, no doubt in the winning, candid manner I know well, that Jews assuredly did not have horns. From my mother's stories I sometimes confuse the two landladies, the horns and the lipstick, and the two trips—if indeed they were separate experiences: Watertown is very near the Thousand Islands, I have since learned. She talked about her travels so often, I imagine, because they were so infrequent. I don't count the Catskill Mountains and Florida: those were not trips but transfers of the corporeal self in a car or an airplane in order to arrive at the same place but with better weather.

Before she was born, her parents traveled halfway round the world at great peril, and whether or not they told her about their travels, she, along with many in her generation, desired nothing more than to stay put where it was safe.

*   *   *

But I always yearned to go on exotic trips and nagged about it till at last, I must have been nine or ten, my mother said all right, we would go to the Thousand Islands. My outlook on life was transformed—I had something to live for beyond the asphyxiating routine of school—and I began making lists, secret lists that I kept hidden in a night-table drawer, of what I would take to the Thousand Islands: 2 pr. shorts, 2 bathing suits, 3 skirts (white w. belt, red print, pleated) . . . Every night I revised the secret lists—for, unlike my mother, I thrived on secrecy— and copied them over, picturing myself in the various combinations of outfits, doing things on my secret agenda: ambling down foreign streets lined with picturesque cottages, or standing on a pier in the salt breeze, gazing over the rippling water dotted with hundreds of tiny gleaming islands. Sometimes I would ask my mother about the impending trip and she would

retell her story about going there as a young woman, the landlady, the horns, and get a nostalgic look on her face which I
interpreted as sweet longing and anticipation. But as weeks
passed, her responses grew vaguer and then dismissive, till it
dawned on me that there would be no Thousand Islands trip
and I would never be packing the clothes on the lists. At first
I thought the plans had fallen through for some adult reason,
then with a kind of gradual shock I understood that there had
never been any trip planned, she had said it only to placate me,
to shut me up, as she did with five-minute spaghetti. When I
was impatient for dinner she would sometimes tell me she was
cooking a special type of spaghetti, five-minute spaghetti, and
in fact those spaghetti meals did seem to materialize more
quickly than most. Only when I was a teen-ager and began to
go to supermarkets alone—for from as far back as I can remember, my mother shopped, pulling me along, in a tiny grocery
with barely room to stand, where she had to ask the waddling
grocer to fetch each item, one by one, which revelation of our
family's intimate tastes and needs seemed a violation of pri-
vacy—did I learn there was no such thing as five-minute spaghetti. I was mortified, not so much on account of having been
duped, but to think that my hunger—evidently an urgent,
abandoned, exposed, unseemly lust—required such strategies.

I forgot about my secret lists and when I found them a few
years later, under a pile of new secret lists and agendas in the
night-table drawer, I studied them with contempt—7 pr. socks,
sneakers, white sndls.—and tore them up. There would come
a time, I thought vengefully, when I could go to the Thousand
Islands by myself, and not need to beg anyone to take me.

*   *   *

One summer afternoon I went on an excursion with a man
I knew. I was going away soon on a long trip, and we wanted
to spent one unfettered, leisurely afternoon together. He said he
knew a place in the country, an old friend's house on a lake; the
friend was away. He picked me up on a street corner in his

car—I knew him well, so it was all right to get in. But when we arrived we found the friend's brother there. We were all very civilized and pretended this was not a tryst, and as we sat on the porch overlooking the lake, eating sandwiches and drinking iced tea, we discussed the troubled politics of the Middle East, where none of us had ever been. After a while the friend's brother excused himself to do some paperwork inside and urged us to enjoy the lake and the house, to make ourselves at home. We swam and lay on the wooden dock in the hot sun, where he caressed my back, and just from that simple motion and from the absurdity of the situation we reached such a pitch of excitement that he wanted to make love then and there, but I couldn't do that right in the middle of a lake with cottages around it, so we went inside to a downstairs bedroom, tearing off our wet suits recklessly and barely in time to fit ourselves together in some frenzied slapdash fashion. Later we told the friend's brother, all of us with composed faces, that we had had a nice swim and a nap, thanked him, and drove back to the city to resume our workaday lives.

Some time later my husband went on a weekend camping trip that wasn't really that, a trip he said he needed for solitude and an imprecise sort of spiritual refreshment which I, of all people, would not dream of challenging—nor of joining him on, not being a camper. He carefully, almost ostentatiously, unearthed supplies like hiking boots and a canteen. Months after, when I found out that the trip had not really been a camping trip—what could I, of all people, say? I would not have been altogether devastated, except for one thing. He had borrowed my knapsack for the trip. "Do you mind if I take your blue knapsack?" he asked, the night before he left, and I shrugged and said, "Sure." That still rankles, that my knapsack was a witness, kidnapped, and on top of that he really didn't need a knapsack (or a canteen) in the city. I don't even like to think of why he did that, even less than I like to think of how mortified and disillusioned I was when I learned, after so many years, that there was no such thing as five-minute spaghetti.

But these are earnest, candid people. It was probably nothing despicably complicated, just for verisimilitude, and again to placate me and any (nonexistent) anxiety or suspicion.

*   *   *

So I became a well-traveled person (though never to the Thousand Islands—I have lost that urge), but unlike my mother, I rarely entertain or lure with travel stories. Nor do I tell about the lists of things to take along the next time and the agendas of things to accomplish. I would never have done a thing like that, taking the knapsack. Not simply because I would not run such risks, fully as mysterious as the risk of the down escalator. But because secrecy has its own proprieties, utterly unknown to those earnest candid people who have to snare others in their travels, who cannot travel alone.

The Infidel

I

Martin Solomon, the well-known painter whose recent work had been called, not entirely to his liking, "an anatomy of entropy," was standing in the bustling vastness of the New York Port Authority bus terminal, a suitcase dangling from one hand, a portfolio of drawings from the other, his raincoat slung over his shoulder. Reflexively, he scanned the crowd for the faces of interesting women, much as an engineer might note structural beams or an orthopedist curved spines. The terminal was undergoing dissection and reconstruction to keep up with modern times: sheets of plastic skirted raw Masonite panels, and makeshift signs and arrows directed the dazed voyager. The usual melancholy of transience was heightened painfully; to Martin the place smelled of desperation, cried out to be left in peace. Martin too, though in transit between the arms of Paula, vacationing in Vermont, and Jess, in a SoHo loft, was in a state of solitary despair. In younger days, he had envisioned himself on these endless treks as a picaresque hero off to meet adventure. But tonight, with the rain battering at the bus windows, leaving a distorting sheen on the gray twilight landscape, he had felt himself an aging man burdened with luggage weightier each year, compelled to wander the earth homeless. There was still the house on the shore, but since Alice had died it didn't feel like home.

"Men are incomplete," he had told Jess months ago. "They need women."

She had rolled her eyes. "Your originality is dazzling. Go on. You can be Sartre, I'll be Simone."

"Listen, my little sourball, I don't mean in all the ordinary ways, socially, sexually, emotionally. . . . They need women psychically. Men are constructed incomplete."

She still looked dubious, hugging her knees to her chest in her big old armchair. She was small, with straight light hair that fell about her face, featherlike, and she was wearing a sweatshirt and blue jeans. She dressed only for gallery openings and meetings with editors. Jess looked like a charming student, but she was nearly forty. Martin was just stretching out a leg to nudge her gently, for she could flay him with words, then throw her arms around him and caress him to distraction, but her son, Max, came in. He was twelve and, like most people, adored Martin. "Wanna box?" he asked.

Martin leaped up and dashed the unruly gray hair off his face. Energy radiated from his big body as, hopping about, he aimed light punches at the boy's jaw. "Do it like I told you, keep alert, that's a boy. A killer. Going to be our next Muhammad Ali, eh, Jess?" He stole a quick glance at her. She had put her glasses back on and was studying the proofs of an article she had written about Duane Hanson, the sculptor whose clothed figures looked so authentic that real people came away feeling diminished.

"Uh-huh." She didn't look up.

Later, while Jess went out to a gallery, Martin made a stew, with Max's help. It had been raining that day too. He felt cozy, puttering around the kitchen with the boy, lovingly stirring the meat and vegetables, while outside the sky was gray with weeping. At last he held out a spoonful to Max. "Taste and see if it needs anything."

"It's great. But don't you feel kind of dumb wearing that apron?" It was Jess's, white with splashes of yellow flowers, a ruffle around the skirt.

"Dumb, why? I don't want to get my pants all dirty. Besides, it's pretty, isn't it?" Martin flicked the ruffle coyly and performed a few can-can steps, singing Offenbach heartily.

Max refused to join in. "Shit, you're weird, man!"

"Tough guy, eh?" He threw a few more punches, sending Max skittering and giggling around the room, till Jess returned and announced she was starving.

"How'd you learn to cook?" Max asked as he set the table. "Your mother make you?"

"My mother? She hardly cooked a decent meal in her life. If she even went to the grocery she had to lie down for an hour afterwards."

"Why, was she sick?"

"Hypochondria. The funny thing about it is you live a very long time. Everyone around you dies young, though, of exhaustion."

"Oh, Martin, cut it out, will you?" Jess called from across the room, pulling off her boots. "Max, I hope you never talk about me like that."

"Okay, forget it. Let's eat. Tell me about the show. What's the little motherfucker up to?"

"Well, he's still under the influence. Yours."

Martin smiled broadly, slapping his large hands on the table. "Good, good! Share and share alike."

In bed that night Jess said, "The way you talk about your mother. She's dead. Doesn't there come a time when you forgive people?"

"Forgive? Forgive is hard. But didn't I do everything a good son should—call her up, send her money, fly to Arizona every time she sneezed?" He reached out for her. "You're very tough, my love. Never let me off, do you?"

He thought even as he kissed her that he had never known a woman as relentless. She took his extravagant words literally, called him to account for every inconsistency, every hasty judgment. Jess thought words were permanent things solidly bonded to truth; holy objects to be used with scrupulous care. But Martin, who liked to be accommodating, spoke to serve the fleeting occasion. Words showered from him, Alice used to say, like puffs of dust rising around a genie. The image amused him. He could see the turban, the broad bare chest, the billowing trousers. But it was the springing from the bottle, he thought, that really attested to the powers of the genie. The dust was a by-product—pretty, but all for show.

"Am I that bad?" Jess said in his arms.

"Merciless."

"It's because I want you to be perfect."

"But I *am* perfect. I keep telling you."

"Show me."

He pulled her on top of him. Just before the climax there came a sinking feeling, his heavy history pressing down on him. His wife dead eight months, who had been barren, and Paula alone. He staved it off until the end. Then, defenseless, crushed, he rolled onto his side, away from Jess.

She drew him back, curled herself under his arm. "Don't go away like that. It's horrible. I'm not your mother, you know."

"I'm sorry. It's not that at all." He held her closer, though it took effort. His muscles felt like stone. "But don't you feel nice, Jess? Didn't you like it?" He made himself smile at her.

"That's hardly the issue, is it?"

"Look, it's been almost six years. You don't just drop someone after all that time, so long, ta-ta, cheerio, ho ho. She depends on me."

Jess pulled away and sat up. "Then why do you come here?"

"I come because I love you."

"No!"

"All right, no. Have it your way. I don't love you."

"No, no, you do love me."

"All right, so I love you."

"You know, Martin, I was a decent person before I got started with you. I was in good standing with myself. Go away, will you? I'll manage fine. Let's part friends."

"Ah, don't be cross, love. Come here. That's right. Tell me a fantasy and we'll do it."

"God, you're impossible! I don't want a fantasy. I like reality—have you heard of it?"

"Come on." He pulled her still closer, stroking in a teasing way. Despite his great weariness he had to be generous and selfless, yet again. Sacrifices were in order, to placate the gods. There was even a certain pleasure in renouncing the self, offering it as sacrifice. This is my body. Eat.

"Okay, baby, think of something—the most exciting, the most lewd, the most lascivious, the most erotic, the most outrageous, the most voluptuous, the most epicurean—"

"Oh, stop already, you nut!"

He had triumphed; she was laughing.

II

At twenty-five, Martin, in his romantic soul, viewed his continental trip as one of initiation, rather like the long, leisurely kind undertaken by sons of propertied British families in the nineteenth century, only Martin did not come from a great family and had to support himself with odd jobs. So much the better: he was nothing if not enterprising, and anyway, property was theft. In Paris, when he was not hauling crates of fruit or repairing the engines of Citroëns, he divided his time among museums, painting, and women. Older women, for the most part. Girls were not as readily accessible to a foreigner. Older women whose husbands were preoccupied and lukewarm with middle age, women to whom a young and boundlessly energetic American artist was a morsel of exotica.

That ended, though, when he found Alice. She was a shy girl from a strict, well-to-do family in Toronto, working for the overseas *Herald Tribune* and trying to perfect her French. She had little experience of men. As they sat in the Bois de Boulogne eating bread and cheese and olives and drinking wine, Martin wooed her with sweeping speeches. He disdained the surrealists, he thrilled to the Fauves and Matisse. Yes to Soutine and all feckless exiles. No to the sterilities of glass and steel, yes to the fecundities of Gaudí. His other passion was history, and his judgments ranged wide (he had read everything), though lingering as if nostalgic on the streak of revolutionary fervor of 1848. He called himself an anarchist. "A lawless man?" Alice laughed in delight. "Not at all! An Old Testament prophet, who bows to no authority but the ineffable! Squash the Philistines!" Eisenhower! Cecil B. de Mille! Coca-Cola inundating the antique splendors of Europe! Well-bred girls made the best audience. Martin pounded a fist on the grass, then sprang up to orate to the poplars. "We shall be drowned in another flood—Coke— for spiritual sloth. Where is the grandeur of mind that gave Samson back his strength? Man was born free, and everywhere he is in chains. So to speak. Life is beautiful, till we mar it by ugliness." He paused to breathe and offered a shy grin. "I was the valedictorian in high school."

When he returned to America he would paint enormous pictures, he told her, not flamboyant like himself, but pictures that showed the meditative, delicate soul within. He would transform the world by vision alone, he promised with a wink and a gleam: Martin was his own ironist. Modest too, in his way. He did not tell her about the scholarships at Yale or the special attentions from the exalted painters there.

To eat, he would dig ditches if necessary. He was huge and had the energy of ten men—that much Alice could see for herself in the way he whisked her in and out of galleries and cafés and, finally, in his lavish love. She followed his lead down erotic byways, querying, "Does everybody really do this?"

Martin too was entranced. He liked the slender toughness of her body, her chestnut hair drawn back in a ponytail, showing the bare, clean lines of her face; more than that he liked her acuity, her ear alive to the slightest nuances of phrase, her rigor in choosing the precise word for her meaning. Sometimes, talking, she would pause for five or six seconds, her face suspended in calm, one hand open and outstretched as if the perfect word were a tactile thing drifting invisibly towards her; intriguing to him, what fevered activity must be hidden within, what flashes scurrying along the circuits of her brain. And still more, he liked the fact of her being—however minimally—foreign, Canadian, nurtured far from the tattered streets of Newark, where Martin's father had been a baker who died young. When Martin told her how relatives had taken him and his mother in, how his aunt had presided over the family candy store while his uncle took bets over the phone, Alice gaped like a schoolgirl. No room for a bulky boy in that apartment where his bed flipped out of a wall. No one had ever asked where he spent his time (the library, and when that closed, the streets), surely not his mother, staring at her blotchy ceiling. There was something crude and primitive and cobwebby and inarticulate about the life in those rooms; not the physical markings of poverty—he was no snob, he assured Alice—but the dismalness lodged in the woodwork. So he developed peripatetic habits; without a roof, he leaned up towards the light. For he earnestly believed life was beautiful. He had to. Could she see? Alice nodded urgently. The abundance he felt within, the very force of those longings bred from books and bleakness, were proof enough. And here was Alice, with her reserve and elegance and precision. Class qualities, bred to deny easy access. Well, he would brook no such barriers.

There was no need to dig ditches. They came home and taught at universities, Alice in Romance language departments and Martin in studio courses. Students loved him, especially when he marched at the head of their ranks protesting racism, and later, war. At rallies, after other speakers unreeled statistics of social injustice, it was Martin, scorning the microphone, who restored everyone's spirits. However much they treasured their indignation, they must treasure their joy equally. He quoted Gramsci on the higher wisdom of optimism. Never cease believing that life was beautiful. After him came the singing.

He organized and exhorted in one university town after another. Alice wanted to settle in and take root; Martin was restless. Not your basic academic type, he told her. He bored easily.

"I see that. People and places both," she said. "You seem to riffle through them and throw them away like newspapers."

"Riffle. That's good, very good," said Martin. "Why don't you write a book instead of doing all those translations?"

They moved partly because administrations found the perils of Martin almost as great as the wonders. Folding her skirts neatly into a suitcase, Alice said, "Even if you're right, you don't have to reveal everything that's on your mind all of the time." That might be all very well for her, but Martin felt natural as a troublemaker, tilting at the status quo, forever urging the needs of blacks, artists, students, and above all, women, for he was an early and ardent champion of their cause. Someone had to do it, he argued. The students needed an example, and could she suggest anyone else among all those stodgy professors? She couldn't. There were days at a stretch so crowded with social agitation, he didn't even see Alice. The day he cast his spell over a townful of Republicans, making them march and even sing "We Shall Overcome," he was so overcome he didn't notice she was not marching at his side.

Alice, tired of seeking new jobs, stopped teaching and devoted herself to translations of novels, at which she was excellent, the best translators being unobtrusive. Martin was proud of her success. His superior Alice. And yet, translations . . . Of course, he did not hint at this to her. They were talking less about everything. When one of the French novels she translated, based on the life of the Renaissance poet Louise Labé, became a campus cult book, it irked him that Alice won little glory. Who ever notices translators' names? He had to tell people. "Please don't make such a point of it," she said, driving home from a party at which he had thrust her forward and announced her credentials. "Why not? One of us around here might as well reap some rewards."

For his paintings wouldn't come right. Not bad, only just below first-rate, the most accursed kind of failure. It was tempting to blame the narrowness of the academic life, but he refused any cheap excuses: better painters taught.

Nor were there children. The doctors found nothing discernibly wrong with either of them. Martin in any case had already fathered a child, or had reason to believe he had, a couple of months before he met Alice. Giovanna, the woman's name was; till now he had all but forgotten. She had come with her three young children to visit parents in Florence and would return to a wealthy husband in Buenos Aires. On the eve of her departure she told him she might be pregnant.

"What do you mean, might? Don't you know?"

"Sometimes I'm a little late."

"How late now?"

"A few weeks."

"But—" Martin stammered. "But what will you do?"

"Un piccolo ricordo." A souvenir. She gave him a coquettish look. He could still remember her earrings, immense, pendulous, gold. He had suddenly found them revolting, but what could he do? She left no address—it was not something that could endure.

"Look, Alice, we could adopt a baby. Six months later you'll be pregnant. That's what happens."

"Maybe later." She lost weight and grew quiet. Martin had never liked silence—it reminded him too much of his mother lying in that close room, or the dinners served on that oilcloth-covered table where the only sounds were biting and chewing and slurping and his uncle's pencil scratching at the racing form. So he filled their rented houses with students who buzzed around day and night. The more they buzzed, the quieter and more unobtrusive Alice grew, retreating to her study to work. But at some point the house would empty out.

"Talk to me."

"It's midnight. Aren't you talked out yet?" She was in bed with a book in a language he couldn't even recognize. Portuguese?

"But you haven't said a word to me all day."

"How could I? You're always surrounded."

Martin sat down at the edge of the bed and smiled, good-tempered as always. "I'm not surrounded now."

"I don't want the dregs."

Every two or three years she set herself to learning a new language—Greek, Russian, Serbo-Croatian. She wore earphones and listened to Berlitz-type dialogues on tape while she cooked dinner, now and then murmuring an odd bunch of syllables. "What are they saying that's so absorbing? You look spellbound," said Martin, tapping at her shoulder.

She turned off the tape. "What? Oh. Stop or I'll scream."
"What did I do! I asked you a simple question. Is it too
much effort to answer? I mean, you're walking around here in
another world, Alice."

"Stop or I'll scream. That's what it's saying. If you're alone
and accosted in Athens."

The intervals at which she undertook these languages,
Martin felt, were intervals at which she might have borne children. Or adopted children. But he could no longer mention such
things. Now all her store of words was in foreign tongues. He
felt faint with loneliness.

"Turn around, Alice. You're not really sleeping." She
would let him make love to her, with never a sound, eyes
closed. Mortifying. "Say something, goddammit," he once
shouted. "Say you hate it, even!" His raised voice shocked him,
but didn't seem to bother Alice in the least.

"What should I say? You just want company on your travels. It doesn't have to be me or anyone in particular. You could
do it yourself and I could watch—it would be the same thing."

The injustice of it! To him, who sought only the perfect
communion of spirits! She was deliberately withholding herself, refusing him what he needed. Just as his mother had done,
but he had not succumbed then and wouldn't now. It all came
clear: his work was failing because she was failing him. Women
were the rich source, the spring, the indispensable path.
Throughout history, Dante to Picasso . . . Poets were not mad
when they wrote of their Muses.

Still, he was never unfaithful to Alice except in the abstract,
though opportunities were near at hand. Students hovered
close, hoping for a sign of his interest; a few were not content
passively to hope and had to be gently deflected. Martin was
surprised, since even in the abstract they were hardly the rich
source he was after. Could it be that his exuberant hugs and
kisses, the long conferences where he allowed them to expatiate
on their private lives, the cups of coffee he offered not only at
home but all over town, his letting his wild hair down at parties
and dancing with the girls, even his occasional ribald remarks,

were misinterpreted? Was he provocative, all unwittingly? The very notion disturbed his pride. Certainly no girl could ever claim his warmth had been anything but paternal, professorial. If he seemed more frankly *human* than the other teachers—well, it was his nature. Not for him that dry aloofness. He had never been an academic type.

It was no more than common courtesy to offer the girl a lift home after their weekly conference: she wasn't feeling well. As they pulled up in front of her house he saw she was weeping.

He put his arm around her shoulder. "What's troubling you?"

It was too awful to speak of. Too embarrassing. Well, all right: she was pregnant.

Martin removed his arm, edged off a bit. "Uh, that's not unheard of. Is it someone you . . ."

"I went out with him a few times, but I don't really want to see him anymore."

"Well, in a college town like this I'm sure there are plenty of . . ."

"Oh, I couldn't do that. I'm Catholic."

"Catholic . . . I see. Look, don't despair. It'll work out somehow. Do your parents . . ."

"You don't understand! It's that . . . I mean . . ." She was hiding her face in her hands. "I'm still a virgin."

"Tracy, really. Catholic, all right, but there are limits. . . . Aren't you getting a little carried away?"

"No, no," she managed to get out between sobs. Her doctor had confirmed it. "It was very fast, do you know what I mean?"

"I think I can figure it out."

"The stuff travels, you know? It doesn't have to be really that near. Just sort of nearby . . . Oh, go ahead and laugh if you want. I know it must seem funny."

"No, I'm not laughing." He patted her hand, lying helpless in her lap. "It's just that it's . . . an unusual case."

"I need someone to help me." She looked at him beseechingly.

"Oh, my dear girl," said Martin after a considerable pause. "You don't really mean that."

"Why not? You always seemed to like me."

"Of course I like you, but . . ."

"Don't you see, I can't go through a whole pregnancy like this!" she cried.

He looked at her and stroked her arm. Paternally, he hoped. At this moment he could hardly distinguish. She put her hand on his knee.

"I've always liked you a lot, Martin."

He thought, while the hand inched up his leg, of the deprivation that had seeped into his life and that he had accepted docilely, so far. Help her. Wouldn't any man?

"Look, uh, Tracy, we'll have to talk this over. This is not just some casual thing." He put his own hand firmly over hers, to halt its progress. "Is anyone home now?"

Have your baby, Martin thought as he returned to his car an hour and a half later. I've cleared the way. First gently but efficiently to get the job done, and then more elaborately, so she might see what it was all about. He felt a trifle exploited, but bore that with patience. Women did, why shouldn't he? At least she was appreciative. So much so, that Martin had felt compelled to leave somewhat abruptly, declining her offer of a hamburger dinner. He drove a few blocks to the edge of town, stopped near a stand of maples ripe with the reds and golds of fall, and rested his head on the steering wheel to weep.

Absurd as it was, the singular event renewed him. He had not fathered a child this time, yet he had had some role in the mysterious process. He felt obscurely chosen, as if he were a larger-than-life character in an ambiguous myth. That winter he worked swiftly, with fresh energy and purpose. He was in his studio one afternoon when Alice interrupted to speak to him, which she rarely did. She had taken to wearing his old sweaters around the house, and her hair was very short now. He couldn't remember when she had cut it, before his encounter with Tracy or after.

"You don't look right. What's the matter?"

She said she had to have a hysterectomy.

Martin laid aside his brushes to listen. Finally he said, "Well, if it's necessary . . . Look, afterwards you'll be better than ever."

"How good is that?"

"Alice." He took her hand. They were sitting on tall stools side by side. "You know how good I think that is."

"We never had any children."

"It doesn't matter."

"You would have enjoyed them. Showing them off. You would have been a good father, too."

"I doubt it."

"Why? Look at you with the students."

"I probably would have suffocated them."

She stared at the floor. In profile, the lines of her face were still clean and young, after ten years. "Maybe. Well, yes, I guess so."

She didn't have to agree so readily! "You would have revived them," he responded gallantly, then paused. "Why? Do I suffocate you?"

"It's not your fault you're so large and . . ." Her hand was stretched out, palm up, but no word came. "Maybe any woman would be insufficient."

"Insufficient! You were all I ever wanted. And still "

"Mm-hm," she said abstractedly, and slid off the stool to look at the paintings. She had a new nervous gesture, he noticed, pushing her hair off her forehead with both hands, fingers outspread. "These new ones are good. Mysterious. Kind of like latter-day Madonnas, aren't they? They're better than anything you've done in years."

Martin grew hot. He realized he was blushing like a girl.

He understood women well enough to know it would be incumbent upon him, after the operation, to show her that it made no difference. Easy enough: to him it made no difference whatsoever; he harbored no old wives' superstitions. No, it was not the presence or absence of any organs that governed his desire, but that gradual shrinking of the spirit. In truth he felt more sorry for himself than for her. What was she losing but a mere lump of flesh? While he had given her his soul in trust, and instead of nurturing it she had starved it.

As he sat in the depressingly plastic waiting room with an atrocious painting of a dancing gypsy girl on the wall—what imbecile's idea to hang it in a hospital?—the idea that there could never be children now for him and Alice struck for the first time as a material reality. Nevermore. Like an attic door flying open, it released a rush of memory and speculation. What might it have been like, how might his life have gone, had he not met her at the American Library in Paris and been captivated by . . . what? By her appreciation of him. He thought of the women he had known during that boyish jaunt through Europe and before, back and back into the past like road markers sliding off a rearview mirror.

From the very beginning, with all the neighborhood girls he had managed to cajole into bed, he had been courtly and gallant, as courtly and gallant as a teen-ager from an inner-city slum could know how to be. Once, a girl had cried out loud, gasping, and Martin stopped short in panic. Maybe he had hurt her, maybe there would be blood. "What is it!" "Oh God," she moaned. "Don't stop." That was how he learned that women might have a personal, noncharitable investment in sex. Once he knew, the fact and the lore surrounding it fascinated him. He was not shy about asking girls questions, and so became a virtuoso. It pleased him to please; it pleased him more to give help to the needy, to girls who had no idea what they were capable of, or to girls who knew but needed a little more time. Of his time and efforts he was unsparing.

How these needy girls had evolved into the sources of inspiration, how his exertions had become sacrificial offerings to the laps of goddesses, was a transsubstantiation even Martin, with his vast learning, could not have explained. He only knew it had to do with art. And that Alice, more than any other, had offered the lure of transformation. He had first watched her bashful face pass through the stages of knowing to finally turn abandoned, and all the times he had made love to her since, or desired her only to be turned away, that progressive image had roused him. It was an image of incomparable voluptuousness, to which he was indispensable.

Now from all their straining nothing could ever spring, and as she lay being eviscerated he thought again that somewhere might be a child of his. Girl or boy? He hoped it was nothing like that lurid gypsy on the wall. The idea engendered no real curiosity or hope, though. What could he hope for? Rather, it opened onto a vista of possibilities—not only all the women there had been but all the women there had not been, trailed by all the possible children. At every nerve ending he sensed the abundance out in the broad world. The doctor who came to tell him Alice was stapled back together found Martin bemused, adrift in transcendent realms, like a youth who has heard the call of the spiritual life.

Still, he strove to do what was right. When Alice came home he hovered over her like a mother, he brought her chocolate turtles and reassured her of his love.

"I know. I know you do," she said wanly. "I just want a little time to myself."

A few months passed. "Alice," he whispered, and caressed her as he used to. "Let it be over. It's long enough."

She felt limp in his arms, and distant. Unfair. Nonetheless, he groped for words befitting the occasion. "It's good to have you in my arms again."

"You look so sad," Alice said in her clever, doleful way. She stroked his hair, beginning to go gray. "My Knight of the Woeful Countenance."

"My Dulcinea," Martin replied obligingly, though as he said it he recognized she was hardly a Dulcinea. He was the street urchin her charmed eyes had once idealized. No wonder he was rejected.

The following month a critic saw his new work in a group show and singled it out. A gallery in New York was interested. As Martin looked his last at the two paintings bought by a nearby museum, it occurred to him that Tracy should be having her baby right around now. She had dropped out of school after Christmas and he had not seen her since. But he hoped all went well—he felt a familial concern. Before long there was a one-man show. He worked feverishly. He was thirty-six, not too old for a fresh start. He traveled, giving lectures, showing slides, showing himself. Everywhere he was such an excellent showman that even without the paintings his charm would have left indelible impressions. Happily, though, he was no charlatan but the genuine article: an artist, with an artistic temperament.

III

A new era dawned, in which Martin became a personage. At each gallery opening, at each university he visited—those trips replete with parties and every variety of chicken dinner—was some woman he knew he might effortlessly possess, and often did, parched and deserving as he was. He was not without scruples or discrimination, would not become one of those middle-aged fools who break the hearts of mere children. They were all so skinny and boyish nowadays anyhow, besides which, a grown man could hardly talk to them. No, give him a mature woman with a fullness of spirit any day.

But he was ravaged by guilt. He thought of his marriage vows, his attachment to Alice, his dependence—for admittedly he was dependent. Was that a crime? She was, after all, his wife, and he needed her, when he returned from his wanderings, to greet him with her cool equanimity, to ask how things had gone at the shows or seminars, to sit up late over cups of honeyed tea, never commenting on his infidelities though it was hardly possible she could be ignorant. The enigma in this friendly civility—*did* she know, and if she knew, how could she not speak?—kept him attached. So that with the others, after the first rush of arousal his spirit would falter. One of his great-grandfathers had been a rabbi back in the Ukraine, his mother had told him. He had always felt, *faute de mieux,* a half-mystic connection to this rabbi—it was the closest thing to an artist his family had ever produced. Now Martin imagined he felt the genes of the rabbi stir within him in revolt and disgust, reminding him of what the decent life was. His spirit would falter, but luckily not his body. For was there not a morality to seduction too? Could one lure a stranger and then desert her midway? Manners were morals, and Martin was a lover of extensive courtesy, until he rolled away clutching a pillow, isolated in a fog of oppression.

When he had had his fill he resolved to give up these ways. This was not the man he was meant to be. Even his work, which by now was praised indiscriminately, seemed to him to have lost texture and to subsist on a surface brilliance. It was only love of a woman, of every plane and arc and fold of her body, every cranny of her spirit, that could open the subterranean chambers.

"Alice," he whispered in bed. "I'm going to change. It's not too late for us, is it? Say it's not."

"Of course it's too late. It's been too late for years." She closed her book, though.

"No! I've never loved anyone else." Moments passed. "You don't believe me, do you?"

"I don't know. Maybe. Why are you suddenly interested in me, Martin? Is the work not going well?" Her finger still marked her place.

"Interested? I've always been interested. You know I'm interested in everything in the world."

"Yes, and it's your world, isn't it, your little garden to drop in on now and then. It's all arbitrary with you. Like God. Who knows why he giveth and taketh away? But I'm not one of your creatures, you see."

He, playing God! When *he* was the humble supplicant, pleading for salvation at her hands! Yet her words did not pain him so much as that thorough calm. He had listened to similar complaints, but they were made in heat and truculence, and never so sharply formulated; he had to hand it to her for that, even as he lay stunned and aching.

"You don't even care anymore, do you, Alice? . . . Do you? Tell me, for God's sake!"

She shut her eyes as if pained. "I have to get up early. A publisher's calling from Madrid."

Then he grasped it. She must have someone else, God knows for how long now. How had he never thought of it before? Occasionally some woman or other had asked about his wife. Do you have an "arrangement"? Does she have someone too? He had always said, with conviction, Oh no, she's very involved in her work. An extraordinary woman. Not once had he made a derogatory remark about Alice to any woman he slept with, or to anyone at all, for that matter. Such was his loyalty. While she, all along, like a snake in the grass . . . That she might prefer solitude he had managed to swallow. But this! Panic broke through his skin in a cold sweat and he pulled the blanket closer.

"Are you saying you want me to leave?"

"Not really. We get along all right. I like watching you, and you like to be watched."

His blood eased. She did need him. Maybe he was imagining it all, exaggerating as usual, yes. He could show her. . . . Summoning his resources, like calling in the diverse troops, foot soldiers, light artillery, cavalry, Martin advanced with cunning on the supposedly impregnable Alice, first setting her book down on the night table, careful not to lose the place. Afterwards he held her close and murmured in her ear, "It isn't so, all you said, is it? Please." She appeared to be sleeping. Her lashes were glistening. A moment or two later she rolled over and curled up, her back turned.

IV

Martin's life became a quest for love. He bypassed ephemera with only a glimmer of regret, for he was pursuing something higher, spiritual. There was a French woman who taught chemistry at a private high school in New York City, where Martin now held a tenured position at the City University. Twice a week, on the days of his classes, he would spend the night at her Brooklyn Heights apartment and return to his house on

Long Island the next morning. Françoise was a woman of firm
and inflexible character: though she was divorced and had two
children she struggled to support, she refused any help he offered. If he would divorce his wife and marry her . . . But this
way, no, *merci*. He listened attentively, but Alice preyed on his
mind. She was losing weight again and having dizzy spells. One
does not desert a sick wife. He did not even need the genes of
a rabbi to tell him that.

When he and Françoise made love, the image of Alice hovered over the bed. Françoise sensed her presence and could not
abide it. Several times she actually stopped in the middle and
fetched a pile of test papers to correct. At last, after almost a
year, she declared she had to think of herself and her children,
her future. Martin was dismayed that a woman he had chosen
could be so pragmatic. She could not love him in "the old high
way of love" (Yeats was Alice's favorite poet), where no obsta-
cle could keep kindred souls apart.

"Well, then . . . ?" Françoise gave a shrug.

"But think," Martin pleaded, at his wit's end. "You're so
logical and scientific. Measure. Which is greater for you in all
this? The pleasure or the pain?"

She was a luscious, plump, dark-haired woman with great
green feline eyes. She was sitting cross-legged in her red flowered armchair, wearing a black satin Chinese robe he had given
her, her breasts spilling out the front. It flashed through Martin's mind that he must keep that image of her, in case it should
be the last.

"The pain. I'm sorry."

He suspected he had not really been in love with her at all,
for parting hurt less than he expected. Quite soon he was distracted by a woman he had noticed during the waning weeks
of the Françoise era, a secretary in the admissions office at the
university, also divorced, with three children. All the women he
was drawn to, Martin couldn't help observing, were mothers.
He liked visiting and finding the children rowdy and ubiqui-
tous; as he bantered with them he grew excited by the prospect
of soon snatching their mother away, locking the bedroom door

against them and seeing her transform from mother to lover, possessing her in a way they would never know. The new woman, Peg, was not beautiful at all. She was tall and thin and moved gawkily—her jutting hips and elbows banging into furniture—and was the most sexually aggressive woman he had ever known. It was she who first suggested they have lunch, and in the restaurant pressed her leg against his. Martin could hardly believe it. His approaches were generally executed with a careful and gracious decorum. "You're far worse than I am," he moaned in bed. "Eat oysters," she advised. "You know what else might work? Sara Lee apple crumb." The latter she ate in bed, a habit he didn't care for. Alice never ate in bed, nor did she leave clumps of hair in the bathtub. Nonetheless something rapacious about Peg's lanky, small-breasted body made him avid. Together they would careen into a world where only flesh and sensation existed; all traces of who they were, and where, were forgotten.

But then at the awakening, the same oppression, the same withdrawal. Peg raged beside him, calling him names. Why did she even bother with him, he was only a stupid old clown who would soon be too feeble to hold a paintbrush, not to mention screw. These were moments when he almost felt the pain was greater than the pleasure, and he understood, to some small degree, what Françoise had meant. At home in his studio, he labored over ungainly images of dislocation and imbalance. When critics called the work startling and original, he decided it was worth the torment.

He discovered she was unfaithful. She would bring home virtual strangers and not even bother to cover her tracks. "Why shouldn't I? What do you want me to do when you're with her—knit you a codpiece to keep it warm? You can drive a person insane, you know? All that wild talk about South Sea islands, then I don't hear from you for days."

"All right, all right, I'll tell her. Tomorrow."

But when he was away from Peg and could think clearly, he knew it would be foolhardy to leave Alice for a woman like that. She would betray him; she was mad; and when she tired of his body she would cast it aside the way she peeled off her clothes in haste and kicked them across the floor.

After a year and a half she exchanged him for someone else. He was in physical agony, had never felt so battered and ready to die. Sexual memories taunted him like furies. Feverish, he thought of escaping into the depths of the Sound. Once he went so far as to drive his car to the water's edge, where he grew lost in dreams of his boyhood; when he awoke with a start he wondered why he was there, and drove home. Alice would find him huddled at the kitchen table and would stroke his hair, nearly gone over to gray now.

Months later, when it passed, he was empty and light-headed, as after a fast. He moved more slowly, his shoulders drooped, and he no longer searched for love. Still, there were women everywhere, and he would sit up talking in bed till the late hours, getting to know all about them—he continued to find so many so interesting.

He never stayed with them long; if he saw they were falling in love with him he extricated himself as best he could. With all his precautions, in some cases he left grief behind him, but what was he to do? He had not forced himself on them. Far from it. And maybe it was only right that a few should suffer, to offset in some small measure the suffering he had undergone at the hands of his mother, and Alice, and Peg, as if there were a great communal balance sheet of suffering to be rendered at the final judgment. Martin was not proud of such feelings, yet didn't the best of disciples sometimes doubt, or wish in vain that vengeance were theirs? Only the untried kept a pure faith.

Sometimes he would glimpse a woman on the street who reminded him of Peg, or of Alice in earlier days, and he felt such acute longing that he would have to follow her for several blocks. His heart fluttered, he stumbled with vertigo, fantasies roiled in his head. He never made any attempt to catch up or to speak, and later, sitting on a park bench to calm his blood, he would fear that he was in his dotage, though he was only forty-five.

Once, on the crowded steps of the Metropolitan Museum,

he came face to face with an old lover. She was graciously polite, even warm, but Martin could tell she had not forgiven his defection. Was she one of those to whom he had sworn eternal friendship? If only he could remember exactly how he had dropped out of her life, he might say something mitigating or soothing, but alas . . . Everything else he remembered vividly. He remembered that though her manner was crisp and lively, in bed she was enchantingly languid. So often they were contrary to the way they appeared. Peg's public behavior was rather severe. Françoise, for all her luscious looks, tended to be phlegmatic, and his own proper Alice in her day, well . . . All this was fascinating, but right now, of no avail. He knew this woman so well, her every expression and mood, the tone she used for each degree of personal connection, that he could have charted on a graph precisely where he stood in her feelings, precisely where the axis of love and the axis of resentment intersected. It was that very knowledge of her that she could not forgive, he well knew, a knowledge painstakingly acquired only to be interred. He sympathized with her veiled disgust; it disgusted him too, that glimpse of his heart as a rank, unvisited graveyard of intimate and varied data about women, once-precious relics, neglected and moldering.

V

When Martin returned from the upstate college where he met Paula—her dance troupe performed opposite the gallery showing his paintings—Alice told him about the lump in her breast. He was dazed by the rhythmic recurrence of events, life grinding in cycles (love, cancer) as though it had but a limited supply of plot. She had noticed it a while ago, she said, but had waited to speak until the doctor was sure. In a manner quite unlike her, hesitant and tremulous, she asked if he wanted to feel it. He didn't want to, but to refuse would be more horrible still. She opened her blouse and offered her breast, showing him the place. He felt it right away, like a berry deep in the flesh. His fingers recoiled but he forced his hand to remain. He was unsure

what to do. He made a gesture like a caress. She stepped back
and buttoned her blouse.

"God," he said. "Well, when?"

"Tomorrow."

"Tomorrow!"

The sooner the better. The doctor had urged an even earlier
day, but she had not wanted to spoil Martin's trip, or to shock
him with a note in an empty house. Tears came to his eyes as
she recounted all this in her even way. Even, yet teetering on
some brink. Martin led her to the sofa and they sat down. He
realized that touch of her breast had been a farewell, and felt
a surge of regret and loss. One flesh, the Bible said. Then shame
crept over him. Men used the word "possess" for a woman's
body, but ultimately . . . no. The word stood for all the advan-
tages of possession, none of the liabilities. It would be her loss.
He had not really possessed her in years, if ever. If they were
truly one flesh he could feel the loss without shame at his
feeling. Who was she, then? In one of those instants when
reality threatens to appear as brutally as a graveyard lit by
lightning, Martin strained to see her, huddled on the worn sofa,
as a being distinct from himself, but it was too arduous. His
imagination shrank back.

He turned with relief to a more practical thought, of Paula.
He had promised to call her. Of course it would be out of the
question to see her this week, perhaps for several weeks. And
he felt a surge of regret and loss over that too, like a distorted
echo.

Alice started to cry and Martin murmured the suitable
words until she was calm again.

"Do you feel any pain? Do you want to lie down?"

"No, I feel all right. I'm hungry, but there's nothing around.
I haven't shopped since you left."

"Let's go out to dinner. How's that?"

"Lobster."

"Terrific."

"My last meal. Don't they give condemned men whatever
they want?" She tried to laugh.

"There'll be lots of lobsters in your future, you'll see. I'll even bring them to you in the hospital if you want. Remember last time I smuggled in a pizza? Nothing is more difficult to conceal than a pizza."

"Last time," she repeated. "What next? What can they take after this?"

"Oh, Alice, don't think that way. Defy it. Go change and make yourself beautiful. Life is still good. It is!"

She smiled wryly, her cheeks damp with tears. "They're cutting off my breast and you're telling me life is beautiful. You really think so, don't you?"

He nodded gravely.

"You're lovable, you know. A lovable jerk."

He beamed like a small boy being appreciated, and for the moment he felt fulfilled again. This was the closest they had been in years. A bitter notion, but what was any pleasure without a dash of bitters? "No." He put his arms around her. He had almost forgotten the feel of her shoulders, square and firm. "Not a lovable jerk. A holy fool."

"Better stop while you're ahead, Martin. This is one show you can't steal."

Alice's recovery was slow. She shuffled groggily through the house in an old bathrobe, and could sit for hours over a jigsaw puzzle of a Rothko painting, adding four or five pieces a day. All the time Martin tended her, his thoughts kept straying to Paula.

She was a dancer. At the reception where they met she had moved lithely through the crowd with a radiant calm. Martin saw her as a descendant of Isadora Duncan, only less dramatic, less self-important. He had not seen her perform, since he was at the time giving his own performance in the gallery, but he felt he knew exactly what she would be like. Watching her, he would know the long-awaited descent of peace.

He had told her all this in a late-night coffee shop, and she had smiled and said it was hard enough to do it, let alone theorize about it, but in any case it sounded lovely. She had crooked teeth, and with each smile they became more endearing; they gave her face an ingenuousness that made him want to protect and cherish her.

Martin did most of the talking that night. Painting was his life, he told her. As he spoke the words, he hoped they were true, for there was something about Paula that repelled myth-making. No doubt his life might be viewed less favorably. Yet wasn't everything he had done ultimately in the service of art?

Paula mostly listened and nodded. She hadn't heard of him, she confessed, her blue eyes apologetic. She had so little time to keep up; dancing was terribly demanding, especially at her age. Thirty-seven. "A kid," Martin chuckled. That was ten years younger than he. Hardly indecent. She had danced ever since she was a child, she said. Halfway through college she left to get married, and soon after had a baby daughter. She had been very happy with her husband, a civil engineer, but he was killed in a plane crash five years ago. These facts she offered shyly, as if a famous artist might find them of scant interest.

Quite the contrary. He was glad she had never heard of him. He had had more than enough of those who had. He loved her single-mindedness, her instinctive dignity. Her happy marriage, that sweet bondage granted to only a few, drew his reverence. Beyond that, she was a mother, and he was enchanted by the tender way she spoke of her daughter, sixteen and a dancer too. Martin envisioned the daughter as a more innocent version of Paula, the same erect body, muscular yet soft and sinuous, the same lush fall of black hair with glossy bangs reaching to the eyebrows, the same olive skin and wide mouth.

"What's her name?"

"May."

"How lovely. I'd love to meet her."

Paula only smiled.

"Will I have a chance to, do you think? Will you invite me over so I can see where you live, what it's like, what you have hanging on your walls?"

"Oh," she said, abashed, "it's nothing special. Just the two of us in this four-room apartment, and we go about our business."

Martin was rapt.

"What about tomorrow? We can meet for breakfast and then take a walk. Are you leaving too? Maybe I can drive you back."

Paula laughed at his grandiose gestures, his voice reverberating in the deserted place. "Thanks, but I have another performance tomorrow night. And I've got to get some rest." She stood up.

"Oh, I wish I could be there. But . . . I can't."

"I guess your wife is expecting you. . . . Look, maybe we'd better say goodbye now. It's been a lovely evening."

"Nonsense! This is very important. Three-fifteen, my God! Come, I'll drive you to your place." He took her firmly by the arm. In front of the white clapboard inn they exchanged a long look, and he leaned over to kiss her lightly on the lips.

"Martin, you must meet people everywhere you go. I . . . I don't live like that."

"I know. I understand completely. That's why it's so wonderful. Till tomorrow. And sleep well."

He watched her walk up the flagstone path. In a filmy summer dress and sandals that laced around the ankles, she was like a mirage receding into the night.

The next morning they ambled on the outskirts of town, then kissed goodbye lightly again. He wouldn't disturb her stillness, not till they were both more than ready, when she would shed layers of calm like veils. He could practically see it, a mesmerizing dance. Underneath, perhaps even in the height of passion, there would be a still center: he would drink from it and be renewed. Saved. But first he would savor the desire, hold it on his fingertips like a bubble, in all its delicacy and iridescence.

After leaving her he sped south towards home and Alice, stirred by the poetry of his discretion. Yes, Paula was assuredly not the sort to be rushed. But Martin rarely rushed in any case; rather, he bided his time discreetly until he could be sure of a favorable response. Instinct always told him the moment. If instinct hung back, he did not make the attempt. Or if he waited long and patiently enough, he might be relieved of the responsibility altogether—they did it. He was more sinned against than sinning, as it were. A few women had even kidded him about that diffidence. His interest, they said, was evident, but . . . "You force women into making the move for you, you big lazy lug." Valerie, he believed that was. "Ah no, love. I'm shy, underneath." "Shy! Don't make me laugh, Martin! You're a tease!" She was wrong. He *was* shy, somewhere inside. Paula would understand. Her appearing in his life could be a sign of grace, pointing the way to those hidden regions. Even in his paintings, there might come a hush, a reticence, all the epicurean joys of quietude. *Luxe, calme, et volupté.* Only Paula, alas, would not appreciate the allusion (as Alice immediately would).

He would revisit these thoughts over and over, like a child rereading a beloved book, while Alice slept heavily beside him. For months, till she recovered her strength, he mesmerized himself with anticipation of the new era.

The four-room apartment was nondescript, as he had been warned, but its plainness only made it a more perfect setting for Paula, who was unconscious of her great worth. Her daughter, May, also lived up to Martin's fantasies, a lissome girl who resembled her mother, though not quite so tall, a good girl in the old-fashioned way, well-mannered, who made her bed unasked and telephoned when she would be late.

"What a dream of a child. Do you think it's upbringing, or are some people just born serene?" Martin wanted to know.

"Born," Paula said. "I don't think I did anything special."

"You both have it and I don't."

"But you have your talent."

"Well, so do you."

"Performing isn't the same thing."

"Are you saying the artist has to be a tormented soul? That's a cliché, Paula. There were countless ones who weren't. Rubens, Van Dyck, Monet, Matisse. Duccio, I bet, was not tormented, but of course that was a different age. Lots of them were monks. Then again there's Vermeer—you'd never think it, would you? And Van Gogh."

Paula had drifted off to water her plants. Well, it didn't matter. He was getting to be an old bore anyway. She was so beautiful, wearing just an open long-sleeved man's shirt, and that curve of her wrist as she tilted the pitcher, nurturing . . . In the slant of buttery morning light on her head and shoulders, she looked like a Vermeer herself.

Twice a week, when he came to the city to teach, Martin would stay overnight with Paula, who rearranged classes and rehearsals to free the time for him. Those evenings he enjoyed the domesticity he had always dreamed of. Often they would all three be in the kitchen, fixing dinner or reading the paper or playing Hearts. May did her homework at the kitchen table— Martin was sure she enjoyed having a man around, poor kid, to have lost her father so young; now and then she would ask him for help with history or trigonometry, or for difficult words in the crossword puzzles to which she was addicted. He would think, This is real life. Ordinary family life. It even pleased him to be irritated by the way May peeled the Styrofoam off soda bottles, slowly, in long curling strips. But of course Paula was not his wife, and May, however fond of her he grew, was not his child, and this was not his home. When Paula gave May grocery lists for the weekends—food to be eaten without him!—Martin suffered pangs of exclusion. May danced in a school production of *Carousel* one Saturday, and as she and Paula relived the evening at the dinner table, chortling over backstage anecdotes, he felt such a sense of emptiness that he had to walk out of the room.

Paula had friends he had never even met. Martin would have loved to talk far into the night with a bunch of dancers— despite his gray hair and the wearied slump of his shoulders, he was still interested in everything. But she said their evenings together were precious, they had so little time. Finally she admitted she felt uncomfortable, being with a married man. . . . She had never intended it. It was happening almost before she knew it. A married man with a sick wife, she added in a whisper.

"Please, my darling, don't torment yourself over it. It's not your doing. It has nothing to do with you."

"I don't see how you can divide things up like that. It has everything to do with me."

"If it weren't you it would be—" Martin stopped himself in chagrin.

She did not talk of giving him up, though. No question of that, by now. No question of Martin's leaving Alice either, nothing to be gnawed over and spit out, as in the era of Peg. Alice was not well. She had never regained her full strength after the operation, and though the doctors with their scans reassured her, Martin could see the wasting. If nothing else, he thought miserably, he had vision. Fading, she turned to him. Too late, she wanted to talk, to spend the time remaining with him. When, silently and hesitantly, she touched him in the night he made love to her, but what he had once yearned for he could do only with pity, and he felt wretched after. What she felt he never dared to ask.

How different from the quality of wonder and luminescence in his love for Paula! And yet he suspected that the wonder existed by virtue of the desolation he felt with Alice, just as the wonder of light exists by virtue of darkness. Even at the extremes of pleasure, when all boundaries seemed to fall away, Martin sensed a pall of darkness. Another presence. He knew then that beyond their marriage, their history, and her illness, something adamant and irreducible soldered him to her. Once, he had chosen her, and so he chose her still. To forsake her would be forsaking the rightness and power of his own will. That he could not do. That would be a denial of his deepest self.

VI

There came a time when Alice needed radiation treatments. The same as five years ago, only worse: it had crept everywhere. This time she did not offer him her breast to feel for the lump. She sank into a solitude. Martin took her for the treatments and did everything there was to do for her, while she looked on, mute. With her thinness, her eyes had become amazingly large; he had the eerie feeling that they saw into him, tracking his every quiver. With contempt? he wondered. Or with pity. Longing, regret? Once, as they were returning from one of her treatments, he dropped his keys at the front door; the ring snapped and they lay scattered on the step, Paula's among them. As he knelt to gather them up he felt her looming above him, her eyes drilling into his bent back. "Why are you looking at me that way? What do you see? Are you thinking I'm clumsy?" "No," she said. "Not at all. I'm not looking at anything at all." It was true, he realized: she was not watching him, she hardly saw him, she had no further interest in him. It came over him with a deathly chill that he was not and had not been for a very long time the center of her life. The center of her life was herself, and she was watching inward.

When Alice died he called Paula and said, "I need to be alone for a while."

"I understand. Take all the time you need. I'm so sorry. Really, I am. I know what she meant to you."

How could she? It was such a secret, pernicious thing. He brooded on it as he stalked the empty house, not so much grieving as flagellating himself. Why had he not let her go when there was still time? She had not been strong enough to leave him—and in a fit of candor he cursed his power over women, wished it shorn away like Samson's—but he could have been strong enough to give her back her life. Instead . . . He tried to conjure scenes of their early days, to feel the balm of genuine regret, but the memories were static pictures, postcard views of Paris, refusing to come to life. There was nothing, nothing. It was all vanity. Even this self-loathing was vanity, for who was he to think of giving and witholding life?

After two weeks, for relief—even mortal sinners deserve some relief, Martin told himself—he went to Paula. They made love, and he wept. He stayed with her for a week: every night they made love and every night he wept, till it was clear he was trying even her saintliness, so he returned to his empty house.

He fell into his old patterns, spending two evenings a week with Paula when he came to the city to teach. The rest of the time he worked. A fierce energy inflamed the paintings, a series of tangled bodies. He could hardly wait to finish each one, to see what he had done.

"What now, Martin?" Paula asked after a few months. It was late at night and they were sitting at her kitchen table, eating cherries. May was all grown and gone, twenty-one, living and dancing in San Francisco.

"What now, what?"

"Well, you're alone now."

"Not really alone." He reached over and stroked her cheek.

"You know what I mean."

"Yes. But I'm not ready to do anything yet."

"You're not ready?" She sat up straighter.

"No."

"I don't understand. I thought when . . . you know."

"I need some time, Paula. The work is going so well, I can't have any disruptions just at this point."

"Disruptions?" She leaned her head back, as if offering her throat to a blade.

"I'm sorry. My darling, you're everything to me. Don't you know that?" He leaned over to embrace her, but she got up and walked away. "Don't, I can't bear it, Paula."

"Please don't touch me right now. Just leave me alone."

He stood by, pained and unable to help her. There was a little mound of cherry pits on the table. He cleared them away, then dried the dinner dishes and put them away, got into bed and lay in the dark by himself.

When they made love now, there was an absence. Alice had deserted him, and alone with Paula, he was bereft. Some nights when he stayed over, Martin simply lay wakeful, restless, ever so slightly bored. This was natural, he reasoned. Longtime lovers must have spells of boredom. He was fifty-one years old and entitled to a rest—God knows he had nothing to prove in that department. He watched old movies on television; *Now, Voyager* he found comforting. Nor was there anything unnatural or clandestine anymore about their being together. The genes of the rabbi dozed in apathy, unperturbed by Bette Davis's tribulations. Yes, a perfectly ordinary situation.

There it was. In the dark middle of the night, with Paula's amiable body curled into his side, he confessed that this perfectly ordinary situation left him numb. To be compelling it wanted the dramatic context: the invisible audience, the betrayal, and the guilt.

Martin squeezed his eyes shut in dread. A vision of himself, such as the Spirit of Time Future brought to Scrooge, took shape in the dark: not dead but doddering, ludicrous, contemptible. He had loved—truly loved—Alice for ten years, Paula for five; soon two and a half, one and a quarter . . . Geometric progressions were swift; he knew perspective. A week, a day, an hour. The nightmare vision sharpened. He saw himself as part of a relay race, a human baton. One after another, his exhausted partners passed him ever more frantically to fresh replacements and retired to observe from the sidelines. Only he was condemned to remain in the game until he dropped. He felt the abyss opening up, and his body gave a great shudder.

But as if somewhere the gods had a drop of mercy left for him (or were not quite finished with him yet), sleep came to his rescue. In the morning he felt better. He studied himself in the mirror, shaving: still presentable. Gray, but firm-fleshed. No jowls. Clear eyes. Thank heavens he was not a drinker—in a man his age it always showed. The terrors of the night evaporated in the steamy bathroom. He resolved, as soon as this group of paintings was done, to arrange somehow for him and Paula to live together. Or at least to spend more time with her.

He began, half unawares, to stare at women on the street again, women of every age, class, race, and shape. When he was invited to parties or openings, he brought Paula along if she could make it—a new and unequivocal pleasure; but when she couldn't, he would strike up conversations with other attractive women. It was amusing to see if the old charm still worked, like digging out and oiling an old baseball glove. Only to stay in practice: use it or lose it, he remembered his uncle and his racetrack cronies joking, and at fifteen he had thought them pathetic. Since he disliked the chitchat of parties, he would invite these women off to a corner for a real talk, or out for a drink, away from the clamor. Once or twice dinner afterwards. But never anything more. Oh no, not again, he cautioned himself. Never mind ethics: it was simple self-preservation. He was, after all, merely satisfying a peculiar little need (less fortunate men were doomed to tie women up or dress them in leather— give thanks for small blessings), adding a little harmless spice to a life now so above reproach it was practically . . . well . . . bourgeois. And he was an artist, was he not?

At one of these gallery parties he was introduced to Jess. Martin had read her articles—she was one of the few decent art critics around.

"So you're Jess Masters! Let me tell you, I'm an admirer of yours. You're extraordinary! When are you going to cast that discriminating eye in my direction?"

"Your turn will come, no doubt," she said pleasantly, not visibly jarred.

Well, here was a woman!

They stood among a crush of bodies and voices. Martin bent closer and touched her arm.

"Look, let's go sit down over there. Okay? We have a lot to talk about." With her this was a risk, he knew. But she did follow him to a quiet nook, where soon they were arguing about de Kooning and everyone after, interrupting, piling challenges one over the other like zestful children piling hands. Her mind was fleet and keen, piercing impatiently through surfaces to the impulse beneath. It was not airy cleverness, either; she was fertile; she *knew* things. How long since he had talked excitedly like this, and to a woman! Martin felt a twinge of disloyalty. Of course he had learned so much from Paula, all about instinct and calm and the harmonious life, but . . . From Jess he was learning something tangible.

She was elegant at the gallery, in a sleek dark green dress belted at the hip, glittering with chains and bracelets, so Martin was surprised, the first time he visited her SoHo loft, to find her girlish, in jeans and a navy blue sweatshirt, and barefoot (narrow feet with a high arch, he noted; also Morton's syndrome, second toe longer than the big toe—this he had learned from Paula). The loft was filled with boys' paraphernalia—bat and glove, barbells, a bicycle; prints lined the walls; there were Indian rugs and large pillows, and on the butcher-block table, a bowl heaped with purple plums. Given her rigorous judgments, Martin had imagined her surroundings would be austere. That they were not suggested indistinct but intriguing possibilities. From behind a closed door came a thumping. "That's my son, Max. He's learning to play the drums. I can ask him to stop if it bothers you. I'm inured." "No, no, that's quite all right."

As a rule Martin found his two days a week quite enough of New York. But to talk to Jess he made the trip. (The second time, he was stopped for speeding.) She loved to unravel everything dark and tangled in the light of reason, whether the subject was serious or the frivolous gossip they laughed over extravagantly. Often their thoughts traveled identical paths, all the same premises taken for granted. And Jess's enthusiasm— its particular mix of fervor and drollery—matched his own, so that listening to her mellow voice, Martin had the faintly delirious sensation of looking in a human mirror. On the street, she might suddenly stop walking mid-speech, the pressure of an idea claiming all her physical energy. When he did this, Paula would wait in puzzlement or take his arm to get him moving again. Jess even hailed buses with his imperious gesture, as if commandeering them for her private use. At last he had met his match!

After about a month Martin invited her out one Saturday to see what he was working on. Paula was away on tour in North Carolina. Since Jess loved to eat he fussed over a lunch of steamed mussels and avocado salad—she always appeared so blithely self-sufficient, so little in need of anything he might offer. His efforts were rewarded. She said it was the first decent meal a man had made her in a long time, but added, lest he grow smug, that the competition was a sorry lot. After she looked at the paintings they walked along the beach. It was a warmish day in November. At the water's edge Martin showed off his skill at skipping stones, and they even tossed a ball back and forth for a while. To his relief, a flaw.

"You throw just like a woman, from the wrist. You're a sight."

"I know. I've been told before. It's hopeless."

"Nothing is hopeless. You just haven't been taught. Come here." He took her arm and made it circle in a wide arc. "Throw from the shoulder, with your whole weight behind it. The whole arm, don't be lazy. That's a girl. Push from the back."

She was an apt pupil. In a few minutes she was throwing yards farther. "Hey, I never could do that before. Thanks!"

Martin, exultant, gave her a quick, one-armed hug. "We'll make a *mensch* of you yet. Next time we bring along a bat."

Back at the house they had a drink—but only one, Jess said. She had to drive home.

"If you'd like to stay on awhile," he said with hesitation, "we could go out to dinner later. There's a good lobster place nearby."

"That sounds lovely, but I can't. I promised to go with Max to see *Aliens.*"

They stared at each other, then burst out laughing. As she left, Martin gazed in through the window of her dilapidated yellow car. "Till next time."

"Goodbye, Martin. Thanks for everything." She zoomed off with an indecipherable grin.

He was confused. She had been in his house, they had had four hours together, and he had acted with a restraint that left him feeling musclebound. Jess must be baffled, if not laughing up her sleeve. It was Paula causing all this confusion. Must he deny himself for her sake? He had been denied so much already. . . .

He visited Jess a few days later. Paula was still away and Max was out at a drum lesson—quiet for once. She was fixing drinks, wearing her jeans and sweatshirt as usual, when he came up from behind and put his arms around her. She turned quickly but didn't retreat. Martin smiled and held her close for a richly triumphant moment before he kissed her. Jess looked more amused than aroused.

"Aha!" she said. "I had begun to wonder."

So she wanted a tone of comedy. Very well. "I'm a Jewish intellectual. I have to think things over." He kissed her again. She seemed to soften in his arms, and slipped her hand inside his shirt.

"And I thought maybe you just wanted an article out of me."

He drew back. "Good Lord! You didn't really think that I—*I* would see a woman for *that!*" He was genuinely appalled.

"I was only teasing, Martin." She reached her arms around his neck. "Resume what you were doing."

He had determined in advance not to let fogs of guilt plague him, but as they lay entwined afterwards he muttered, "Oh God, I can't do this."

"But you already did."

"I mean I'm incapable of this. I'm torn apart."

"You seemed capable enough. Are you allergic? Wait, I know. Anhedonism."

"This is no joke, Jess. Really." He told her about Paula. Naturally he had mentioned her before; he had—with a sickening sense of his own treachery—presented Paula as an old friend with whom he had a warm and intermittent sexual liaison. Now he winced at that version and gave her the truth.

"I see." She had moved across the bed as he spoke. "You might have thought of this before."

"I did! I agonized for weeks. Why do you think it took me so long to—"

"You might have thought of me, I mean. Or do you like having one in reserve? Like a backup system."

There was a long silence. Jess got out of bed and put her clothes on. "Let's eat something. I have a meat loaf."

While they ate they got into a heated discussion of the work of Gregson, a conceptual artist whose bare compositions Martin despised. Jess behaved as though they had never been

in bed, and Martin followed her lead. As he was leaving she
relented and gave him an intimate grin. "I think I've figured out
why women like you. They sense the presence of others.
There's a feeling of camaraderie. Sisterhood." She kissed him,
with a gentle shove towards the door.

But he wouldn't keep away. He dreamed of spending the
rest of his life with her (despite the pounding of the drums). It
was inconceivable that his interest would flag—everything
about them together was so right. Jess loved him too, she confessed. "And I hate it. You're part of someone else. This is
disgusting. It reeks."

Hearing her lurch into despair, Martin felt tortured. He had
done this to her, brought her down to his level. By possessing
her he had shattered that splendid self-possession.

They dragged on through the bitter winter and into the
spring. The pleasure, Martin assumed, must be greater than the
pain. He taught Max how to box and cook and skip stones.
Meanwhile he saw Paula as usual, but there were moments
when he could not look at her face, whose serenity reproached
him for the commotion he would soon cause. If she suspected,
she said nothing. She was in Alice's place now, haunting Jess's
bed, dimming his joys. Martin was worn out. He hadn't enough
time for his work. Sometimes on awakening he wasn't sure
which bed he was in. The flowered pillowcase he could glimpse
from a slit in his eye, that was Paula's. The hard mattress on a
wooden board—Jess's. And when his arms stretched out to
empty space—his own, at home.

It could not continue. Surely he had learned something
from Alice's slow death. He could redeem his life. "It's not fair,"
he told Jess in bed, one night late in June. "She needs me. That's
all there is to it. I'll sacrifice myself."

"A martyr! What next?"

"Please be serious. You know I'm in torment."

"Yes, I know who you're sacrificing too. Okay, if she needs
you then go to her. You're probably right. Here, put on your
pants and go." She began tossing his clothes at him.

"I don't mean this minute. Jesus Christ, you're so literal."

It was two-thirty in the morning. "I mean needs me in general."

"I don't understand in general. I only understand specific. If she needs you she needs you. Go. Here. Here's your socks, here's your shoes. Do you need a subway token? Oh, she's away, I forgot. Clever timing, Martin."

"Would you calm down? You're a hellion, do you know that? Get these shoes out of the bed, they're getting it filthy. I'm only trying to say, if Paula had any idea of this—"

"You bastard, of course she knows about it. You think she's dumb, don't you? With all your devotion, you ain't got no respect. Well, listen, she's probably lying awake right now, knowing what you're doing. And take your hands off me—you don't have to do it while I talk about it! Big-shot stud! You complain about Gregson, so stingy in his work, but look at you! It's how you live! You think you love women, but all you really love is yourself, seeing yourself. My God, it's not even selfish. Without them you wouldn't have a self!"

"Stop, stop! I don't want to hear any more!" He rolled over with his face in the pillow and yearned for instant death. It would serve her right, too, a big hairy naked corpse in her bed.

"Listen," he said the next morning. "I was up all night thinking. I'm going to tell her this time." He had promised to spend a week with Paula in Vermont, where she had rented a cottage. May would be there too—her first trip east in a year. "When you see me next week I'll be finished and we can start leading a normal life."

Jess kept brushing her hair in front of the mirror with brisk strokes, as though she hadn't heard.

"What's the matter? Don't you believe me?"

"Whether I believe you or not is immaterial. Only don't come back here unless you've made your choice. I mean it."

In the thick summer heat, Martin shivered.

VII

The rain was persistent. Martin sat down on a plastic chair in the terminal and watched people enter, dripping, shaking water from their umbrellas. Outside, it would be dark by now: in a few moments he would be out there hailing a taxi to Jess's. First he would rest for a while. It had been a trying week.

Not the first few days, when, in glorious sunshine, the three of them had gone swimming and canoeing and, to indulge May, even ridden in a chair lift over the mountains. May's skin was sleekly tan now and she walked with an easy West Coast swing, yet from time to time the ingenuous child flickered behind the sophisticated manner. In the evenings they sat drinking tea while she regaled them with stories of her dancer friends in San Francisco. Paula listened proudly. Martin too, as if he had had a share in raising her. For hadn't he sat around the kitchen table helping her with logarithms, explaining articles in the newspaper, supplying words for the crossword puzzles? "Seven-letter novelist starting with *D*, author of *An American Tragedy?*. . . Nine letters, Martin, a prince of an anarchist, starting with *K?*" He had given more than she asked, supplied all the history. In a small way, he could claim she was his.

Caught up in the family, he almost forgot Jess. Or rather her image performed an odd dance in his head. At night she receded nearly to the vanishing point, as he and Paula gloated over May and made love much as in the old days. Then in the morning she would loom very close and large. He put the ordeal off. This was a vacation, after all, the days long and full of light. He wished them longer, wished they would never end. If only it could be the present forever—Jess in abeyance far away, Paula contented, May young and eager, and he himself harming no one. But by the fifth day he was heavy with anxiety. He lay down after dinner and Paula came in to ask if he was feeling all right.

"Yes, fine."

"No, there's something. You might as well say it. I think I know, anyway."

"You do?"

"If it's all over, I wish you would tell me, Martin."

"What a thing to say! It's not all over. With us, it could never be that."

"But as far as, like, the day-to-day, it's over, right?"

"No. I just thought . . ." Martin paused because it hurt to breathe. The weight on his chest was crushing. He was too old for this, his heart . . . "I thought it might be best if we . . . saw each other a little less." It was out! He had done it! Immediately the pain in his chest eased.

"A little less?" said Paula in her serene way. "We don't see each other that much as it is. I really don't think I want that. I think I might want . . . well, more or nothing at all."

More . . .? More he could not give her. But the prospect of nothing at all was suddenly devastating. How could he forsake her—she was a haven of peace, she was so familiar, she needed him. . . .

"I can't . . . I can't . . ." A strange and terrible thing was happening. He could locate no words. He couldn't locate a thought, a wish—there was only a dark clot in his head. Time stopped, leaving him wedged in its warp. When he tried to swallow, his mouth was as dry as a desert. An eyelid twitched. "I don't know. I can't—I don't want to end. . . . I can't face that."

"But, Martin, it's not really fair, you know? Why should I live that way, when I know you're involved with someone else?"

He started to cry. "Don't do this to me!" It was all unexpected, all awry. "Please. Think it over."

For the first time since he had known her, she seemed quite without pity or solace. "I've thought and thought. I didn't like to say anything when I wasn't sure, but now . . . What do you expect me to do?"

"All right." He composed himself. "I understand your position. This is not the end, though. Not so fast. We'll have to talk about it in the city. Maybe I'll . . . I just don't know."

She didn't object when, hours later, in the middle of the night, he reached out for her. Martin tried to recover his old ardor. Maybe, in the end . . . But it was impossible: her responses were muted those last few days, her love-making elegiac.

She and May drove him to the bus when the week was out.

Thoroughly exhausted, he said, "Thanks for having me up. I'll call as soon as you get back. When is that, the Monday after next? I'll be over." She sighed. "Call if you like. But I can't see how things will change." He couldn't pursue this with May standing there. It was too mortifying. "Goodbye, May darling. It's been marvelous seeing you. Drop me a line, don't forget." As he hugged her, May held herself rigid. That hurt.

Martin could envision exactly what awaited him at Jess's. After the pleasantries, dinner, maybe some fooling around with Max, maybe some art world gossip, sooner or later she would say, "Well . . .?" His muscles went limp. No, he really wasn't up to it just yet. What sorts of men sit alone like this in bus terminals? he wondered. Frankly, right now he didn't especially desire either one of them. He desired only to be rid of his burdens, to slump over on the unyielding seat. No, he had to pull himself together. If he lived with Jess . . . But could he ever actually live with those drums? He was very fond of the kid, but six more years of drums? In earnest, if he lived with her, would he eventually grow tired of her unfailing brilliance, her energy so like his own, her trim body? And then what? He glanced around. Directly opposite him sat a soft, honey-skinned Indian woman in a sari, her shining hair pulled back in a knot, a red teardrop on her forehead. She must be around thirty-two or -three, he imagined, and she was surrounded by four young children. The sari was something like the robes Madonnas wore. In fact, the pattern the group of them made—the woman with her head tilted towards one child in particular—reminded him of one of Raphael's Madonnas. Where could she be going? There was only one large suitcase. Was her husband off buying the tickets or was she alone? And how did a sari work, anyhow? She had full, curving lips. Martin smiled at her tentatively. Respectfully—he might have been smiling in appreciation of the children, as strangers do. Her eyes seemed to smile back, then she bent over the smallest girl, fixing the barrette in her hair. A dark man in a white shirt approached, holding a handful of tickets. The woman smiled a welcome while the children clustered around him.

Oh, Martin, he thought, looking on at them, you are a sad case.

It was very unfair. He had served and worshipped all his life, while other men reaped the rewards. Nevertheless, one must go on. Take the next step, whatever that might be. He got up slowly, gathered his things, and headed for the exit. In a few minutes he would be at Jess's. It would be dry and warm, at least. She would be glad to see him, for a while, at least. He must remember what he used to tell his students, in the days of strife and idealism. (Of wine and roses.) No matter how great your anger at injustice, never let it embitter you. Don't lose your sense of joy. Remember that life is . . . But the word wouldn't come.